How to Build a
Real Estate
Money Machine

How to Build a Real Estate Money Machine

Money Machine

An Investment Guide for the Eighties

WADE B. COOK

ITP Inc.
Distributed by Kampmann & Co.

Published by
Investment & Tax Publications, Inc.
P.O. Box 1201
Orem, Utah 84057
1-801-224-3500

ISBN 0-910019-00-2
Library of Congress Catalog Card Number: 83-81764

Distributed by Kampmann & Co.
New York (212-685-2928)

Manufactured in the United States of America

This new and revised edition
is dedicated to my wife, Laura,
our girls Brenda, Carrie
and Leslie:
a family that is a new and wonderful
revision to my life.

"This publication is designed to provide accurate and authoritative information in regard to the subject matter covered. It is sold with the understanding that the publisher is not engaged in rendering legal, accounting, or other professional service. If legal or other expert assistance is required, the services of a competent professional person should be sought."

Contents

Preface

WOULD YOU LIKE to have a million dollars, or would you rather have what a million dollars could do for you? Several years ago my economics professor asked this question. He told us that a million dollars would earn $167 a day in the bank. "I could live on that," he joked, "if I didn't eat so much." We all talked about having the million dollars, but out of our discussions came the conclusions that, even though having the money would be nice, having the income created by the million dollars would be even nicer.

A while ago, I read of a publisher giving some advice to a new author. "Look," he said, "We have enough books on how to make a million dollars. Can you write a book on how to make a living?" I'm taking his advice. This book is a guideline for building a monthly income. The equities will be there, but you can LIVE on the monthly payments.

In this book I present an investment idea for the eighties that could increase your income and net worth if you're an investor, or help create an income and net worth if you're a novice. The reason I use the word IDEA is because this is not a "magic, get-rich-quick formula." It is a sensible, attainable approach—with new answers to old questions. There was a time when I needed new answers, a lot of new answers, because the old formulas weren't working for me.

My story back then was just like that of many investors. When I was in my early twenties and a little disenchanted with middle income America, I, like many others, went in search of something—some way, some formula—to get ahead. The time was the early seventies and all the talk centered on real estate. I picked up a few of the books popular at that time and started reading. The theories seemed good and I was excited to get started, but I didn't have a thousand dollars. It wasn't until a few years later that the opportunity came.

I lived two doors down from a small house that went up for sale. It was a cute little place and I thought it would make the "perfect rental." After a few bargaining sessions with the owner, the house was mine. I spent a few days cleaning and painting and by the weekend it was rented. It almost seemed too easy to be true. That adventure whetted my investing appetite, so I dug out the old books and read them again. At that time, when the economy was good and interest rates were lower, these books seemed to offer some realistic advice.

I kept my eyes open for other houses and, sure enough, *doors opened*. I looked at many and bought a few, and then realized that I had become an investor through and through.

About one year after my first investment I was making enough money in real estate to quit my job and devote all my time to investing. It seemed odd that all day, every day, I could look at houses, talk to real estate agents, call on homesellers, and be a full-time investor. It was exciting. Never before had I been in so much control of my time.

Everything was going well until one day some of my bills came due and I didn't have the money to pay them. This was upsetting to me, but more so to my wife (as most of you self-employed people can verify). How could this happen? I had EQUITIES! I soon realized that ownership doesn't mean cash flow—that having assets is not synonymous with having money in your pocket. I didn't realize when I went on my own that most of what I did was going to be controlled by someone else.

During this period I experienced time problems that almost drove me crazy—the seller that was out of town until Tuesday and was tying up my money because I was not willing to make other offers; the escrow company that was waiting for something to come in the mail; the bank that wouldn't send the assumption papers; and the attorney who looked over the final papers and wanted to make several changes. These problems seem small compared to the problems created when buying or selling through some government agency. Endless months would go by and all of my energies would become exhausted just trying to get one deal closed. These delays took some of the excitement out of investing because I was being controlled by someone else—working within their time frame, meeting their requirements, etc.

One day I was about to sign another earnest money agreement to sell a house FHA. I didn't have much cash and I was looking at two problems: the additional cash I would need to fix up the house to meet FHA requirements, and the extremely long time it would take to close and receive my money. I asked myself, "Wouldn't it be better to sell on contract? (For a definition of the word contract, please see the page following this preface.) Couldn't I make more money in the long run if I could close sooner and reinvest the down payment in one or two more places?" I knew I could close the house on contract by that Friday. All day I penciled out this idea on paper and could hardly believe the figures.

Had I sold the house FHA it would have taken about five months to receive my $12,000 profit. My figures showed that, in the same time period, I could take a $4,000 down payment and turn it into $150,000 in equities with about $1,200 a month coming in on my net monthly payments. I put it to the test and the results surprised me (even though I had written it down five months earlier). My actual equities were $151,000 and my net monthly payments were $1,290. As I continued to invest using this approach, it got even better.

When friends and other investors asked me about these ideas I began giving seminars—in my home, in my office, at the community college, and at many real estate offices. This investment idea soon caught on and seemed to work for anyone who tried it—anyone, that is, who didn't live to cash out. It was a way for these novice or experienced investors to have a cash flow in the present, equity growth for the future, and tax advantages for both time frames, all at a rate faster than they ever thought possible.

Now, the economic climate is stagnant and tight money makes it necessary to change the nature of investing. Many of the old formulas don't apply, and while everyone is waiting for a new game plan, the institutions with the money just continue to say, "NO." Buying and selling real estate isn't what it used to be, and everyone is sitting on the sidelines waiting for something to break.

I've realized that NOW is the time the information in this book is really needed. The theory is sound. The rate of equity growth will astound you, and the tax advantages of selling on installments will pleasantly surprise you. There is obviously a great need for new ideas in the real estate market today—and that's exactly what I have to offer. Ideas are stimulating and what's more important to you is that these ideas will stimulate your mind—creating even more ideas; hopefully ones that will work for you and solve your problems.

The contents of this book will help any investor. If you think you're past the stage of the average small investor, I suggest that you glance at the first few chapters, (Chapter 8 is a must) then skip to the last chapter which is written for the investor with some excess cash flow.

I tested this investment hypothesis and it worked. Now, let it work for you and in less than five years you could have what a million dollars would do for you. The ideas presented here are easy to understand and just as easy to implement. By reading this book you can learn *How to Build a Real Estate Money Machine!*

Contract: A definition

Throughout the book I use the word contract. My definition of contract is *any type of owner financing.* It is an agreement for purchasing or selling real property. You may use a Uniform Real Estate Contract, a Land Contract, a Contract for Purchase, or as is becoming popular now an AITD or All Inclusive Trust Deed. When I buy I give the seller a Mortgage or Trust Deed for the equity. This Deed of Trust (or Trust Deed in some states) or Mortgage is accompanied by a note which states the terms.

PUBLISHER'S NOTE: Mr. Cook has authored a new book entitled *The First National Bank of Real Estate Clauses* with over a thousand clauses and phrases for effectively buying and selling property. There is one phrase, an exculpatory clause, which will help assure that the only collateral for the note is the real property and does not extend to your other assets. This one phrase alone would make the purchase of this valuable book worthwhile. Look in the back of this book for information on how to order this and other books.

How to Build a
Real Estate
Money Machine

Chapter 1

The Problem

BEFORE this investment idea can be fully appreciated, one must understand the questions it answers, the problems it solves, and the headaches it avoids.

In my first twelve months of investing, I was able to purchase nine different houses and not one of these transactions was handled in the same way. Each was unique, having a new set of circumstances requiring new solutions, but I managed to get them all sold or rented. My investing really picked up and I thought I had found my niche in life so I quit my job. Then, about this time, something happened to my plans—I was losing control of my cash flow.

The investment books I'd read were written on the sole premise of buying and fixing up in order to eventually cash out and reinvest in larger units. I must admit I made money, but in most instances cashing out created several problems: I had too much money buried in each property for too long, and the time factor in waiting for the cash-out caused a fleet of hardships. Also, on April 15, Uncle Sam was going to be waiting with a noose because of all the cash I'd received at once. In order to save my neck I decided to change my tactics.

I searched for information to make my investing more effective. I spent countless hours reading and asking questions of professionals who knew anything at all about real estate. There were plenty of people who knew bits and pieces of the investment game, but very few had a comprehensive knowledge that could be depended on for all types of real estate transactions. It became increasingly obvious that I was getting only pat answers because they were all investing under the same investment formulas. It took a year of dealing with these problems before I asked myself the question, "Isn't there an easier, more profitable way?" The answer to that question didn't come overnight. As you read the following examples of the problems I experienced you'll understand why I decided it was time for a new approach. In chapter two you'll read how I solved these problems.

Problem # 1:
Government Financing—FHA/VA

"I think I've just sold your house."

"Ahhhh, who is this?" I asked, talking into the phone.

"This is Sue at Bingo Realty. I have a buyer for your house. May I come over and present this offer to you?"

Sound familiar? I hadn't had the house on the market very long and already offers were coming in. When Sue arrived and laid the earnest money agreement down in front of me I was surprised, because it was for the exact amount I was asking ($50,000). She said the people were extremely qualified and that they'd breeze through the buyer qualification the VA requires for loan approval. That was too good to be true; *I was going to get exactly what I was asking for*. That last sentence is not the whole truth. (Boy! I didn't know what I was asking for!) What happened over the next several months seemed like a mini-nightmare.

"Well, first of all, they'll have to qualify."

"Who takes care of that?"

"I do. As a matter of fact, I'll take care of everything." Then she walked out the door with the next four months of my life in her briefcase.

Instead of two weeks to qualify, it took four. A part of their income wouldn't count because he was self-employed part-time making "pot" holders (not the kind one uses to handle hot pans) and he, obviously, didn't keep the best set of records. But, after a few adjustments here and there, they finally qualified.

About this time the inspection report came in on the house. I wasn't worried that it was five pages long. What hurt was they didn't even double space when listing all the things that needed repairing and the list still filled up every available space on the inspection sheet. I figured that the additional work would cost close to two thousand dollars and take an extra month. It did, and two more house payments later I had my second appointment with the VA House Inspector. I was about five minutes late. One word of advice—don't be late. Hell hath no fury like an inspector scorned. It took about fifteen minutes before we were talking again. Actually, I was talking the whole fifteen minutes trying to get him to smile. He took a few notes and left.

About two weeks later his reinspection report came in and all it said was to remove a little dirt touching one of the basement window sills. I drove all the way over there and kicked the dirt away with my shoe. The inspector probably spent more time writing that on the report than it would have taken him to do it himself. (It seems they either like you or they don't.) Another house payment came due.

After this, I finally thought I was getting somewhere. The buyers were so anxious to move in and I was anxious to get my money, so, naturally, I thought everyone was on the same team. How uninformed I was. There was one other party in this transaction that hadn't played a big part until now. You guessed it—the banker. Apparently, this certain banker thought he was doing everybody a favor by making this loan and felt he could act in his own best interest. What that means is that he's going to close the deal when it's in his own best interest. Pardon the pun, but *interest* is the name of the game. FHA and VA loans have a little thing called "points." Frankly put, points are the amount the bank is *going* to charge the seller for making the loan.

Why the seller you ask? Good question. After all, it wasn't his idea to get the loan or use the bank. Why should he have to pay even one cent? VA to the BUYERS rescue. There is a rule which states that the buyer can only be charged so much for loan fees, and because the FHA/VA dictate how much interest the participating banks can charge, the banks have devised a system to collect—up front—what they figure they'll lose over the course of the loan. What frustrates me more is that if the house is resold at any time before the loan is paid off, no points are ever returned to the seller and they are charged AGAIN to the new seller at the new selling price. These loans are guaranteed by the FHA/VA which means, in case of foreclosure, the government would pick up the tab—paying off the house. See how the banks watch out for their own *interest*? Have I made my *point*? The banks cover their. . . .

The points at the time I signed this particular earnest money agreement were one and a half—meaning 1½ percent of the selling price, or $750 that would be paid to the bank by me. The interest rate the buyer was going to pay was 9½ percent.

I was told several times by one of the escrow officers that everything was ready to close, so I couldn't understand the continued delay that dragged on over a month more. I was getting tired of their excuses, but it was ". . .supposed to close any day now." It was now two weeks before Christmas and if it hadn't been for my wife and children being so happy in spite of the bank, Christmas indeed would have been bleak.

One day about mid-January, the phone rang. "You can come in and sign the papers now," said the escrow officer. I could hardly believe my ears. Inside of two minutes I was in the car heading out to pick up my money.

"Why is this amount $2,000 less than what I planned on?" I asked, expecting an apology for the error. The answer was on the closing statement which was pushed in front of my face. Closing statements are usually fun, but this one had some strange figures on it. During the time it took to close, the points rose to SIX, which doesn't sound that bad until you realize the other 4½ percent added another $2,250 to my costs. (There was also a "Warehouse Interest Adjustment Fee"—which I'll talk about in the next section—and a few other costs.)

The buyers' costs were not affected by this, although the interest rates on their loan had gone up to 10 percent because the original agreement had passed the interest rate commitment date. Decision time. Do I go through with it or do I back out? That was no easy decision. I knew if I backed out now, I'd probably be sued for performance. (This means that I'd probably be forced legally to go through with the deal. Meanwhile, I'd still be making the monthly payments.) It was ready to close now and I desperately needed the money. The decision was made. I signed the papers and stood there waiting for the check. "Not now," said the girl. "The papers have to be recorded and it's too late for that today. We'll record tomorrow and you can pick up the check Monday." I was rather upset with this whole set of affairs and upon leaving I looked the loan officer in the eyes and said, "I know you've been postponing this until the points went up." Silence. He looked at me and smiled.

Monday—I thought I could finally make offers on those two other houses that I thought I had lost because this deal had taken so long for me to get my money. I drove out to pick up the check only to be told that it was ". . . in the mail." It arrived Thursday.

This was such a raw deal that I started asking myself some important questions. There had to be better ways of doing the same thing. I was determined to get back in control and find those ways, or create them.

In spite of the problems they cause, I feel there's a place and a time for government lending agencies, FHA/VA financing is too important to the home owner just to dismiss them because they're cumbersome. They have given a chunk of owning America to the Americans. Originally, government financing came along at a time of great distress in our economy. Banks were afraid to loan money and most people couldn't qualify anyway. In comes the federal government with nothing but good intentions and a lot of other people's tax money; and after all they wouldn't actually be loaning the money, they would just guarantee the loans. Now, the banks and mortgage companies had nothing to lose but a little interest. But, with a little creativity (like adding a few additional charges here and there, i.e., points) they were also able to eliminate this deficiency and lose nothing.

The FHA/VA not only set up rules for the banks and mortgage companies but they also dictate loan approval requirements for the buyers and the properties. This can be a big problem. From remodeling an "old beater" to new construction they are there with their mountains of regulations and paperwork. For the private home-owner much of this is to his advantage. If I didn't know the contractor and the quality of his work I, too, would much rather live in an FHA/VA approved home, knowing at least the house met up to some standards.

Many of the buyers out there can only purchase a home under FHA or VA terms. These plans offer low down payments and lower interest rates, keeping the monthly payments lower. They also stipulate foreclosure provisions which are weighted in favor of the buyer. Because so many buyers want these benefits, the loan demand has put a heavy burden on FHA/VA offices causing great delays in processing time.

These problems of regulations and time delay create several other problems (if you are the seller) which invariably involves money—*your money*. If the house you're selling needs repairs you must understand their regulations, follow the written requirements, search for the proper materials, and make sure that whoever is doing the work does it right. Complying with all these regulations can cost dearly. It also creates a time problem, adding to the misery created by the FHA/VA in-house delays. Remember the monthly payments; I know everyone would like to forget them, but they march on. My longest closing took about six months, and with payments of $240 per month (totaling $1,440) it's a good way to wipe out any cash flow you have coming from other sources.

If you can overlook the problems of regulations and time delays (which you can only afford to do if you're the buyer) there are some FHA/VA benefits for the small investor. Most of their loans are readily assumable by anyone, even corporations. That means a lot when you can take over payments with interest rates far below what you would be paying the bank or the current seller.

For example, I made an offer on a house which included the assumption of an older FHA loan. The agent told me it was about 7½ percent so I was pretty excited. When I arrived back at his office I was told it looked more like 6½ percent and my excitement grew. About a week later I was talking to the seller and I mentioned the 6½ percent. He said, "Oh, no. I think it's 5¾ percent." When I heard that, I called the escrow company. The girl said the assumption figures had just arrived from the bank. I was really anxious for her to read and verify the 5¾ percent. She chuckled and I held my breath. "Ahhh . . . it's not quite that; he lied to you. It's 5¼ percent." I wanted to hear that again! Actually I wanted to hear it several times again. I was so excited I could hardly drive.

Maybe you think it's crazy to get excited over assuming $4,400 at 5¼ percent, but there are certain things investors are allowed to get excited about. Assuming low interest rates is one of them. We had a celebration party.

The next benefit will be most understood by investors who consider themselves builders. Construction financing is almost always short term (six months, more or less) and the interest rates are a healthy cut above regular mortgage rates, so the builder needs to cash out. And, because so many buyers want FHA/VA benefits, the builders need to sell this way or many of them would be out of business. Usually, all excess interest costs and the time factor for selling FHA/VA are taken into account at the beginning. To anyone absolutely needing to cash out (assuming they have the time and money to wait) this is one way to go.

Last Benefit

The last benefit is based on more than just figures or time. It's partly because of these programs that America has become a nation of homeowners. Put whatever value you want on that (there are several) but to me as an investor it means there are a lot of people who want a piece of the rock. Their desire to own their own home is strong, but in today's economy that desire can't always be met, so there needs to be a new approach.

Be smart. Use these plans to your best advantage. *Stay one step ahead by being educated*—knowing what these plans will or won't do for you.

Problem #2:
Conventional Financing

Conventional financing simply means someone goes to the bank to get a loan to buy their house. The problems here are nothing like government insured loans, but there are some things to be aware of.

Once again, the first consideration is money—your money. The bank stays in complete control, and sometimes to their *disadvantage*. The following story is so incredible that even I find it hard to believe.

I made an earnest money offer on a house my wife and I wanted to live in. It was a beautiful brick home in a nice neighborhood. My offer was very close to the asking price; the owner wanted $33,000 and I offered $32,000. This was accepted so I went to a savings and loan to borrow the money. We spent several hours filling out all their forms and then they ordered an appraisal of the property. Within a couple of weeks the bank said the loan was not approved. I couldn't understand why because everything had seemed so right. I was informed that the computer kicked it out because it didn't fit their formulas. I inquired further and found out that the property had appraised at $60,000. According to their formula the selling price couldn't deviate more than 20 percent from the appraised value.

Now, no reasonable person would refuse a loan with DOUBLE collateral if all the other conditions were met. Apparently, though, this company was not reasonable. I really wanted the house, but only on my terms. We argued back and forth for about three weeks, but because the strain was getting to be too much I just dropped it. I wanted to take their computer and dump it in the ocean with an epitaph on it reading, "May you *rust* in peace."

Now all savings and loan companies are not this bad, nevertheless, they do want to keep control. For instance, suppose the appraisal comes in lower than the selling price you and the buyer have agreed on. The loan would be adjusted and you would receive the lower amount.

Suppose your buyer qualifies for a loan but the bank will not guarantee the interest rate. Four weeks later, when it's ready to close, the interest rate has increased which, in turn, increases the house payment. Now, because his "income to payments" ratio doesn't fit their formula, your buyer no longer qualifies. The deal is off and you are out looking for a new buyer. Guess who gets to make all the house payments in the meantime? YOU.

On another deal I was sitting in the bank getting ready to sign the closing papers. When I was going over the closing statement I noticed an extra charge for $80 with the title, "Warehouse Interest Adjustment Fee." (Have you ever seen a bank's warehouse? Neither have I!) That meant $80 less to me, so I questioned the agent.

She said I'd have to take it up with her supervisor. When he came in he explained that the charge was there because they were having to borrow money at a higher rate than they were when they started processing this loan. I said, "Listen, I'm the SELLER here. I didn't come in for this loan—my buyers did. Why are you charging me loan fees?" He said, "Well, we can only charge the buyers so much and we need more to pay for the higher costs of our money." I said, "I don't care what you have to pay for your money. The buyer is borrowing the money from you to get into my house. We had an agreement in writing and I don't want to pay this $80." He said, "Well, we are doing it to everyone."

I said, "Gary, let's suppose one day your employees go to lunch and while they're gone you take $80 out of their purses. When they come back they notice that their money is missing and they say, 'Gary, what's going on here?' You answer, 'Well, we're running a business here, but we're just not making enough money. Sorry, I just had to take it. I had to take a little bit from all of you so we can keep the business going.'" Gary just looked at me and smiled.

Then I said, "Gary, let's bring it to you a little more personally. Let's say Friday you get your paycheck and there's an extra $80 deducted. You're a little upset about this so you call the payroll officer and say, 'Hey! Why has this $80 been taken out of my paycheck?' And she says, 'Well, look Gary, we know you're a nice guy and a good employee, but we're having to pay a little bit more for our money then we'd planned on. Business costs are going up, but hey, don't worry. Gary, we're doing it to everybody.'" I think he was getting tired of my logic, so he gave me two choices: Sign the papers or back out of the deal. I was looking at a $13,000 check coming to me and I really didn't want to back out. So, I said I would sign the papers under protest. I wrote down on a piece of paper, "I do not agree with this charge. If it is with-held from my proceeds it is against my best interest and against my will."

I thought, possibly, I could go back and sue them, not realizing at the time how naive I was. They were the largest bank in the state and it probably would have cost me ten times that amount to take them to court. So I signed the papers and took my money and, again, learned a lesson: Investors shouldn't do business with banks.

The banks want to control everything; the selling price (they usually have their own appraisers); the necessary down payment (controlling who can or cannot buy); interest rates (which tend to fluctuate upwards during the processing time of the loan); closing time (the faster you want it to close, the longer they take); the length of time the loan will run (this amortization time determines the monthly payment amount so again the bank controls who qualifies and who doesn't) and pre-payment penalties on the loan if the buyer decides to pay it off early. If you would really like to see more of the controls they take, read over their security agreements the buyer must sign.

Another thing: if you want to buy or sell a house with an existing bank loan, they can raise the interest rates at the time of sale (which would then raise the monthly payments) or call the loan due (so they can get their money back and loan it out at higher rates).

A Friendly Banker?

I had a friend who worked at a bank. Knowing that I was investing heavily in real estate, he approached me at a time when they needed someone to take over payments on a foreclosure. They made me an offer I couldn't refuse. The house appraised at about $160,000, but for $10,000 I could take over the payments with a balance owing of $70,000. I told him I didn't have $10,000 at the time. He said they'd loan me the $10,000 plus $9,000 to fix it up, with the payback at the end of the year. I was thrilled with the equity. He drew up the papers and when I went to sign I noticed the contract stated that the $19,000 was to be paid back in six months. I mentioned this to my "friend." He put his arm around me and assured me saying, "If you can't do it by then, we'll work with you." Well, at the end of six months they weren't in a position to work with me, so guess who lost control? (Not the bank!) I also lost most of the equity in that house. I lowered the price drastically and sold it quickly to get the bank out of my life and get myself back in control.

When staying in control is the name of the game you must "stay away from the banks." There's a lot more I'd like to say about banks, but enough is enough.

Problem #3:
Cashing Out and Uncle Sam

Other problems caused by cashing out are concerned with income taxes. Most small investors need to be turning their properties in order to make a profit to live on. If he makes about $10,000 on each of three properties within a year, his income soars up into a higher tax bracket. The IRS has given some relief to the investor who holds a property over one year. (This is called "long term capital gains"—see Chapter 8.) Sometimes, though, it's not in his best interest to do this. So, he sells and makes a healthy profit and reinvests the money into another place. Then, when he sells that, he makes more than he was planning on. Now *both* profits are taxed at an even higher rate. Trying to get ahead this way can be very painful. If he decides to rent for a year to take long term capital gains he has accompanying problems that he may not want to handle. Without a doubt, this is one of the most difficult problems and is one of the main reasons why I've written this book. I will discuss tax benefits of investing with a new approach in Chapter 9.

Problem #4
Rentals

On a cash-out investment, all of the profits must be claimed. But in order to save on taxes some people retain their properties for a year to take advantage of long term capital gain. Of course a house, or larger unit, can't sit vacant for one year—the payment would destroy most investment plans. The only alternative to this approach is to become a landlord with all of its problems and headaches. As a landlord I realized that this was just another problem that I wanted to avoid. (For more information on renting see Chapter 8.)

Problem #5
Cash-Out Promises

Another problem is that of "balloon" payments. This happens when the seller absolutely wants his cash, but is willing to sell on contract with the whole balance (or a portion of it) due after a certain length of time. Ostensibly this doesn't sound bad, but I have seen many people not able to sleep at night because they felt so out of control. (This could be compared to the story I told about my banker "friend.") No one knows what the economy will be like when the balance becomes due—whether it be a few months or a few years. You may be able to stay in control if the balloon payment is not an extremely large amount or if you have enough assets which you can use anytime.

My advice here would be not to make any promises you're not certain you can keep, because you could lose that investment, and a lot more.

Problem #6
Inflation

Inflation itself is not really a problem when dealing in real estate. The problem that concerned me was, as an inexperienced investor, I centered my investment plans on it. Inflation can't be controlled, therefore it's one of the problems I feel needs to be mentioned in this chapter. There were times I would invest in property with high hopes that it would increase in value just so much by a certain time. When that time came, I found myself in a dilemma because inflation didn't always do what I expected it to do. If I was counting on inflation to meet my promises, I was counting on something I couldn't control. Even if it increased beyond my expectations I learned that this equity growth was not the same as cash—no matter what the increase. In other words, selling the property and getting at some cash is better than hanging on and hoping that inflation will increase your equity.

I got tired of being controlled by this uncertainty, so, as I considered the profits in a piece of property, I only allowed inflation to be the icing on the cake.

Instead of trying to make money hoping that inflation will do what I want, I'd much rather find a good deal on a house. A deal to me is one where the owner *must* sell (for whatever reason), or a house that needs a good cleaning (I'm surprised at how many people turn these down), or one that needs minor repair and cosmetics. This way, I am in control.

Conclusion

There seems to be a direct ratio between the amount of investing most people do and the control they relinquish to someone else.

With someone else in control the investor is playing an "away" game on *their* field and by *their* rules. An investor needs to play "home" games on *his* field and by *his* rules so he can control his money.

During the first year of my investing I was involved with all these problems—FHA/VA, banks, high taxes, rentals (tenants), and balloon commitments. These were the "away" team and I was way out of my league. I needed a new ball game with a new set of rules that would let me be a winner. The name of the game is: **AVOID COSTLY ENTANGLEMENTS,** which will be referred to throughout this book as A.C.E.

Chapter 2

The Solution

HAVE you ever been up against a brick wall? There's no budging it! That's the way I felt when dealing with the problems mentioned in the last chapter. I suppose I could have continued and I might have succeeded, but I kept thinking that there had to be a better way. I didn't have all the answers, but I knew enough to know that I wanted more out of my investing.

The investment plan I wanted had to answer the following questions:

1. Could I be in *control?* I didn't want any banks or government agencies telling me what, when, or where I could buy or sell.

2. Would it *build* a money machine that would give me a *continuous* monthly income?

3. Would I be able to *slow down* later? I needed something that would keep growing with relatively little effort.

4. Would it give me and my family *security?*

5. Could I *measure* my net worth and see my growth (without someone else's appraisals and conjectures)?

6. Could I leave my assets behind for my family? I needed something that would be:
   a. steady
   b. inflation resistant
   c. able to increase with little effort
   d. easy to handle

7. Could I spread my assets around and not have them tied up in just a few properties or in one place?

8. Could I do it quickly, taking advantage of current prices and conditions?

9. Would I need to know everything there is to know about real estate or could I concentrate everything, even my learning, so that I could become effective?

10. Would it challenge me and be exciting?

I looked at what I had done with my first nine properties and at what other investors were doing. I realized that if I kept going that way it would be a long hard road to meet my goals. Sure I had made money, but I also paid a lot of taxes and was concerned about the future. The money I did make was at a great time cost. Then I asked the question, "What else could I be doing with my money or time?" The answer pointed me in the direction of reaching my goals.

Simply stated, the solution was **TO BUY AND SELL ON CONTRACT—ALL THE TIME.** If it sounds too easy to be true, it is—easy, I mean, and that's the truth! My properties and contracts have proven this approach to investing.

When I was forced with the decision of whether or not to sell another house FHA I had to make a decision on what direction I wanted to go.

Had I sold the house FHA I would have received about $12,000 five to six months down the road. My figures showed that I could sell the house on contract, get the down payment, invest it *again and again* and, in the same time period, make it mushroom into $150,000 in equities which would *net* me $1,200 a month from the monthly payments. This idea demanded testing. It was a race to see what I could do with the next five months.

At first, business was as usual. I took a $4,000 down payment and used it as a down payment and fix-up costs on the next house. Within a week I had it back on the market. It sold for $10,000 more than what I had paid for it and on the resale I received $6,000 down. I also created an equity of $6,000 with a net income of $60 a month. It was five weeks from the day I made my offer to *buy* the house until the day I *closed* it. Incredible you ask? Not at all. Many investors have done this before; the difference is that I committed myself to doing it this way continually.

If you'll remember, the previous chapter tells a story of my playing "away" games and being out of my league. I wanted to take on someone my own size. After this deal I realized who that someone should be—not the banks, not the government, but other people— people who were having *people* problems. If I could work with *people* I stood a much better chance of controlling my progress.

There were four months left to see how many more times I could do it. With this $6,000 I paid some bills and purchased two more houses. Because we were dealing with people, and not institutions, we closed each of these transactions within two weeks.

I had an offer from someone wanting to purchase one of these houses, even before I signed the final purchase papers. They offered only $500 more down than what I had put down, but they were willing to pay $6,000 more than what I had just paid. I accepted their offer.

The other house needed a cleaning job. In addition, it also had a few broken windows, and the yard was atrocious. Within four days it was manicured and ready to sell. That weekend I took an offer and closed the deal the following Wednesday. Both of these houses were also sold within two weeks, only this time around I had $8,000 cash from the down payments and I had created another $17,000 in equities with $150 a month coming in from these two contracts.

I was back out looking for more houses to buy, and over the next three months I repeated this process eleven more times. I don't want to bog down this chapter with the specifics of these transactions; I'll cover many case histories in the following chapters.

At the end of the five months I had about $151,000 in equities and I was netting $1,290 per month. This investment idea passed the test with flying colors. (See chart below.)

Let's see how it answered my previous questions:

Solution # 1
Control

As you can see from the preceding stories, dealing with people let me bypass growth steps that I would have had to go through if I had dealt with banks, etc. I controlled everything and I could sleep at nights without worrying.

Solutions # 2 and # 3
Spin Off Income / Keep Growing

As you can see, each of these properties (contracts) was giving me a net *spendable* monthly income. With a little creativity I knew that eventually the plan would support itself. The hardest aspect of what I wanted out

A.C.E.

Avoid Costly Entanglements

			Accumulated:	
			Equity	**Monthly Payment**
1st Month Start $4,000	Selling Price $30,000 Purchase Price 20,000 Capital Improvement 2,000 Profit $ 8,000	Results: $24,000 Receivable 18,000 Payable $ 6,000 Equity $ 60 Per Month	6,000	60
2nd Month Start $6,000	$26,000R 18,000P 8,000E $70.00 per month	$20,500R 11,500P 9,000E $80.00 per month	+ 17,000 = 23,000	+150 210
3rd Month Start $8,000	$29,000R 21,000P 8,000E $65 per month / $35,000R 25,000P 10,000E $80 per month	$45,000R 25,000P 15,000E $125 per month	+ 33,000 = 56,000	+270 480
4th Month Start $10,000	$39,000R 25,000P 14,000E $125 per month / $42,000R 30,000P 12,000E $100 per month	$44,000R 34,000P 10,000E $80 per month / $28,000R 17,000P 9,000E $75 per month	+ 45,000 +101,000	+375 +855
5th Month Start $12,000 (Excess of $8,000)	$37,000R 18,000P 19,000E $185 per month / $40,000R 24,000P 16,000E $130 per month	$20,000R 13,000P 7,000E $55 per month / $19,000R 11,000P 8,000 $65 per month	+ 50,000 $151,000	+435 $1,290

R = receivable contract   P = payable contract

of a plan was accomplished—that is to have a perpetual monthly income and to have these assets spinoff enough income so I could slow down. The equities between my receivables and my payables did keep growing. (This will be discussed in detail in Chapter 10.)

Solution # 4
Security

The fourth aspect was another aspect that I thought would be very difficult because:

A. Questions about the economy kept coming up.

B. Rental units had their advantages (which I'll cover in Chapter 8), but it wasn't steady enough and dealt in too many variables. I found that the contracts provided me with everything I was looking for. They were secured by real property. In every case the person making me payments had something to lose if he walked away. (This is an incentive for them to keep up their payments.)

Solution # 5
Measure

In real estate I've never found any form better for measuring your net worth than with contracts. I had receivables, (overriding contracts) payables, (underlying contracts, mortgages, deeds of trust, etc.) monthly payments, and a way to delay my taxes. (See Chapter 9 for details.) I could measure to the penny what my net worth was.

Solution # 6
Leaving Assets for My Family

Probably the aspect that gives me the most peace of
mind is the way this plan answers this question. It is
answered by:

A. The steadiness of the monthly income (the bills
come in every month and it's nice to know they would
be paid if something happened to me).

B. The amount would increase as the underlying
mortgages were paid off, plus purchasing more contracts is relatively simple (see the last chapter) and my
family could have my "team" help them to do this. Setting up collections through a good contract collection
agency is a way to make contracts easy to handle—my
family would just receive one check. See back of book
for details.

Solution # 7
Spreading the Assets

The answer to question # 7 is yes. As a matter of fact,
I've found that in order to keep up the speed of the plan
I had to stay where the biggest market of buyers and
sellers were. I would have gone for one big unit, but
instead I processed five smaller ones in the same time
and spread out my assets and liabilities.

Solution # 8
Do It Quickly

The results of my actual investing proved to me that it
could be done. How well it has worked in tight money

conditions shows that it is a tenable plan—a great one for the times.

Solution # 9
Being Effective

In Chapter 17 I talk about being a monomaniac. Success comes from targeting your efforts. I might not have had the success I did have, had not my efforts been zeroed-in on this one method. The simple aspect of believing in the plan and working to make it succeed created lucrative opportunities.

Solution # 10
Challenging and Exciting

Because this approach to investing answers the last nine questions so well it is probably the most exciting thing I have ever done. When you've tried it and experienced the growth you, too, will agree.

Keep on Track

This investment approach does not preclude you from handling your houses in other ways, but I find almost strict adherence to this plan will bring success. Once again, my approach is to process houses by always buying and selling on contract. Once in a while you will be tempted to deviate from this. If you do, make sure your reasoning is sound. For example:

I found a fixer-upper for $30,000 with $3,000 down. By putting $1,000 into it I thought I could get the value up to $37,000 (an additional $4,000 would get it to $45,000). Following my own method I should have sold the house for $37,000—getting $4,000 down—and going onto the next one. But I thought that finding another good deal would be too hard, so I decided to pour in the other $4,000 and gamble that I could get all $8,000 back when I sold the house for $45,000. Let's look at what happened to my thinking: (Usually in my seminars, I catch a lot of people smiling when I list the following. I think a lot of people have been here before.)

1. I felt that, because I had put so much money into the house, I was justified in asking $50,000. The problem is the increase in purchase price made it harder to sell.

2. Consequently, I had to make three more house payments before I could find a buyer.

3. I ceased to look for other good deals because my time was taken up and my money was gone.

4. To get my money back ($8,000), I had to require almost 20 percent down, thus limiting the amount of people that could possibly buy it.

5. I was left with having to sell it to some people who got conventional financing, and it took over six weeks to close. Also, I lost whatever else my money could have been doing for me, plus I lost the right to claim my profit by the installment sales method.

Make Decisions from a Position of Strength

Once time and money were depleted in this project, I started making decisions from a position of weakness. Most wrong decisions are made at such a time. *A house will take control of you when a chunk of you is in it.* I thought this house would be the exception to the rule, but look what happened to my thinking process once I was deeply committed.

THE REAL ESTATE MONEY MACHINE

Get in control! Traditional concepts are okay, but a real punch is needed to quickly build up a lot of cash flow.
BIG PROFITS ARE REALIZED WHEN WE SELL!

I. Try to assume everything:

Example:

What you do:

1. Assume the first
2. Assume the second
3. Create third mortgage (deed of trust) to pay sellers equity
4. Spend $1,000 and fix-up

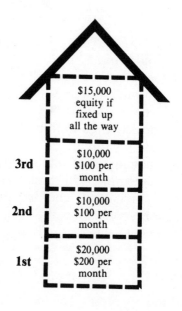

3rd	$10,000 $100 per month
2nd	$10,000 $100 per month
1st	$20,000 $200 per month

$15,000 equity if fixed up all the way

Purchase Price	$42,000
with down payment of	2,000
loans payable at $400 per month	$40,000

II. Now sell on a wrap around. Try to get all of your down payment, fix-up cost, and closing cost back.

House worth $55,000, but let's sell for $53,000 with $3,000 down.

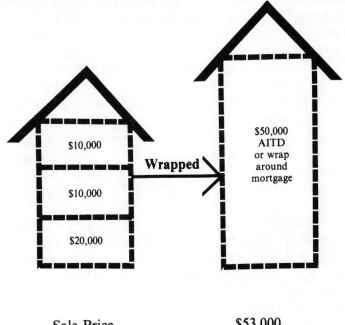

Sale Price	$53,000
Down Payment	3,000
Note Receivable at $500 per month	$50,000

RESULTS:

A. Down payment returned and ready to go to work again.
B. $10,000 equity note created
C. $100 a month coming in. This will increase as senior loans pay off.
D. We're in control. All payments—coming and going are funneling through us.

After a few years of using this new approach the results were electrifying. Suppose you could maintain buying and selling about two houses a month (it's easier than you think). It would mean that within two years you would have a net worth of just under $500,000 with an approximate net yearly income of $40,000. Before I write what the figures would be like in five years, let me state again—I was after the income that a million dollars could give me. All I needed to do was create the equities that would give me that kind of income. Sure enough, within five years there would be equities of approximately one million dollars and the net yearly income would be over $80,000 or $219 a day—including Saturday and Sunday.

I know this investment idea can bring you as much growth as it did me. The following chapters offer much of what I have learned over the past several years. It is given as support for this plan, constantly keeping in mind the ten questions, and the need to "avoid costly entanglements."

Chapter 3

". . . Act, Act in the Living Present . . ."

THERE IS one quality that I've noticed in all successful people and that is the ability to make decisions and be willing to take risks. "He who hesitates is lost," is too harsh for investors because there's always another deal. It is true to a certain degree, though, because there is only a certain time period that deals can be acted upon. An investor has to be ready to move—sometimes on gut feelings. A few times, good deals ended up not being quite what I anticipated, but in my worst deal of 45 transactions, I made over $4,000. I'm not saying that I couldn't have lost on any deal, but anyone who understands the fundamentals—and several alternatives—will not lose. (Unless there is really a bust in the economy, but even prophets of doom are buying real estate.)

Let me compare investing to a torpedo. Once the enemy ship is in range, the torpedo is fired. The currents affect it and the enemy ship moves, but the torpedo stays on target. Why? Because it's constantly sending out radar signals that bounce back. When the torpedo receives this new information, it adjusts and corrects its direction. The battle would be disastrous if the captain of the ship said, "Why waste the torpedo? The ship will probably move and the current may be too strong for it," or gave a hundred other reasons.

Life is like this, but to the investor, waiting can be cruel. If a person wastes time trying to gather all of the facts, the deal will be snapped up by someone willing to move on it, having only the general facts and a feeling about the place.

One occasion I saw a house for sale for $22,000. I called immediately and made an appointment to see it the next morning at 10:00 A.M. I made my offer which was $20,000 with $1,000 down. He wanted $2,000 down, so I agreed to pay him an additional $1,000 in a year. We drew up the papers and went to the title company to have them notarized. While we were there I checked the status of title and seeing everything was okay, we recorded and said our goodbyes. I went back over to the house a few hours later and there were five or six people in the kitchen. I said, "Hi, can I help you?" They asked me if I was the owner and I said I was. Then they said they were the ones that had called the night before and would like to make me an offer. I said "Oh, I'm not that owner. I just bought the house a few hours ago."

To say the least, they were quite stunned when I showed them the papers. They couldn't believe it because they couldn't understand 1) how it could be done so quickly, and 2) why I was willing to buy a place that needed so much work—at least without getting bids to do the work.

These people had apparently come over the night before and, feeling good about the place, called a few contractor friends. That explained the other people in the kitchen. They were taking a magnifying glass to the house.

The man said, "But how could you buy it with all the work that needs to be done under the kitchen sink?" I asked him how much he thought the house was worth. He replied, "About $30,000." I told him I agreed. Then I asked him how much he would pay for it. He said about $20,000. I showed him that figure on the contract. Then I asked him how much it would take to repair under the sink and he said, "$500." I asked if he needed a contractor to tell him that—(he didn't want to answer because that particular contractor was standing right there). I told him I estimated that the plumbing under the sink would cost the $500 but I was going to put in a new counter top and sink which would bring the total repair to $1,000. I concluded with the question, "So what if I only make $8,000 instead of $9,000 on the house?" He stood there scratching his head.

On another occasion I was standing in the yard of a vacant house with my heart pounding. This property was in foreclosure and I could get it at a fantastic price. I thought to myself, I've made between $8,000–$10,000 on all of my deals up until now. If this lady, the former owner, comes to sign these papers, I am going to make up to $20,000 on this house! Even though I had not seen the inside of the house (except through the windows) everything looked fine. (I had some questions though—I couldn't tell whether it had three or four bedrooms, or how many bathrooms it had, nor could I tell if it had a full basement.

I made an appointment to meet this lady at the bank at 10:30 A.M. and sign in front of a notary public. I left the house and drove across town, arriving about 15 minutes early. I sat there in my truck and waited. I tried to read a magazine but couldn't concentrate because my heart was still beating too hard. I started getting really nervous when it was 10:30 and she still wasn't there. I started thinking that she might not even show because she knew she wasn't getting anything out of this except ridding herself of the hassles of being foreclosed on. After waiting about 15 more minutes, with my heart sinking, I started to get really depressed. I thought this would be my one chance of breaking over the top and have enough money coming in each month to live fairly comfortably.

I decided to wait just a few minutes more. At ten to eleven I reached for the keys to leave, then I heard a knock on my window. I looked and rolled down the window as she said "Are you the man that is interested in the house on Adams Street?" I said, "I sure am," and I almost knocked her over getting out of the truck. I had the papers all filled out and had previously checked the title status to see if there were any other liens on it.

I was ready for her to sign. She showed her I.D. to the bank officer and signed the papers. After he notarized them we walked out. I said, "Listen, are you sure you don't want anything for the house?" She told me she didn't. I said, "Well, when you purchased it a few years ago you put $98 down. How about if I at least give you your $98 back?" She said, "Okay," so I gave her a check for the $98.

I jumped in the truck and was singing and hollering all the way back to the house with the keys in my pocket. As I walked through the house I was pleasantly surprised. It was a five-bedroom house, instead of the three or four bedrooms I'd expected. It had two full baths and a full basement. All this took up the value of the home and I figured it would sell for a price in the $50,000 price range with $5,000 down.

I called some people who were looking for a house like this and they agreed to meet me there that afternoon. Because the house did need some new carpeting, the people offered me only $4,000 down, so they could keep the other $1,000 for carpeting. I accepted their offer. We sat there and drew up the earnest money agreement, took it to the escrow company and three days later we closed the transaction. They moved in the following weekend.

This is a deal where I put about $2,000 out of my pocket, (to cure the back payments) and took a little time to check the title status of the property. I took over loans on the house of about $17,200. When I sold it for $4,000 down, I had net monthly payments coming in of $140. Had I waited to gather all the facts, the foreclosure proceedings on this house would have finalized. The risk was there, but so were the profits.

Volume Breeds Higher Volume

Moving on deals like this quickly put me into a different category. I knew that speed was important so I hired a few employees and a subcontractor to do the work on some of these houses. Each house was a race against time.

Right when I decided to slow down, a Realtor called and said she knew of eight good houses. I told her I was too busy and couldn't handle any more, but she persuaded me to go look. We spent the afternoon checking them out, and I made offers on all eight. Because I was so busy, and only wanted to handle them if the deals were *really* right, my offers were almost ridiculous.

She went to work and within three days she had five of them locked up. Two others had minor changes that didn't affect the deals very much, and the last one was sold by the time she got there.

I knew that I needed a big exit if I was going to buy this many. I needed to be able to sell them quickly (some of them needed to be sold before I finished buying them). When she told me I was the proud new owner of seven more houses, I was shocked. At first I didn't know what to do—I never thought they would accept. Now I had to work quickly so I could turn them into profits.

Before I tell you what I did with them, let me tell you some of the terms on the seven houses. My average down payment was about four percent. They let me assume over $100,000 in less than eight percent money—$40,000 of it was less than six percent. Not one house had a "due on sale clause;" for that matter, there weren't any clauses that would restrict me when I went to sell them, either.

Five of the seven houses were livable right then, needing very little work, and all five of them were sold within three weeks. The other two took two months to fix up and sell. When they were all sold I had $84,000 in equities and was netting $750 a month. I paid the realtor out of some of the down payments and I still had $6,000 cash left over.

The tide rose in my life right then and I felt it was time to ride it. I was able to squeeze in all this excess activity because I learned how to process and sell them. That was information that is still valuable today and no book anywhere contains it. One learns it out there by doing.

Let me illustrate this point: I had a friend who wanted to do what I was doing so he spent a week with me. During that week I rented one apartment and one house, put ads in the paper to sell two houses, looked at ten more houses to buy and made earnest monies on four and bought two of them, evicted a tenant, met with three subcontractors on a number of jobs, fired an employee and hired a new one and towards the end of the week I picked up a house on foreclosure for about one-third of its value.

At about 4:30 P.M. on Friday we walked out of the courthouse where we recorded several deeds and I said, "Well that's about it—you've seen what I do." He clasped his hands together and said, "Boy! I've got to take some college classes and learn how to do this!" I looked at him and smiled, knowing that he missed the whole point. There isn't such a class—you learn by doing, by acting, by taking chances and by being aggressive.

To summarize this chapter I'll quote the last stanza from the poem that started this chapter.

> "Let us then be up and doing
> with a heart for any fate . . .
> Still achieving, still pursuing
> learn to labor and to wait."
>
> WILLIAM WORDSWORTH
> *A Psalm of Life*

Chapter 4

This One's On the House

FOR the past two years, I have had the distinct pleasure of traveling the width and breadth of this country. In every city, there are people really trying to get ahead. Some trying to make a little extra to cover bills, some looking imminently at retirement and almost all discouraged by the huge tax bite taken out of their paychecks.

I've listened to their problems, their concern and their success. I've seen literally hundreds, possibly thousands become wealthy. Everyone did so by taking his own life into his hands and making things happen. Nobody handed any of these people anything on a silver platter. They worked hard for everything. The free enterprise system is alive and well for anyone enterprising enough to stick his neck out.

I hope that I have been a help to some people. My original goal in turning to this field of education was to help people see new ideas, try new avenues and find a more excellent way of doing things. People from all over have consulted with me by phone, in letters and in person and I take this responsibility very seriously. I've always tried to make sure what I teach and write is useful, pertinent information.

Often times I'm asked, "What do I do now?" "I've heard you and I'm excited Mr. Cook, what do I do first?" "Mr. Cook, can you give us some advice in just a few words?" To all these questions, there must be one good answer. Yes, every person is different but is there one piece of advice that underlies and gives support and direction to everything else we do.

Think Big

I've searched long and hard for such an idea. I've watched the good, the bad and the ugly that real estate investors go through. Finally I thought I was getting close in the early part of 1983, but before I wrote about it I wanted to try it out on audiences in many states. I really got into this idea and my desire to express it sharpened as the economy started to recover. People are confused. "Is now the time?" "When do we get started?" "What area of investment is best right now?"

The idea was well received. It is not for the high rollers but for the average person who wants his actions to mean something. And I've also discovered it was consistent with everything else that I've been writing and teaching about. It's amazing how the puzzle fits together. Well here it is in all its simple glory. THINK BIG IN A WHOLE BUNCH OF SMALL WAYS.

Many of you have heard me and know the emphasis I put on the "Z" of any system. The Z is the end, the retirement. It is where we want to end up. Once we know where we want to be, we can set up systems to get us there. The "think big" of this idea is that, but a little more. We need to think ahead. Plan and then work. We need to know what we want each property to do for us. How it fits and what we are trading off by buying, renting or selling it. The alternative to thinking big isn't a very comforting thought.

I can only say that in this book, because I can pretty well guess the type of person who is reading this book. Many people are content to live mundane lives or to be victims rather than participants in life. But not you. You want to get ahead as fast and cautiously as you can and I commend you for your desires.

Thinking big—at least dreaming big is a way of life. It's easy to get bogged down and lose sight of our goals, but we are in control of our destiny and that's the place we need to be. So let's make the most of it. Thinking big is what gets us out of bed earlier in the morning and it's the element of our character that gets people to follow us. You'll learn quickly how important those other people are. Think high and fly.

The Numbers Game

The next part of the idea is the "whole bunch" concept. Whatever you're doing successfully is strengthened by doing it time and time again. The one thing that I've learned about business success is that there are no secrets. Success is achieved by obedience to certain principles. There are hundreds of laws but they all fit into three categories: 1) Fill a need; 2) Hard work/ hard thinking; 3) Play the numbers game.

This third idea is what I want to write about the most. It doesn't matter what business you are into, all you need to do is figure out the numbers game for that business and you'll be a success—eventually. Once you've figured out the game, then figure out your *modus operandi* and get to work making it happen.

You've probably all heard something like: I look at 15 houses, make offers on 6 and buy one. The numbers may change but the concept is the same. You cannot control the "one," only the fifteen. If you want the "one" to happen you have to look at the fifteen and make offers on the six.

Playing the numbers game also keeps you in control. You're not just spending all your time looking and negotiating on one house but on many. The good deals will come.

What does this mean in the context of this book? I will present many ideas in this book on the beauty of investing in single family houses. I'll explore extensively the idea of creating systems and only doing that which can be duplicated. It is sufficient to say here that repetition breeds success. No athlete will ever win a gold medal without first doing the training exercises time and time again, beforehand.

I read a statement by the president of Whamo (Hula hoops-frisbees) that I like. I do like making money though so I'll temper what he said a little for myself. He said, "I'd rather lose money and know how I lost it than make money and not know how I made it." Pretty heavy stuff, and meaningful to us as we realize the importance of being able to analyze what we do.

If we are doing a whole bunch of things and creating systems that help us duplicate our successes then we have a jump on our future. Not only is the repetition bringing in money but doing whatever repetitiously allows us the opportunity to refine the system. It gets better and easier with practice.

Let's get down to the end of the ideas—"small ways." I think we're all convinced that real estate is the best vehicle for wealth accumulation. (If not then may I suggest your reading *Real Estate: The Best Game in Town,* formerly entitled *Real Estate on Trial,* by this same author.) We need more real estate to solve our problems. Thinking big doesn't mean think about big deals. It means thinking of attainable goals, which means attainable properties that help us accomplish our goals.

For those people who ask me questions about where to start and what to do, I answer emphatically, "Invest in single family houses." Single Family Houses (SFH) or small rental units should be the backbone of our investing. All the following chapters answer the whys and hows and what nows.

I sincerely hope these ideas bring back into focus so many of the ideas that have left people befuddled. Now is the time to be investing. Suit up and it's time to hit the waves—not tidal waves but the little ones that we can handle. Think big in a whole bunch of small ways.

Why Single Family Residences?

It would be good to ask the question: Why single family houses? There are many good answers—many are pat but most are well founded and thought out. We'll explore those answers, but it would be beneficial for you, not to mention cautious on my part, to admit that there are many great forms of investment. An investment is as good or bad as the problems it solves or creates for the investor.

With this in mind the first question that needs answering is not "why" but "for whom does the doorbell ring?" If you have lots of money and are in a "preserving mode" then single family houses may not be for you, although you'll see several aspects of investing in SFH that will help even you. If you are in a growing

mode or accumulating mode then read on, these words
are for you.

Let's break investors into two groups: big and small.
The big investor hopefully is usually where he is because he or she has accumulated too much. He may be
on to bigger things. Notice I didn't say "bigger and
better" because most big investors are where they are
because a lot of small investments were used as stepping stones. Moving from these investments to other
investments is usually a matter of time management.
Once wealthy, the return on one's money is great but
only in a dollar sense. The rate of return is probably not
as great. This is as it should be. No sense monkeying
around in the minors if you're ready for the majors (but
please read on).

The other investor is the small investor and all the
rest of us fit into this category. We are they who need
more income, more wealth accumulation and more tax
write offs. We've read a book or two on how to get
ahead. We may be making $10,000 a year or $100,000 a
year and it's still not enough. Our investment assets are
usually under $100,000 but more commonly in the
$150,000 range.

I'm writing this chapter to those people or companies
who need to grow as fast as possible with as little cash
involvement and risk as possible.

Now to get to the why of single family residences.
The first reason is an outgrowth of the fact that there are
more small investors than large. If I can establish the
fact that Single Family Residences are good for the small
investor (and that will be easy to do) then it naturally
follows that investor demands for SFR's helps increase
their value, even causes them to be a great investment
in all other SFR areas.

The demand for such dwelling goes much further
than just investor demand. Indeed this demand is an

after effect of most people's desire to own their own piece of earth. I think most people are aware of this so I won't belabor it here. The simple phrase "they ain't making no more land" will suffice.

But why single family residences rather than multi-family residences? The next reason hones in even more on the small investor's own knowledge and locale. It's just down the street. It's next door or across town. It's easy to quickly gain a working knowledge of areas, prices, and institutions to deal with. It's everywhere and good deals are everywhere. I've covered this subject extensively in *Real Estate: The Best Game in Town* (formerly entitled *Real Estate on Trial*) and the gist of my writing there was that you can be in control. You're not waiting for the Dow Jones Chemical average to come out or the London Gold exchange to close to know how you're doing.

This aspect of investing for the small investor means even more when this idea is added to the fact that most small investors already know a great deal about real estate. Most people have bought and sold a few of their own houses. If not, they have been tenants. All of us are surrounded every day with the good and the bad of real estate investing.

But whatever the case, we've gotten some training and though many of us have not done anything about it as investors this knowledge will only help. And one other point pops out here. Because so many people know a little about real estate a lot of them invest in small ways. There is a lot of movement. Even when times are sluggish as they have been the past few years there was some movement and many fortunes being made.

If this book is to be successful it must be timely and the most timely aspect of all that I've written in the past several paragraphs is that the demand for individual housing is still there. Obviously the culprit in slowing down housing was high interest rates. Look what happens when long term mortgage rates get close to 12 percent. If and when interest rates hit down to around 10 percent and under this demand will show its head like never before. Bad times force people to get smart and the one thing everyone learns is that congress loves real estate. This has extensive applications for the investor.

The homeowner realizes these savings and so does the real estate investor. The underlying fact that this demand exists, and the continuing fact that unless Americans change the value they put on ownership this demand will always exist, makes real estate the best possible form of investment—bar none. And the smaller the unit the greater the number of people wanting it. Single family residences stand head and shoulders above its closest competitor.

More Benefits

There are many other areas of discussion that explain further the benefits of investing in single family residences.

- A whole industry is set up that deals with single family residences. Bankers, builders, real estate people, title and escrow people, lawyers and CPA's; not to mention the industry that supplies material and services. This helps the small investor greatly. Prices are protected. Laws are created. Tax incentives are installed. These businessmen need each other. Anything you need to know is yours for the asking.
- With the current creative purchase techniques in practice today—especially those that let you maximize the laws of leverage—an investor can buy several different

properties to solve different problems. He can buy a
duplex for tax write-offs, three houses to build cash flow
on the money machine concept, and a four-plex to fix up
and cash out of. It's great to be so diverse with so little
money.

· Once you have purchased many, you learn many ways
to keep doing it. We need to be able to analyze our
methods. The only way to do that is to only do things
that can be duplicated. I'm not saying to only buy du-
plexes or three bedroom houses, but to set up systems
that can be recreated. For example: every morning from
7 to 8 A.M. you will look at the paper for good deals and
at least call on five ads. Every afternoon from 2 to 4 P.M.
you will meet with an agent to look at and make offers
on properties. It may be enough at first but when you
can refine these systems, success is on the way. No area
of investing lets us do this better than single family residences. And once you get the goose that lays the golden
egg don't kill it by changing.

· The last point that I'll mention here is that once you own
any investment and then decide to unload it you need to
have all of your options open for doing just that. With
SFR you can cash out and get your equity, trade your
equity for a different property—perhaps a larger unit
that you can start depreciating over at the new price.
Maybe you want income without the rental headaches
so you take your equity on a note. This way is also good
if receiving the cash would force you into a higher tax
bracket. You could lease it on a long term lease option
and hold onto the tax write-offs but possibly get higher
than average rents in the meantime.

If you need cash you may want to refinance and pull
out your money that way. Later on you can sell, trade,
refinance again. You may even want to keep it as is and
try to get the rents; if so, all of these other things are
better if and when they do happen. You have so many
things that can be done, regardless. So many other peo-

ple want your little investment so they can do the same thing.

Yes, these aspects are available on larger units but for the small investor these small properties will allow him to build up assets faster, and take advantage of these diverse reasons for owning and selling more than anything else. Think big in a whole bunch of small ways and think big in a whole bunch of diverse ways.

Chapter 5

You Have to Buy Right to Sell Right

HOW ANGRY would you be if your foundation collapsed and your house was ruined? A proper foundation is essential to buildings. It is also essential to any investment plan. Investing in real estate can do one of three things: It either saves money (on depreciation expense, tax shelter, etc.) or makes money (by finding good deals, improvements, inflation, etc.), but if the proper foundation is not laid, you could lose money.

If the following conversation happened in a store we would applaud the store owner.

"But nobody buys anchovies anymore."

"Come on, you only have to order a case to get this special price and they'll never be at this price again."

"I don't care what price they're at—nobody buys them, so I don't want them."

The salesman leaves. The store owner *maintained control*—he knows what sells and what doesn't. Should investing in real estate be any different? Should we be any different than this store owner and not know the *exit* before we go in at the *entrance?* Investing in real estate demands that we do know the exit. If not, then we will flounder, and not move deliberately and quickly enough to succeed.

Let's compare the selling of the property to getting a rebound in basketball. After all, the house is on the rebound. You need to be in the right place to get an offensive rebound to make a basket. In real estate there are several things you can do to get yourself in a wrong place—a place where it's hard to shoot from. Then you might have to: 1) take a bad shot, 2) pass off, 3) lose the ball. The best thing to do in real estate, like basketball, is to eliminate the obstacles.

The foundation to my idea is simple and solid. George Washington probably said it best when he said, ". . . avoid costly entanglements." Most investment formulas that I've read keep the aspirin companies in business. But by following this advice we will all have fewer headaches.

Avoid Promises You Can't Keep

The most common costly entanglement is making promises that can't be kept. Don't think that you have to buy everything you see—good deals are always there. If a certain house has an uncertain future—avoid it. The most common promise (which will cause a foreclosure if not kept) is agreeing to pay additional cash at some future time. This is not too bad if all your bases are covered, but if you are relying on some future event, especially inflation, or the hopes that banks will have more money next year, then you might end up behind the eight ball. I've been there several times.

One time I found a house for the really low price of

$10,000. I was to give them $1,000 down and $90 a month on contract. At the last moment they received an offer for $10,000 cash. I thought I was going to lose it (I knew the house would be worth $30,000 all fixed up) so I offered them $15,000 if I could pay them in one year, and pay nothing down at the beginning. They accepted. $5,000 additional dollars sounded good to them. I got the house habitable and rented it. When it came time to really fix it up and get it sold to cash them out, I didn't have the money. They started legal proceedings. I was finally able to save it and make a little, but it was a totally unenjoyable experience. As a matter of fact, looking back over the several years of my investing, every really bad experience I had was when I committed myself to performing in a market I couldn't control.

Short vs. Long

It reminds me of a football game where all the pass receivers go short, the quarterback drops back and passes long—and no pass is completed.

Property investments are usually for the long run, not the short run. If an investor gets caught borrowing short and selling long, he will get trapped. Or if he invests his short term money into long term projects he will soon run out of cash.

Many times I would borrow fix-up money from a bank. Almost invariably something would go wrong. Some delay—some change, that I had no control over. The loan would become due and I would have to get extensions and sell other properties. It got to the point that I wanted no short term money. It caused too many headaches.

I know this sounds harsh. After all, there are all kinds of books on using OPM (other people's money). If you are just getting started, go ahead, but be careful. Remember, *their expectations* are probably different than *your expectations*. Stay in control. Be prudent. Promise only what you can control.

Proper Foundation—Part I

The number one concern is that the property is being purchased at a good price. You're investing to make money and build a future. Keep that in mind. If the price is too high—even if all the other factors are okay—reconsider the purchase. Does it fit into your plans?

If it needs to be resold quickly this requirement is compounded when you go to sell it. Selling quickly will happen only if you can resell it at a fair price—Selling where the biggest market (number) of buyers are—in the medium income housing bracket. If you can stay just below that it will sell easily. My economics professor had another good story. A little facetious but with a good lesson. He said, "If you want to be successful, sell food or women's shoes. Everyone needs to eat and the average American woman owns 26 pairs of shoes." He had thought about real estate because everyone needs shelter. His lesson is to go where the market is.

One other important point needs to be covered here. I'm a firm believer in not overcharging. When I price my houses, I leave enough room to raise the price if the prospective purchasers come in with less down. For instance, I had a house that was worth $50,000 tops. I put it up for $48,000 with $4,000 down. A young couple wanted it. They offered me $50,000 with $2,000 down. This *is* sound investing in that you're having to trade the other things your money could be doing for you and leave it tied up in the house—for a long time.

Don't Bury Your Cash

Buy with low down payment so you can sell at a fair price and recover your money. Don't compromise, hoping inflation will bail you out. Make sure it's worth your while. It takes a long time for great terms to make up for an overpriced house or too large of a down payment.

Keep your cash turning. Don't bury too much of it. In the preceding example I had put $3,500 into this property. Sure, I now had $9,000 in equity with $80 a month coming in, but I buried $1,500 of hard cash ($3,500 minus the $2,000 down payment). I went through a four month period when I did this seven times. I was putting too much emphasis on equities and not on what it takes to continue growth. By the end of this time I had run out of cash. It was all buried somewhere in equities.

Proper Foundation—Part II

Make sure all of the terms are agreeable and assumable.

Either on the Earnest Money Agreement or on the contract, you will make promises to the person selling you the property. He might want all kinds of things. Some of them might not seem bad at the point of purchase but at the point of selling they could destroy the deal.

Some glaring clauses to watch out for are:

1. Due on Sale clauses.
2. Payment Acceleration Clauses.
3. Clauses limiting your right to sell or encumber the property.
4. Usurious interest rates.
5. Excessive late payment penalties or early payoff penalties.

Most of these are reserved to the banks, but as they get more prevalent, many people begin to act like banks and want some of them. Read the details carefully, *even if you are told that it's a uniform contract.*

Proper Foundation—Part III

Payments should be kept low, as should interest rates. If someone wanted to change bank rates I would remind them that they weren't a bank and therefore should look at what the banks were paying, not charging. This is good advice. When selling the same basic principals should be followed. (I've met people who tried to get every last penny—they didn't last very long as investors.)

The process of deciding on the payment amount always starts with questions because nobody knows how much to give or take. If I'm asked, I say jokingly, "I would like to pay a dollar down a dollar a month for the rest of my life." It might sound stupid but at least he knows where I stand. Once again, if the interest rates and monthly payments are too high, (even assuming all else is okay), it will be hard to sell and generate any kind of cash flow. For instance, if you are paying $300 per month on a $20,000 loan and sell the house with a $30,000 balance with payments of $300, you'll have no cash flow (but a great equity growth). Only do this after you've built your income and have a lot of experience.

Proper Foundation—Part IV; Low Down

This can't be exaggerated enough. The more money you sink into a place, the less control you have over your selling options. Having to recover large amounts could even dictate to you the way you will have to sell, even when the taxes will kill you. Guard your cash.

Sometimes you'll need to rent. We'll cover that in Chapter 8—if you do, the best rentals (tax wise—leverage wise) are the ones with the least amount of money tied up.

Location in Perspective

The phrase "What's important to business? Location, Location, Location," takes on a semblance of importance, but it is so subjective that the only comment I'll make is this: anything will sell at the right price. Of course, different houses will sell for different prices in different parts of town, but profits can be made anywhere. I've made just as much in the poorer areas as I have in the wealthy areas. You should be aware of this intangible information and know what you are getting into.

Don't Make His Problem Your Problem

I went to look at a house that was for sale by a guy who had to "unload" it. He purchased it for $20,000 and started making extensive repairs. This may seem like a low price in light of today's prices, but the house was a wreck. Nothing worked, not the plumbing, electricity or heating. I realize really low prices are harder to find but they are out there and there are fewer people looking for them. He ripped out walls, started lowering the ceilings and began stripping all the trim back to the wood. To this point he had made it uglier in order to make it more beautiful, but it was uglier. He had already spent $5,000 fixing it up, but then ran out of time and money. After listening to this story I said, "Look, I really sympathize with you. I'm sorry that you read someone else's investment formula and then couldn't make it work, but the house is still worth only $20,000." That's what I offered. He wanted to try to sell it for more, but after two weeks he called back and accepted my offer. It would have been easy to let his problems become mine. We all want to help, but *I didn't want to make his problems my problems.*

Conclusion

In summary, get all the terms compatible with the ability to quickly resell the property. Even one catch or out of proportion promise could jeopardize you. If all the terms are not in line with your best interest, get on to something else—don't compromise.

Note

I have traveled extensively all over the country, and spoken before thousands of real estate investors. Many have asked if this same plan can be worked in today's market.

Before I answer this question let me preface the answer with this comment. When I travel to some states some people say the houses I talked about in the $30,000 to $60,000 range are too low. The next week I'm in middle America and people complain that I'm talking too high. Several people I know are buying 2 to 5 houses a month and have never paid over $25,000 for any of them.

Does it work? The answer is emphatically, "Yes." As a matter of fact, other investors are making what I've done look like kid's stuff. People have taken these ideas and started fresh or have used these ideas to fine-tune what they were already doing and done so well.

They have done it with nursing homes, shopping centers, apartment complexes, condominiums, and storage units. Several have devised ways to get back several thousand dollars on the down payment turn around.

It's like anything else; it is the active doer that achieves success. There are plenty of reasons for failing in real estate investments and many dwell on those reasons. They don't do anything but get good at excuses. Investors who continuously proceed will win the prize.

It is gratifying to see so much happening with these ideas. It worked for me and to see it work for others adds a special dimension.

Chapter 6

Tips on Buying—Part I

Give Them What They Want, But In A Different Way

A CONCEPT to help you buy right to sell right is *give them what they want, but in a different way*. This assumes that the purchase arrangements are not exactly compatible with your plans and rather than lose the deal you need some alternatives to present to the seller. Once again, your only limitation is your own imagination.

I developed this concept over a period of time by trial and error. Developing it was a necessity because deals slipped away when I couldn't satisfy the need of the seller.

A Seller That Knew What He Wanted, and Would Settle for Nothing Less

A case in point. One summer day I came across a fiveplex that was just what I wanted. The selling price should have been around $30,000, so when the seller said he would like to get $17–$19,000 out of it, I said,—"It does need a lot of work, but $17,000 sounds like a good price." "But I have to get $3,000 down," he demanded. I didn't have that much cash but this was no time to walk away. Stupified, I asked why, "Because I have $2,200 in back taxes on the place and I need $800 to pay some bills." Now, I had a bargaining point. In that county, taxes could be five years delinquent before there would be a tax sale. I had plenty of time before that so I asked, "Would it be okay if I pay the back taxes later and pay you the $800 now?" He said, "Okay, but I have to get $200 a month on the balance and not a penny less." "That's a good payment, but how would it be if I give you $150 a month for a year, then $175 a month for the next year and then $200 a month for the whole balance of the loan?" He said that was okay.

We drew up papers that weekend and it was mine for $800. I had given him what he wanted, but on terms compatible with my plans. And because I bought right, I got by putting a mere $2,000 into it, and after 15 months I sold it for $50,000 with $8,000 down. My payment coming in was $425 and the next year my payment going out was the $200.

He felt satisfied because he made me give him what he wanted. I hadn't disagreed with him, but had agreed quickly and then changed it a little to suit my plans.

The Seller Had Plans But Could Wait for the Money

Another time I received information about three houses for sale on one piece of property. The owner wanted $30,000 for all three, but she wanted too much down. I asked her why she needed so much and she said she was buying into a dog kennel partnership and would need $5,000 on January 1 of the next year to do it. Add that to the $2,000 for closing costs and the required down payment was at $7,000. She also had a $7,000 underlying loan with a $250 monthly payment at 8 percent interest. (This was too high a payment for that loan amount.)

After brain-storming with the realtor we came up with the following offer: The purchase price would be $27,000. I would pay the $2,000 up front. Then on December 1, I would pay the other $5,000. I would assume the $7,000 loan and pay her equity of $13,000 at $200 a month starting 30 days after the $7,000 loan was paid off. Interest at 9 percent would also start the day it was paid off. In other words, she would let $13,000 sit dormant for five or so years with no interest at all. She thought this was great and for her it was. First, she was going to get her money in time, and second, she wouldn't have to be a landlady anymore, which she hated.

The foundation was in place for a good resale. I put $3,000 into roof and minor repairs, and then sold all three a few months later for $59,000 with $5,000 down. Payments coming in were $550 per month. My payment was the $250. I could have used the $5,000 down payment to pay her off, but there were other uses for it right then, and there still were four months before December 1 rolled around. In November a few other deals fell through that I was to use to pay her. This contract was too good to sell but her money was due, so I had to sell it. The people that bought my contracts ate this one up. They couldn't believe $13,000 was sitting dormant. My equity was $34,000 which was the difference between my receivable of $54,000 and my payable of $20,000 ($7,000 + $13,000). I received $24,000 cash for this equity and after paying her $5,000 note we cleared $19,000.

Everybody—the lady, the realtors, my buyers and I got what we wanted—*just in different ways.*

Find Out Why They are Selling

People sell properties for good reasons. It's so important to find out the "why" behind their selling. You won't be able to offer alternatives until you know what they need. A friend of mine made an offer on a house that required $2,000 down which was more than he wanted to put into it.

Upon inquiring why that much was needed he found out that the seller wanted to get his daughter a car for about $1,000. He quickly offered his wife's car, which the man took as credit for $1,000. His wife was angry for a few weeks until he sold the house and bought her a newer station wagon which she loves. He also made enough to get two more houses.

Are There Alternatives to What They Think They Can Get?

A realtor called about a possible triplex. The zoning was right, and each possible unit had an outside entrance so it wouldn't take much to turn this turn-of-the-century house into three separate units. They wanted $22,000. I offered $20,000. I hadn't yet learned at this time to **assume all underlying loans,** so my financing was a straight contract payable at $175 per month. The morning it was to close I thought I'd be back home in an hour or so.

I arrived at the escrow company first and found out about an existing underlying loan which I hadn't known about. Then I found out she was having all kinds of financial problems. I wanted nothing to do with making a payment to her and then hope she would pay the underlying payment. (Even though there is plenty of protection against this in the contract, I just didn't want to be bothered with it.)

We changed the papers for me to assume the loan and pay her the difference. Her equity payments were going to be only $40 a month at 5 percent. Because the underlying payment was so high, her payment had to be smaller, and in order to get the payment this small the interest had to be substantially reduced. She agreed and was even relieved that she wouldn't be responsible for making that payment. But she started crying when she saw that the whole of my $2,000 down payment was eaten up in closing costs and all she would get was $71. After making these changes we were all ready to sign, but then her agent felt that all these changes should be reviewed with his broker. We all agreed to meet at his office and close there.

While driving, I kept asking myself, "Why was she crying? What does she want?" By the time I got to the office I figured out that she must need more cash now. After the broker agreed with the changes I offered a different plan that I had devised in the car—which was for me to pay a) all the closing costs, b) her back payments and back taxes, and c) give her $1,000 right then. They wanted to talk it over.

I sat out in the car for 30 minutes and when the broker came out he said, "She accepted your second offer, but with one change." Reluctantly I asked what it was. "She wants the $1,000, but because she is going through a divorce she wants $500 of it now and $500 in 60 days." Of course I accepted. The price was lowered to accomodate this change and therefore so were the closing costs. As a matter of fact, the money required to close right then (partially because I delayed the taxes) was $200 less than the previous plan. She was elated to have the money and I returned home four hours later with the place for $13,050—not the $20,000 I was willing to pay for it.

Excellent financing was now in place. And because such a low price and terms had been negotiated, I wouldn't have to put that much more into the place for a good profit. I had the lawn mowed and the home cleaned up and then put it up for sale one week later as a "triplex fixer upper." It sold in two days for $26,000 with $3,000 down. I made back my original capital plus the $500 to pay her. Then my contract equity was $12,000 with a net monthly payment of $105. Everyone got what they wanted.

Ads in the Paper

Home for sale advertising usually tells very little of what's important to put a deal together. Occasionally you'll see a "Leaving town, must sell" clause, but even that is rare. Also, only a few of the acceptable terms are in the ad.

I have made some of my best deals from what looked like hard financing. Read past the words. Don't be afraid to call and make suggestions. You never know what someone will take. And what they won't take to-day they might take next week.

Once I offered a man his $2,000 down payment at $200 each month for 10 months above the regular pay-ments. He balked at first, but two days later he called and said, "Make it $225 and you've got a deal." I did and we had a deal. At other times, I would go to a seller on contract and he would agree to sell it that way even though he originally demanded cash. For a detailed brochure of many of those techniques, see the book section in the back of this book.

Make Wording in Their Favor

Sometimes, people think that they will not be able to enforce the contract terms, or maybe that the implication of certain words are more in the buyer's favor than in their favor. The normal wording in an earnest money agreement and contract could be changed to make them feel much more comfortable, i.e., "It is mandatory that the purchasers make this monthly payment on the due date. If not they will have to pay a late charge of $15." Compare that to "A $15 late payment will be assessed if payment is not received on or before the due date." Yes, they do both say exactly the same thing, but the first one sounds a lot more comfortable to some people.

Conclusion

Continuously look at houses and the deal will be there. Of course you won't be able to get compatible terms on every house you look at. If not, move on to the next one. But if you are creative and persistent you'll make good deals where others can't. Giving them what they want but giving it to them your way will lay the foundation for success.

"If there's a way, take it, if not, make it."
ANONYMOUS

Chapter 7

Tips on Buying—Part II

Get There Before the Crowds

THIS SUBJECT is probably written about more than any other concerning real estate. Whole books are written on it, so I don't want to belabor it here. I will just cover the basic premise and then give a few tips.

Common sense tells us that if several people are bargaining on the same house, the price goes up. It's the old law of supply and demand. In every city there are different ways to get there first. Do some research and find the system that works best for you. For a long time I chased foreclosures. A few of the best deals I made were on foreclosures, but after pursuing several of them it got to be very nerve racking. Some other investors I knew specialized in them and were extremely successful. It wasn't comfortable for me, so I went in other directions. Here are several suggestions for any investor.

Real Estate Agent

An agent can be an investor's best friend.

A. A good agent who is *looking out for your interest* will probably be your greatest asset. I had one agent that knew what I was looking for. He combed the city, watched the paper, called other real estate agents and offices, knocked on doors, and kept going over the MLS computer (see note on MLS computer). Within three months I bought eight properties through him, and they all met most of the requirements that I asked for.

B. I've had several different agents working for me at one time, but once in a while it caused friction. One good one is more valuable than ten mediocre ones.

C. Get a good agent, then make sure he understands exactly what you're looking for.

D. Let's see how they can help you get there first.

It's the nature of their work to search and look for properties. Each real estate office fluctuates between:

1. Having all kinds of listings (and therefore they should have a few good deals), so they're looking for buyers. When there is a glut of houses on the market, good deals can be made.

2. Having no listings—then they're out looking for sellers and they uncover the good deals.

E. If you want to find a good real estate agent, call a real estate office and ask to speak to the broker. Tell him, or her, that you would like to work with them or one of the more experienced agents. This way you have a better chance of getting someone who knows what they're talking about. After all, if they help you accomplish your goals, they'll be accomplishing theirs.

Remember, there are good and bad in every profession. If you find yourself with someone who is slowing you down, you need to move on to someone else. Once you find a good realtor who recognizes your needs and your goals, hang on to him—make him your friend. His help will be invaluable.

F. Real estate agents are able to hold a listing for a few days before it has to go into the computer, so during that time they might try to find a buyer on their own. If the financing arrangements require new money then they'll probably put it in the computer right away but if I could find a realtor that had a property he was holding, it usually represented a good deal.

I would walk into an office and ask them if they had any good deals in their back pocket. If they tried to get me over by the computer I would leave—knowing that they had nothing. I found several good houses that were being held in back pockets. Some call them pocket listings.

Note on MLS Computers

Be a little leery of the MLS computer. Remember it's only as good as the information that's fed into it. Real estate information is hard to keep current. People forget to update and because of this, current information is not in there all the time.

Let me explain:

One day a new realtor showed up with a computer printout containing thirty houses. I couldn't believe that there were so many. I spent the next two days looking at all of them. The terms weren't right on most of them, but I was ready to make offers on six. Then I found out that four of them were sold—one of them three months earlier and one two months earlier. One of the six had an offer on it that was better than mine, and the last one didn't accept my offer.

Neither the agent not I did the right homework. About two hours of phoning would have saved two days of hard work.

Foreclosures

Probably the best deals come from distress sales. There are several ways to find them, i.e.:

1. Watch the legal notices put out in your paper. In larger cities, there is usually a paper dedicated to such notices. You'll find them under "Trustee's Sale," "Sheriff's Sale," "Foreclosure Notice" or "Tax Sale."

2. Another way of finding these houses is through attorneys. More specifically, the attorneys who handle trustee sales, or probate. There aren't that many of these attorneys. You'll see their names in the trustee notices. Sometimes they are reluctant to give out information on other foreclosures, but if you're nice and persistent, you'll find them.

3. Realtors sometimes know of them.

Once you find a foreclosure, follow these steps:

Step 1: Go look at the property—the address should be in the notice, but if it's not, call the attorney and ask him or get it from the title company. Seeing the property will tell you if the value is there or if it's in a good neighborhood, etc.

Step 2: Call the attorney in charge. It may have been "cured." If not, he'll point you in the right direction and reaffirm the cure and sale dates.

Step 3: Find out from the bank, or the attorney, the balance on the loan and how much cash is needed to cure the deficiency, back payments and costs. Most of this information is in the notice, *but it is not current.*

Before going on, let's review what will happen if the mortgage is not brought current. On the appointed day the attorney, acting as trustee for the bank (beneficiary), will stand in the courthouse lobby or on the steps and announce his intentions. He will then bid the total amount (balance of mortgage and costs) in behalf of the beneficiaries. If no one else bids, the sale is over and the bank can then take possession and dispose (sell, hold, etc.) of the house to recover their money.

Any excess money received on this sale goes to the owner. Also, any other bidded amount needs to be in cash (or cashier's check) right there at the time of sale.

One other point: Each state (and sometimes counties) gives the homeowners a certain period of time to redeem his interest. It could be six months to a year. During that time, he could come up with the previous amount due plus current charges and interest and get the house back (even if it had been sold). *This redemption right is usually only on sheriff's sales,* but check into it. Basically it means the investor could have his money tied up for that period of time. If the previous homeowner comes up with the money then the investor's money would be returned to him (plus a modest amount of interest). Also, the previous homeowner could convey that right of redemption by using someone else's money and then sell the house to them. These could be good deals, but be cautious.

Step 4: Check the chain of title to see if any other liens are on the property. Also, check the person's name at the title company to see if he has the right to convey ownership unencumbered.

Step 5: Get to the homeowner before it goes past the cure date. Before that time, you could pick it up for the back payments, plus a few hundred dollars in costs. Buying it at the trustee's sale will be the whole loan balance, foreclosure costs, etc.—in cash.

Once you meet with the homeowner you will see the frustration of this system.

Usually the house is vacant and it takes some detective work to track down the homeowner. If you can find them they're usually willing to convey the house because it will protect their credit rating. A few times people would only convey if I would give them a few hundred dollars. The most I've ever paid was $800. Point out to them that they have probably already lived in the house for the last four to ten months free (not making the payments). Also, that you're using your cash to cure the default and do the cleaning and fixing up the house needs.

If the people are still living there, it's even sadder. They can't believe they're losing their house. (One foreign speaking lady wasn't even aware of what was going on.) I usually explain the situation, state my intentions, and then leave, giving them my card so they can get a hold of me. I've seen it so often where they won't do anything and then, after the sale, they're evicted—still not believing that this could happen to them.

Step 6: Have the homeowner sign a Quit Claim or other appropriate deed. Also, draw up an agreement stating what both of you will do, i.e. move out, clean-up, hold harmless, etc.

Step 7: Notify the bank and the attorney that you wish to cure the default and they will tell you what you need to do from there.

Publisher's Note:

Mr. Cook has now written a book entitled "How to Pick up Foreclosures." This book explains in great detail all of the facets of the foreclosure process. This new book also contains a questionnaire that will help you zero in on the process used in your individual state. This questionnaire alone could save you thousands of dollars. The goal of the book is to get you to the purchase point of these houses long before the auction. We're confident it will really help your investment process. You can order this book by sending $19.95 to ITP, Inc., P.O. Box 1201, Orem, UT 84057 or call 1-801-224-3500 if you have a Mastercard, Visa or American Express number. The price includes postage and handling.

Newspapers

This is probably the most often used service for selling houses, so it could be your best place to find good deals. Don't be misled by thinking that there will be a hot deal every day. Maybe once a week a real good one will come along, but keep looking all the time.

Call and ask questions about the financing. See if you can make a good deal out of one that ostensibly doesn't look too promising.

I go through the whole section on Homes for Sale and circle all the ones I'm interested in, then I go back and start calling the ones that I get excited about. Call first, even if the address is there; it will save you a lot of gas.

If you're actually looking for your next house, try to get the paper as soon as it comes off the press and act right away.

Advertise Yourself

Put out some form of advertisement to let people know that you are in the market for buying houses.

I once put an ad in the paper which read, "I'm a young investor looking for houses to buy to fix-up and sell, or use as rentals. Call _____." I didn't get a lot of calls, but the ones that did come in were rewarding. I ran that ad for about two weeks. I cancelled the ad effective Thursday and that Wednesday evening a man called and said that he had seen my ad in the paper. He had a house that had been in a fire, and wanted to know if I would like to come and look at it. I went out to see the house and to talk with him. He had already received his insurance money and basically just wanted me to take over the mortgage.

I took over the mortgage of about $30,000 on the house which was in one of the nicest neighborhoods in the city. I realized that this house had a lot of potential and that this would be a great one to fix up and get some cash. So I poured about $8,000 into the house to fix it up, and all of my costs, including the monthly payments that elapsed from the time I started until the time I fixed it up were $10,000. I turned around and sold the house for $77,000. So that ad did work. All it took was one phone call to make a small fortune. I ran the same ad now and then, and once in a while I'd receive a profitable phone call.

There is another ad that has gained some popularity lately. *"I will pay full price for your house if you will be flexible on the terms."* Even though I like the way it reads I think it would do a safer job if it read, *"I will give you good terms if you will be flexible on the price."* The first has a guarantee that you'll pay the price which might increase by the time you get to the house. The second ad only guarantees good terms and because terms are arbitrary, you can go out and negotiate a good deal.

Even when you aren't actively looking, keep something going. *Good deals usually don't come looking for you, you have to go looking for them*—**all the time.** Keep the gears in motion and the wheels greased.

Once You've Found the Property

The next step is to make certain all the terms are compatible with your plans. Don't think that the seller should be deprived of his rights in order to go along with yours. Be fair, and realize that sometimes a good deal can't be made. Never buy a property without an earnest money agreement, or some other agreement stating what is expected of all the parties.

One of the biggest headaches I ever had was on a deal with no earnest money (or agreement). The buyers were supposed to do certain things, but it happened so fast that we just drew up the final papers. Then when they didn't perform, all I had were verbal promises. I thought they would come through so they could keep the property, but they didn't. They walked and I was stuck with a much worse situation than before.

I've purchased several places for little or zero down. In many cases, though, the seller is only willing to take a small down for some kind of trade—say, a cash out provision, a higher price, or higher payments, etc. I know of some investors whose best deals in terms of low downs turned out to be their worst deals in the long run. They made promises they couldn't keep. Guard your cash. Be careful not to promise that which you can't give. Other people's money is usually short term, and if not repaid promptly, their patience is also short term.

Speed is the word. Do what it takes to get the property sold (or rented) as soon as possible. The following might help. When you're going to sell it right away, the one thing that will hold up the transaction 'is getting' title insurance, so order it immediately after you purchase it. Then all you'll have to do is get an update and you could close in a matter of days (or hours), rather than weeks. Also, remember that it could sell at any time, but it is very unlikely to sell if it's a mess. So, after you've ordered the title report get the lawn mowed and clean up the yard. If the grass is long it takes two to three weeks after cutting before it's green again. Mow it even before you finish buying it—that's not too much of a financial risk to take. Even if it needs repair it could possibly be sold right away if it's clean—inside and out.

I bought a house once that was so *cluttered and dirty* that literally, all the floors had to be raked before it could even be swept. And a 100 percent improvement in the place occurred when fifty large sacks of garbage were taken to the dump. After this, I took another look at the house and knew I'd made a much better deal than I'd originally thought. The seller had even admitted earlier that he'd had a hard time finding a buyer because it was so filthy.

Most of us go through a thinking process that takes a while. When there are so many possibilities for every house, we need as much time as possible (preferably someone else's time). If the house is vacant, get the keys upon acceptance of the earnest money. I strongly advise that you don't put any money into the place until it is legally yours, but at least you'll have the keys to look at it (and possibly find someone to buy it from you). A clause for the earnest money agreement should read "Purchaser gets keys upon acceptance of earnest money."

I used to go over to a house early in the morning and lay on the floor. It was quiet and I could look all around and go over *all the possibilities*. I missed those experiences when I was processing so many houses that I didn't have the time to do that. Less mistakes were made at that time. During that time I could also get bids on doing any work that needed to be done and get everything ready to go.

Gut Feelings

I've written on this in a previous chapter, but it is so important to be a little intuitive when buying places. Other people's formulas have to become yours—adapt them to fit you, because you're the one that wins or loses. Sometimes certain things about a property outweighs the figures in some formulas. Gather as many facts as time will allow, then trust your feelings. If you have properly prepared yourself, things will go well; probably even better than you expected.

Chapter 8

A Comparison of Investment Strategies

"WAIT a year, then sell it," has been said so often that it seems like it's the only answer to protecting one's money. While the IRS had done some rather interesting things to make investing in real estate very lucrative, it would be a limited point of view to invest with only tax ramifications in mind. I'm not saying that you should ignore the IRS and plunge headfirst into any type of investment and then in the past tense look and see what tax implications your actions have had. What I am saying is that everything should be in its proper perspective.

Let me give an example: If you were to buy and sell a place and make $10,000, you might have to pay several thousands of dollars in taxes. Should you not do it then? Proper tax planning is important to minimize your tax liability but when tax considerations keep you from acting in your best interests then it's time to step back and take a look at your progress.

This chapter will help put all of this in perspective and hopefully it will help you get the answer to the question, "What else could I be doing with my money?"

The IRS and You

Note: I'm going to try to make the following information on the IRS sound as good as possible. Don't stop reading, though, until you've finished reading the three projects at the end of this chapter.

Depreciation Expense

The first consideration is depreciation expense. Basically, it means you can recover the total cost of a building over its useful life. For example, if you purchase a building for $100,000 with a useful life of twenty years, you will be able to take a $5,000 a year depreciation expense which will help you shelter your rental income plus any other income. This example is figured on the straight line method.

$$\frac{\$100,000}{20 \text{ years}} = \$5,000 \text{ per year}$$

If on this building you have a net profit of $2,000 for the year, the $5,000 will be applied to that and the difference (a $3,000 loss) will show up on your 1040 and offset other income.

If you do repairs to the building which add to its value, this will be added to the cost basis and will also be depreciated over the useful life. This is a problem to some people in that they want to deduct all of these repairs in the year they were done, but if they are considered capital improvements they will have to be added to the cost basis.

Leverage

 Probably the biggest benefit to real estate investing as compared to the other forms of investing is the fact that one can purchase property with only a portion of the sale price as a down payment. Ten percent financing is common but there are many cases of purchasing properties with little or zero down. In any case, these tax benefits add to the rate of return you'll earn on your money. The less money down the greater the return. For example, let's say you put down $5,000 to purchase the previously mentioned $100,000 building. The first year you recover $2,000 of the $5,000 in cash. That's a great return, and if you are in a 30 percent tax bracket you will save another $900 (30 percent $\times$ $3,000) by being able to deduct the excess depreciation expense against any other income you might have.

Long-Term Gains

The second consideration is long-term capital gains. If you hold this property for over one year and then sell it, all you will have to claim is 40 percent of the gain. (Watch for a change to go either to 30 percent and possibly 20 percent.) Let's go back to our $100,000 building. By the end of the year, you have put $2,000 into fixing it up. The cost basis is now $102,000. Let's say the value has increased to $112,000. If you sell it you'll make a $10,000 profit.

Before you claim that you'll have to adjust the cost basis to account for the depreciation expense that you've already claimed. You're not going to be able to deduct it and then not figure it back in. This depreciation expense reduces the cost basis to $97,000 so your profit is actually $15,000 and because you have held it over a year you'll only have to claim 40 percent of that, or $6,000. That's pretty neat—you've made $10,000 profit and all you have to claim is $6,000. There are even other forms of depreciation which will enable you to claim even larger amounts in your early years of ownership. They even make it more exciting, but remember when you recapture these amounts, any amount claimed over the straight line method will have to be recaptured at 100 percent—as ordinary income.

If you hold on to this building for several years you will keep taking the depreciation expense each year, and whenever you sell it the profit will be claimed at long-term ratios. It is necessary to note here that turning properties as fast as I did made it impossible for my gains to qualify for long-term ratios. This was not a major concern because of the great advantage for claiming these gains on the installment sales method. This is a point that most investors overlook. They continually subject themselves to the headache of landlording when with hardly any tax liability ramifications at all they could be on to making more money.

Increase in Value and Rents

The third consideration, which we have already covered to some extent with our previous building, is the increase in value and, more than likely, the increase in rents (if rent controls don't kill these increases). The value is increased by improving the building and by inflation. All of this is a tax advantage while you own the property, in that this increased value is only figured in at the time you sell the property.

You can see why so many people buy rental units—there are so many advantages. The few negative aspects can be taken care of with caution and planning.

Negative Cash Flow

The first negative aspect to rentals is cash flow. If the expenses eat up your income it could cause hardships. Make sure you can financially handle more going out than is coming in. Even if the tax advantages are available in the future make sure the financial situation won't harm you in the present. Yes, even with a negative cash flow, the other tax advantages are there, and your tax advantages are *probably heightened*, but this negative cash flow will eat into the money you've had targeted for other things. Also you will have an increased hardship if your tenancy rate fluctuates.

On Being a Landlord

The second negative aspect to holding for a year is being a landlord. I've spent many hours tracking down tenants, fixing toilets at 2 A.M. and trying to figure out who's growing those funny weeds in an upper unit, etc. I don't like being a landlord. Fortunately, there are property managers around who can handle this and free up your time so you can be an investor. Be sure to find a good firm to handle this—they should help you "Avoid Costly Entanglements."

There are excellent books written on all of these aspects—both positive and negative. It's not my intention here to go into the details, but only lay the foundation so when we get to project number two (dealing in rentals) the result will be understandable.

Projects for Comparison

We're going to hypothetically invest some money three different ways. The time period will be one year. All three projects will start with $4,000. The first project will see how much cash we can turn by buying, fixing up, and cashing out as many properties as possible. The second project will be to take the $4,000 and buy a rental unit. The third project will be to buy on contract, fix up and sell on contract as many times as possible. All of the properties are actual transactions of mine—I've used all three of these approaches. *After you study the following it won't be hard for you to see which approach I use exclusively now.*

Project # 1

Cash Out

Purchased: Jan.	Purchased: May	Purchased: Sept.
Sold: May	Sold: Sept.	Sold: Dec.
Net Profit: $7,500	Net Profit: $8,500	Net Profit: $9,000

Results

1. Profit $25,000.
2. Taxes to be paid at 30 percent—$7,500 netting $17,500.
We won't figure in what effect this tax bracket had on other income. It should be figured in real life though.
3. All three were handled through banks, with their attendant problems.

Project # 2

Buy A Rental Unit

Purchased duplex for $60,000
$600 Monthly rents
− $550 Monthly expense

The payment mentioned here doesn't include the principal part of the monthly payment. The principal is not expense.

$$\$50 \times 12 \text{ months} = \$600 \text{ net income}$$

Results

1. $600 cash in pocket (principal paid totaled $400 so actual taxable amount equaled $1,000).
2. Property value had increased to $66,000.
3. Rents should increase next year.
4. Depreciation expense of $3,000 (twenty year

straight line) offsets the $1,000 profit and the $2,000 excess depreciation expense can offset other income (30 percent tax bracket × $2,000 = $600 additional savings).

5. If, and when sold, the amount over your adjusted basis of $60,000 + Capital Improvements is taxed at long term rates.

Sounds good, doesn't it? But wait until Project 3!

Project # 3

Months	Equity	Monthly Payment
1.	$ 6,000	$ 60
2.	$ 23,000	$ 210
3.	$ 56,000	$ 480
4.	$101,000	$ 855
5.	$151,000	$1,290
6.	$184,000	$1,560
7.	$222,000	$1,970
8.	$244,000	$2,280
9.	$298,000	$2,800
10.	$340,000	$3,200
11.	$364,000	$3,420
12.	$392,000	$3,680

Buy and Sell on Contract—All The Time
Avoid Costly Entanglements—A.C.E.

(Author's note: The results of this project are so superior to projects one and two that had I not made it happen myself, I would find it hard to believe.)

Before we determine our final equity the following needs to be considered:

During the year three of the people that purchased my houses fixed up and sold them—cashing me out. I used that money plus sold two other contracts to invest further and pay the taxes.

Results

1. Equity of $310,000
2. Monthly payments (net) = $2,800
3. Cash on hand $17,000—generated from our excess down payments and a few of the cash-outs.
4. Actual net cash received from the monthly payments during the year totaled over $12,000.
5. Equity growth each month now totaled $890 (the increasing difference between our receivable balance and our payable balances).

I started investing by borrowing $500 from a friend, and at the end of one year I actually had this $4,000 and started the A.C.E. Plan. I was building a *Real Estate Money Machine!* I never realized that such a small amount of money could grow into so much. All that I ever wanted in an investment plan was knocking at my door.

What About the Tax Benefits of Rentals

I surely don't want to diminish the importance of depreciation expense, long-term capital gains, etc., because during this time I also had several rental units that helped me avoid paying taxes on the small amount

I had to claim by qualifying for installment sales consideration. (See Chapter 9 for more details on taxes.)

You might be asking yourself, "If buying and selling on contract all the time is so great then why would you want to have any rentals at all?"

The answer is simple. I want to retain as much of my profits as possible. I do believe in paying taxes, but I want my tax burden to be as light as possible, so I structure my investments to avoid and defer as much tax as possible.

In order for my tax load to be light I needed to take an "eight-cylinder approach" (Chapter 13) using all appropriate deductions to my advantage. I'm not saying by this that I went out in search of rental units. I actively worked only my plan, but when I came across a good property for renting I would buy it for that purpose. What constitutes a good rental? There must be hundreds of answers to that question because so much is written about it, but my answer centered on "avoiding costly entanglements."

High Leverage

First, I wanted hardly any of my money tied up in a rental unit. So the down payment had to be small and the fix up cost inexpensive. If this were not the case I would borrow against the property to free my money up again. If this couldn't happen it was back on the market for sale. Remember the results of the three projects. Having my money dead end into a rental project for over a year in no way compared to the advantages of keeping it moving.

Positive Cash Flow

Second, it's becoming increasingly hard to find properties where the rents cover the expenses, but they are out there. As I said before, I wouldn't go looking for these units but if they came along and all the monthly figures were right, then and only then would I buy it as a rental unit.

Property Management

Third. I'm an investor—not a landlord. *The property had to be easy for someone else to take care of*—with all the traditional rental aspects being in line, i.e., vacancy factor, location, yield rate, etc.

Conclusion

One just needs to look at the results of the three projects to see the differences. All the projects were successful, but to increase your success even above the normal lucrative aspects of real estate investing *use the A.C.E. concept as your primary focus of attention.*

I say this because I've never seen any other investment plan work so well. However, I am not asking you to change anything you're doing or forget anything you've learned; what I am suggesting is that you "up" what you're already doing.

If you're just getting started then "go for it," but if

your plan is already in motion, then use these ideas to get your investment elevator to the top floor. Add it to what you're doing for synergy.

Chapter 9

Tax Advantages

ALL THROUGH this book I mention the tax advantages of selling on contract. When I started using this approach this wasn't one of my major considerations, but after setting up several good contracts, I questioned the method of claiming profits. I know I would have to claim the profits but since I wasn't receiving that whole amount at one time I wasn't sure what to pay. About this time my accountant was reviewing my financial situation. He said, "You really like this, don't you? You get to buy a lot of places and create these great contracts, and you get your money back so you can do it again—not to mention these monthly payments."

The answer to his question was "yes," but it became an emphatic YES when he said, "Wait until you see the tax advantages you'll receive for doing it this way." I wanted to shield as much as I could from the IRS but I didn't think it was going to be this good.

The best way to explain these advantages and have it easily understood is to go through the details in question and answer form. The following are typical questions asked in my seminars, augmented by a few of my own to help clarify a few points. (Please refer to Appendix for examples.)

Q. What is an installment sale?

A. The sale of real property priced over $1,000 where payments are made in two or more tax years.

Q. Can I receive more than 30 percent of the sales price as a down payment and still qualify for these tax advantages?

A. Yes. The law has been changed so that now the seller can receive any amount as the down payment and still qualify.

Q. Why is claiming my profits this way such an advantage?

A. Because it lets you spread the payment of your taxes out over the whole length of the contract.

Q. But how do I know how much to claim?

A. On any sale that qualifies for installment sale consideration you claim only the *portion* of any principal payment received which represents profit.

Q. That sounds exciting. Tell me how much I will have to claim this year on the following sale: I purchase a house for $30,000 (nothing down) and put $3,000 into fixing it up. My selling expenses came to $2,000. I sold it for $50,000 with $5,000 down. I received payments of $450 for 12 months of which the PRINCIPAL portion totaled $1000 for the year.

A. You will pay that portion of the $6,000 ($15,000 down payment plus $1,000 monthly principal payments) which represents profit. (See example 9-1— Appendix.)

Q. But won't I have to claim my whole $15,000 profit?

A. Yes, but over the whole course of the loan.

Q. How do I figure that?

A. The easiest way to figure it is to use the IRS form 6252 that you'll see in example 9-1. In this case, your profit on the house is $15,000. You divide that profit by the contract price of $50,000 and you will get the ratio to use when figuring how much to claim. $15,000 divided by $50,000 = .3 or 30 percent. This year you will claim 30 percent of the $6,000 that you received. (You claim only $1800.)

Q. Do you mean that I was able to recover my invested money, create a $17,000 equity contract netting $170 a month (12 × $170 = $2,040 each year) and all I have to claim is $1,800?

A. Yes.

Q. What about next year?

A. That 30 percent ratio will continue for the length of the loan. Let's assume that the portion of the monthly payments which is principal totals $1,200 next year. You then would claim 30 percent of that, or $400.

Q. Are there ways that I could avoid claiming even these modest amounts?

A. Yes, even though you'll have to claim it, there are ways to shelter it. In Chapter 8 we went over rental units and long-term capital gains. I'll let my explanation there answer the question.

Q. Where do I put this on my tax forms?

A. Come up with the figure each year on Form 6252 and transfer that amount to Schedule D.

Q. Schedule D—isn't that the form for Capital Gains?

A. That's right. This transaction could also qualify for long-term capital gains, which means that if you held this property for over one year you would have to claim only 40 percent of the gain. Back to your example: This year you would only have to claim 40 percent of the $1,800 or $720!

Q. Will I only have to claim 40 percent of the 30 percent each year?

A. Not necessarily. Even though your profit ratio doesn't change, the IRS might change the capital gains exclusion. Each year could be different. (See examples 9-2 and 9-3).

Q. What happens if my buyer makes additional principal payments?

A. Those payments are treated just like regular payments. The portion representing profit is claimed.

Q.   I've just figured the ratio on the sale of a house and it involves a lot of numbers after the decimal point. How many numbers should I use?

A.   Seven or eight. That might seem strange, but in order to get the figure on line 17 correct, you'll need them all. (See example 9-5.)

Q.   When I sold my house I maintained the underlying mortgage. A friend said my profit was the difference between my payment coming in and my payment going out. Is this true?

A.   No. The amount of monthly payments coming in and going out has nothing to do with the profit of this transaction. They also have nothing to do with the ratio. These amounts (profits and ratio) need to be calculated according to the simple way explained on Form 6252.

Q.   But is the interest paid out deductible? And doesn't the interest received have to be claimed?

A.   Interest is interest and has nothing to do with capital gains. Interest income is treated as ordinary income and must be claimed. (The amount goes on the front page of your 1040.) The interest expense can be a deduction and is reported on your Schedule A.

Q.   What about the amount of principal coming off the underlying loan?

A.   It has no tax bearing.

Q.   What do I do if I have claimed depreciation expense already?

A.   That amount would be subtracted from your cost basis. You won't be able to claim it twice. (See line 5 on Form 6252.) One additional note: Take all the depreciation expense you can. Being able to reclaim it here, especially if long-term, is a great way to avoid paying taxes.

Q.   I bought a property and refinanced it. When I sold it my cost basis was $33,000. The amount of the refinance loan was $36,000. I did this to free up some cash. Then when I sold it I let my buyer assume the loan and pay me my equity on a second note. What do I claim now?

A. Like the previous example, you'll have to figure your profit ratio and apply it to any principal payments received. But in this case you will also have to claim the amount by which the assumed loan is greater than your cost basis. In this instance it will be $1,000 ($36,000 assumed loan and $35,000 cost basis). (See example 9-4.) In this example, you still are able to spread out your tax liability but you will have to claim 100 percent of your principal payments as received.

Q. How can I avoid having to claim this excess assumed amount?

A. Don't let your buyer assume it. Carry a "wraparound" contract for the whole amount. Note: Line 2 of form 6252 takes for granted that the buyer assumes the underlying mortgage(s). If this is not the case write in "mortgage not assumed." (See examples 9-1 and 9-6).

Q. Can you give me an example of a transaction where more than a 30 percent down payment was received?

A. Yes. (See example 9-6.)

Q. What happens if a subsequent buyer cashes me out?

A. Your ratio has been established. Basically, all your profits at the percentage would then be claimed.

Q. What happens if I use my contract equity for a trade?

A. It is added to the cost basis of your new property no matter what ratio it is traded at. For example, the person selling you the property may only give you 70 percent of the contract value.

Q. How do I claim my profit if I buy a contract? I purchased a $10,000 mortgage for $6,000.

A. You figure this the same way as before. Divide your profit by the contract amount—$4,000 divided by $10,000 = .4 or 40 percent—Forty percent of all PRINCIPAL payments will be claimed as they are received.

Q. A man owed me $5,500 and couldn't pay. I agreed to take a $10,000 real estate note as payment in full. Do I have to claim the whole amount?

A.   No. Your cost basis is the $5,500. Just like in the last question, you figure your profit ratio which is $4,500 divided by the contract amount of $10,000 = .45 or 45 percent. Forty-five percent of each principal payment would be considered profit.

Q.   What if I sell my personal residence on installment sales?

A.   Selling on contract is only one of the tax advantages private homeowners have; there are several others. Sit down with a good tax consultant and go over all of your possibilities.

Q.   If my buyer doesn't assume my loans and the amount of equity between my receivables and my payables is growing, will I have to pay taxes on the growth?

A.   No. You claim profits according to the computation. Your equity growth has nothing to do with this.

Q.   Do I have to use the installment sales method if I sell on contract?

A.   No.

Q.   When would it be advisable to claim the whole amount in the year of the sale?

A.   This is a hard answer. I want to say *never*, but I guess there could be a situation for someone, somewhere to claim it all. I've never seen anyone wanting to do it once they understood the ramifications. Let me explain. Suppose you had a modest income one year and decided to claim it all right then. Let's look at some things that are pertinent:

1. What would it be like if you only claimed part of your profits which were received on installments? (In our first example you would be claiming $1,800—if short term—instead of $15,000.) Could you get refunds (minimize the tax due in other years) with income averaging or loss carry backs and carry overs?

2. When you claim your profit five, ten, and fifteen years down the road you'll be paying your taxes with inflated dollars. Why pay with current dollars when it can be spread out?

3. What happens if you have to foreclose on your

buyer a few years from now? You've already claimed
your profit so now you'll have to back up, figure the
new value basis, etc., and do a nice song and dance
routine to get your money back.

Conclusion

Q.   How can I benefit from this way of claiming my
     profit?

A.   There are several answers to this, but they all center
     on controlling your money. Computing taxes this
     way and spreading the liability over a number of
     years instead of one, allows you to turn large quan-
     tities of property by keeping more money to invest.
     The installment sales method lets an investor be just
     that—an investor—and not have to feel like he is
     working for the IRS.

Form **6252**	**Computation of Installment Sale Income**			
Department of the Treasury Internal Revenue Service	▶ See instructions on back. ▶ Attach to your tax return. Use a separate form for each sale or other disposition of property on the installment basis.			**1980**

Name(s) as shown on tax return				Identifying number 123-45-6789	

A Kind of property and description ▶ Single Family Residence
B Date acquired (month, day, and year) ▶ 1-10-80   **C** Date sold (month, day, and year) ▶ 1-25-80
D Was property sold to a related party after May 14, 1980? (See instruction C) . . . . ☐ Yes ☒ No
If you checked "No" to question D, complete Part I (if 1980 is year of sale) and Part II (if you received a payment in 1980).
If you checked "Yes," you must also complete Part III.

Part I Computation of Gross Profit and Contract Price

1 Selling price including mortgages and other indebtedness	**1**	50,000	00
Note: *If $1,000 or less and this is a casual sale of personal property before October 20, 1980, do not complete the rest of this form. You cannot elect installment sale treatment.*			
2 Mortgages and other indebtedness purchaser assumes or takes property subject to "mortgage not assumed" . . . . . **2** -0-			
3 Subtract line 2 from line 1 . . . . **3** 50,000.00			
4 Cost or other basis of property sold **4** 33,000.00			
5 Depreciation allowed or allowable . . . . **5** -0-			
6 Adjusted basis (subtract line 5 from line 4) **6** 33,000.00			
7 Commissions and other expenses of sale **7** 2,000.00			
8 Add line 6 and line 7	**8**	35,000	00
9 Gross profit (subtract line 8 from line 1). If result is zero or less, do not complete rest of form . . .	**9**	15,000	00
10 Subtract line 8 from line 2. If line 8 is more than line 2, enter zero.	**10**	-0-	
11 Contract price (add line 3 and line 10)	**11**	50,000	00
12 Gross profit ratio (divide line 9 by line 11)	**12**	.3	

Part II Computation of Taxable Part of Installment Sale

13 For year of sale only—enter amount from line 10 above	**13**	-0-	
14 Payments received during year	**14**	6,000	00
15 Add lines 13 and 14	**15**	6,000	00
16 Payments received in prior years . . . . **16** -0-			
17 Taxable part of installment sale (multiply line 15 by line 12 for year of sale)	**17**	1,800	00
18 Part of line 17 that is ordinary income under recapture rules (see instructions)	**18**	0	
19 Subtract line 18 from line 17. Enter on Schedule D or Form 4797. Identify as from Form 6252 . . .	**19**	1,800	00

Part III Information and Computation for Related Party Installment Sale

Complete this part only if you answered "Yes" to question D.
E Name, address, and taxpayer identifying number of related party
- -

F Did the related party resell or dispose of this property, acquired from you after May 14, 1980, during 1980? . . ☐ Yes ☐ No
G If the answer to question F is "Yes," complete lines 20 through 27 below unless one of the following conditions not check only
   applies).

Example 9-1

In this example, a home was purchased for $30,000. $3,000 was put into it as capital improvements. When sold, the selling expenses totaled $2,000. The profit is $15,000, but all that will have to be claimed this year is 30 percent of the $6,000 ($5,000 down payment plus $1,000, which is the principal part of the monthly payments). This totals $1,800 (or $720 if this property were held for over a year).

Form **6252**	**Computation of Installment Sale Income**	**1981**
Department of the Treasury Internal Revenue Service	▶ See instructions on back. ▶ Attach to your tax return. Use a separate form for each sale or other disposition of property on the installment basis.	

Name(s) as shown on tax return	Identifying number 123-45-6789

A Kind of property and description ▶ Single Family Residence

B Date acquired (month, day, and year) ▶   **C** Date sold (month, day, and year) ▶

D Was property sold to a related party after May 14, 1980? (See instruction C) . . . . ☐ Yes ☐ No

If you checked "No" to question D, complete Part I (if 1980 is year of sale) and Part II (if you received a payment in 1980).
If you checked "Yes," you must also complete Part III.

Part I   Computation of Gross Profit and Contract Price

1 Selling price including mortgages and other indebtedness	**1**		
Note: *If $1,000 or less and this is a casual sale of personal property before October 20, 1980, do not complete the rest of this form. You cannot elect installment sale treatment.*			
2 Mortgages and other indebtedness purchaser assumes or takes property subject to	**2**		
3 Subtract line 2 from line 1	**3**		
4 Cost or other basis of property sold	**4**		
5 Depreciation allowed or allowable	**5**		
6 Adjusted basis (subtract line 5 from line 4)	**6**		
7 Commissions and other expenses of sale	**7**		
8 Add line 6 and line 7	**8**		
9 Gross profit (subtract line 8 from line 1). If result is zero or less, do not complete rest of form . . .	**9**		
10 Subtract line 8 from line 2. If line 8 is more than line 2, enter zero	**10**		
11 Contract price (add line 3 and line 10)	**11**		
12 Gross profit ratio (divide line 9 by line 11)	**12**	.3	

Part II   Computation of Taxable Part of Installment Sale

13 For year of sale only—enter amount from line 10 above	**13**		
14 Payments received during year	**14**	1,200	00
15 Add lines 13 and 14	**15**	1,200	00
16 Payments received in prior years First filed 1980	16	1,800 00	**16**		
17 Taxable part of installment sale (multiply line 15 by line 12 for year of sale)	**17**	400	00
18 Part of line 17 that is ordinary income under recapture rules (see instructions)	**18**	-0-	
19 Subtract line 18 from line 17. Enter on Schedule D or Form 4797. Identify as from Form 6252 . . .	**19**	400	00

Part III   Information and Computation for Related Party Installment Sale

Complete this part only if you answered "Yes" to question D.

E Name, address, and taxpayer identifying number of related party

F Did the related party resell or dispose of this property, acquired from you after May 14, 1980, during 1980? . . ☐ Yes ☐ No

G If ~~answer~~ to question F is "Y~~es~~" complete lines 20 thro~~ugh~~ below unless one of ~~the~~ following conditions i~~s~~ ~~met (check only~~ ~~one applies).~~

Example 9-2

This example shows what will have to be claimed the second year of the sale which was explained in Example 9-1. Note that the 30 percent stays the same.

Form **6252**	**Computation of Installment Sale Income**	**1999**
Department of the Treasury Internal Revenue Service	▶ See instructions on back. ▶ Attach to your tax return. Use a separate form for each sale or other disposition of property on the installment basis.	

Name(s) as shown on tax return	Identifying number 123-45-6789

A Kind of property and description ▶ ... Single Family Residence ...

B Date acquired (month, day, and year) ▶ .... **C** Date sold (month, day, and year) ▶ ....

D Was property sold to a related party after May 14, 1980? (See instruction C) . . . . ☐ Yes ☐ No

If you checked "No" to question D, complete Part I (if 1980 is year of sale) and Part II (if you received a payment in 1980).
If you checked "Yes," you must also complete Part III.

Part I — **Computation of Gross Profit and Contract Price**

1	Selling price including mortgages and other indebtedness	1	
	Note: *If $1,000 or less and this is a casual sale of personal property before October 20, 1980, do not complete the rest of this form. You cannot elect installment sale treatment.*		
2	Mortgages and other indebtedness purchaser assumes or takes property subject to **2**		
3	Subtract line 2 from line 1 . . . . **3**		
4	Cost or other basis of property sold **4**		
5	Depreciation allowed or allowable **5**		
6	Adjusted basis (subtract line 5 from line 4) **6**		
7	Commissions and other expenses of sale **7**		
8	Add line 6 and line 7	8	
9	Gross profit (subtract line 8 from line 1). If result is zero or less, do not complete rest of form . . .	9	
10	Subtract line 8 from line 2. If line 8 is more than line 2, enter zero	10	
11	Contract price (add line 3 and line 10)	11	
12	Gross profit ratio (divide line 9 by line 11)	12	.3 or 30%

Part II — **Computation of Taxable Part of Installment Sale**

13	For year of sale only—enter amount from line 10 above	13	
14	Payments received during year	14	4,200 00
15	Add lines 13 and 14	15	4,200 00
16	Payments received in prior years First filed 1980 . . **16** 38,000 00		
17	Taxable part of installment sale (multiply line 15 by line 12 for year of sale)	17	1,260 00
18	Part of line 17 that is ordinary income under recapture rules (see instructions)	18	0
19	Subtract line 18 from line 17. Enter on Schedule D or Form 4797. Identify as from Form 6252 . . .	19	1,260 00

Part III — **Information and Computation for Related Party Installment Sale**

Complete this part only if you answered "Yes" to question D.

E Name, address, and taxpayer identifying number of related party

----

F Did the related party resell or dispose of this property, acquired from you after May 14, 1980, during 1980? . . ☐ Yes ☐ No

G If ... to question F is "Y..." complete lines 20 th... below unless one of ... following conditions ... check only ...ies).

Example 9-3

After several years, the ratio stays the same and even then only a
small portion would have to be claimed.

Form **6252** Department of the Treasury Internal Revenue Service	**Computation of Installment Sale Income** ▶ See instructions on back. ▶ Attach to your tax return. Use a separate form for each sale or other disposition of property on the installment basis.	**1980**

Name(s) as shown on tax return	Identifying number 123-45-6789

A Kind of property and description ▶   Single Family Residence

B Date acquired (month, day, and year) ▶   3-12-80   **C** Date sold (month, day, and year) ▶ 4-5-80

D Was property sold to a related party after May 14, 1980? (See instruction C) . . . . ☐ Yes ☒ No

If you checked "No" to question D, complete Part I (if 1980 is year of sale) and Part II (if you received a payment in 1980).
If you checked "Yes," you must also complete Part III.

Part I   **Computation of Gross Profit and Contract Price**

1	Selling price including mortgages and other indebtedness	**1**	50,000 00
	Note: If $1,000 or less and this is a casual sale of personal property before October 20, 1980, do not complete the rest of this form. You cannot elect installment sale treatment.		
2	Mortgages and other indebtedness purchaser assumes or takes property subject to **2** 36,000 00		
3	Subtract line 2 from line 1 . . . . **3** 14,000 00		
4	Cost or other basis of property sold **4** 33,000 00		
5	Depreciation allowed or allowable **5** 0		
6	Adjusted basis (subtract line 5 from line 4) **6** 33,000 00		
7	Commissions and other expenses of sale **7** 2,000 00		
8	Add line 6 and line 7	**8**	35,000 00
9	Gross profit (subtract line 8 from line 1). If result is zero or less, do not complete rest of form . . .	**9**	15,000 00
10	Subtract line 8 from line 2. If line 8 is more than line 2, enter zero	**10**	1,000 00
11	Contract price (add line 3 and line 10)	**11**	15,000 00
12	Gross profit ratio (divide line 9 by line 11)	**12**	100%

Part II   **Computation of Taxable Part of Installment Sale**

13	For year of sale only—enter amount from line 10 above	**13**	1,000 00
14	Payments received during year	**14**	5,200 00
15	Add lines 13 and 14	**15**	6,200 00
16	Payments received in prior years . . . . . . **16** -0-		
17	Taxable part of installment sale (multiply line 15 by line 12 for year of sale)	**17**	6,200 00
18	Part of line 17 that is ordinary income under recapture rules (see instructions)	**18**	0
19	Subtract line 18 from line 17. Enter on Schedule D or Form 4797. Identify as from Form 6252 . . .	**19**	6,200 00

Part III   **Information and Computation for Related Party Installment Sale**

Complete this part only if you answered "Yes" to question D.

E Name, address, and taxpayer identifying number of related party

F Did the related party resell or dispose of this property, acquire from you after May 14, 1980, during 1980? . . ☐ Yes ☐ No

G If the answer to question F is "Yes" complete lines 20 through 24 below unless one of the conditions ... check only ... applies).

Example 9-4

This $6,200 might seem high but we did only put $3,000 into the property. The $5,000 down payment that we received was enough to cover selling expenses of $2,000. When we refinanced the property we freed this $3,000 plus $3,000 more. The results are $6,000 cash in our pocket; we have an equity contract of $9,000—netting $90 a month; and all we have to claim is $6,200 (which can be offset by other deductions).

Form **6252**	**Computation of Installment Sale Income**	**1980**
Department of the Treasury Internal Revenue Service	▶ See instructions on back. ▶ Attach to your tax return. Use a separate form for each sale or other disposition of property on the installment basis.	

Name(s) as shown on tax return	Identifying number 123-45-6789

A Kind of property and description ▶ Duplex

B Date acquired (month, day, and year) ▶ 3-11-81 **C** Date sold (month, day, and year) ▶ 4-5-81

D Was property sold to a related party after May 14, 1980? (See instruction C) . . . . ☐ Yes ☒ No

If you checked "No" to question D, complete Part I (if 1980 is year of sale) and Part II (if you received a payment in 1980).
If you checked "Yes," you must also complete Part III.

Part I   Computation of Gross Profit and Contract Price

1	Selling price including mortgages and other indebtedness	**1**	50,000	00
	Note: *If $1,000 or less and this is a casual sale of personal property before October 20, 1980, do not complete the rest of this form. You cannot elect installment sale treatment.*			
2	Mortgages and other indebtedness purchaser assumes or takes property subject to	**2** 36,000 00		
3	Subtract line 2 from line 1	**3** 14,000 00		
4	Cost or other basis of property sold	**4** 37,000 00		
5	Depreciation allowed or allowable	**5** 0		
6	Adjusted basis (subtract line 5 from line 4)	**6** 37,000 00		
7	Commissions and other expenses of sale	**7** 2,000 00		
8	Add line 6 and line 7	**8**	39,000	00
9	Gross profit (subtract line 8 from line 1). If result is zero or less, do not complete rest of form . . .	**9**	11,000	00
10	Subtract line 8 from line 2. If line 8 is more than line 2, enter zero	**10**	0	
11	Contract price (add line 3 and line 10)	**11**	14,000	00
12	Gross profit ratio (divide line 9 by line 11)	**12**	.7857142	

Part II   Computation of Taxable Part of Installment Sale

13	For year of sale only—enter amount from line 10 above	**13**	0	
14	Payments received during year	**14**	5,200	00
15	Add lines 13 and 14	**15**	5,200	00
16	Payments received in prior years	**16** -0-		
17	Taxable part of installment sale (multiply line 15 by line 12 for year of sale)	**17**	4,085	71
18	Part of line 17 that is ordinary income under recapture rules (see instructions)	**18**	0	
19	Subtract line 18 from line 17. Enter on Schedule D or Form 4797. Identify as from Form 6252 . . .	**19**	4,085	71

Part III   Information and Computation for Related Party Installment Sale

Complete this part only if you answered "Yes" to question D.

E Name, address, and taxpayer identifying number of related party

F Did the related party resell or dispose of this property, acquired from you after May 14, 1980, during 1980? . . ☐ Yes ☐ No

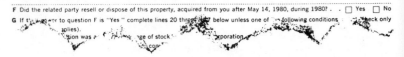

G If t... ...r to question F is "Yes" complete lines 20 thr...... below unless one of ...following conditions ... ...eck only ... ...plies).
...tion was ... ...ge of stock ... ...xporation...
...con...

Example 9-5

In this example the underlying mortgage was assumed by the buyer but the amount assumed is lower than the cost basis. Only amounts actually received then would have to be claimed.

Form **6252**	**Computation of Installment Sale Income**	**1980**

Department of the Treasury
Internal Revenue Service

▶ See instructions on back. ▶ Attach to your tax return.
Use a separate form for each sale or other disposition of property on the installment basis.

Name(s) as shown on tax return	Identifying number
	123-45-6789

A Kind of property and description ▶ ....

B Date acquired (month, day, and year) ▶ .... **C** Date sold (month, day, and year) ▶ ....

D Was property sold to a related party after May 14, 1980? (See instruction C) . . . . ☐ Yes ☐ No

If you checked "No" to question D, complete Part I (if 1980 is year of sale) and Part II (if you received a payment in 1980).
If you checked "Yes," you must also complete Part III.

Part I   Computation of Gross Profit and Contract Price

1 Selling price including mortgages and other indebtedness			**1**	50,000 00
Note: *If $1,000 or less and this is a casual sale of personal property before October 20, 1980, do not complete the rest of this form. You cannot elect installment sale treatment.*				
2 Mortgages and other indebtedness purchaser assumes or takes property subject to . mortgage not assumed	**2**	–0–		
3 Subtract line 2 from line 1	**3**	50,000 00		
4 Cost or other basis of property sold	**4**	33,000 00		
5 Depreciation allowed or allowable	**5**	–0–		
6 Adjusted basis (subtract line 5 from line 4)	**6**	33,000 00		
7 Commissions and other expenses of sale	**7**	2,000 00		
8 Add line 6 and line 7			**8**	35,000 00
9 Gross profit (subtract line 8 from line 1). If result is zero or less, do not complete rest of form . . .			**9**	15,000 00
10 Subtract line 8 from line 2. If line 8 is more than line 2, enter zero			**10**	0
11 Contract price (add line 3 and line 10)			**11**	50,000 00
12 Gross profit ratio (divide line 9 by line 11)			**12**	.3 or 30%

Part II   Computation of Taxable Part of Installment Sale

13 For year of sale only—enter amount from line 10 above			**13**	0
14 Payments received during year			**14**	16,800 00
15 Add lines 13 and 14			**15**	16,800 00
16 Payments received in prior years	**16**	–0–		
17 Taxable part of installment sale (multiply line 15 by line 12 for year of sale)			**17**	5,040 00
18 Part of line 17 that is ordinary income under recapture rules (see instructions)			**18**	0
19 Subtract line 18 from line 17. Enter on Schedule D or Form 4797. Identify as from Form 6252 . . .			**19**	5,040 00

Part III   Information and Computation for Related Party Installment Sale

Complete this part only if you answered "Yes" to question D.

E Name, address, and taxpayer identifying number of related party

----

F Did the related party resell or dispose of this property, acquired from you after May 14, 1980, during 1980? . . ☐ Yes ☐ No

G If the answer to question F is "Yes," complete lines 20 through ?? below unless one of the following conditions ... check only ... plies).
... ition was a s... nge of stock t... rporation.

Example 9-6

In this example $8,000 was invested, but the $16,000 down payment received, more than returned the $8,000, plus an additional $8,000 was received.

A $7,000 equity contract was created—netting $70 a month. All that has to be claimed is $5,040.

Chapter 10

More Information on Contracts

BEFORE we get into the particulars of what contracts can be used for, let's cover the two types of contracts. (Once again contracts mean mortgages, trust deeds, real estate contracts and other notes.)

The first type of contract is created by taking one's equity in a piece of property on installments. All underlying mortgages, if any, are assumed by the buyer. It only has payments coming in or a promise to pay at some future date. For this definition, it doesn't matter whether it's in first, second, third, or whatever position on the property.

The second type of equity contract is that equity which represents the difference between a receivable contract and a payable contract. Some refer to it as a "wrap around" mortgage, which is in common usage, but I prefer to call it an "over-riding" contract or mortgage. If we refer to it this way, then when we refer to underlying loans and over-riding loans, it makes more sense. This kind of a loan takes the premise that the buyer does not assume the underlying loans; the seller maintains all underlying responsibilities.

The amount of difference between the over-riding loan and the underlying loan 1) increases, 2) decreases, or 3) stays the same (which is hard to do). It is mandatory that one understands this principle before buying or selling on installments. Look at the following examples for a further explanation of this.

Example I
Equity Increase

$60,000 receivable @ $600 per month ($540 interest/ $60 principal).

$40,000 payable @ $400 per month ($360 interest/$40 principal).

There is a $20 equity increase because there are $20 more going off the underlying loan than there are coming off the over-riding loan. All contracts should be set up like this so that the underlying loans pay off before the over-riding loan, at which time there will be assets but no liabilities.

Example II
Equity Decrease

$60,000 receivable @ $600 per month ($520 interest/ $80 principal).

$40,000 payable @ $400 per month ($360 interest/$40 principal).

There is a $40 equity decrease because there are $40 more coming off the over-riding loan than there are going off the underlying loan.

It would be easy to think that the only adjustment to influence the amount applied to principal would be to raise or lower the monthly payment, but could also raise or lower the interest rate. If the interest rate was lower on the over-riding loan, then more would come off as principal payment, and if too much is applied to the principal, then it will cause your equity to decrease.

There is one other way to influence how much of the payment will be interest and how much will be principal and that is to raise or lower the purchase price. I would suggest not altering the purchase price. Alter the interest rate and/or the monthly payment.

Example III
Equity Stays The Same

In order for this to happen there would have to be a great amount of manipulation on somebody's part. The chances of it happening are rare, but if it does happen, it won't stay that way. Even if both amounts applied to principal were the same this month they would change the next month due to the difference in the total balance.

Of these three types of equity situations Example I is best. Example III is nearly impossible and because Example II is unfavorable, it needs to have some further explanation and some possible remedies.

In an equity decreasing situation there is a risk that the over-riding loan will catch up to and pass the underlying loan (especially in loans with small equity splits, i.e. a $95,000 receivable and $90,000 payable). This would be a very awkward situation. Think about it. You would not only have a negative equity growth, which is bad enough (every month your net worth would decrease and look bad on your financial statement), but also the deed you would be required to give your buyer (or satisfaction of mortgage) would be due before you received your deed.

If a mistake is made and you find yourself in this position (maybe you assumed a loan that had a negative equity growth with the loan underlying it), there are two remedies. First, you could renegotiate one of the mortgages and rerecord it. Second, and this is probably the easiest way, you could exercise the payment clause that contains the words "or more" and make a larger payment on the underlying loan. The additional amount would be applied to principal. Make sure this extra payment is large enough to set it straight. This does not have to be done each month. It can be done when you feel like it. And just because an over-riding loan is catching up to the underlying loan, it doesn't mean that it will catch it. For example, you may have an $80,000 receivable with a $40,000 payable. The negative equity growth could be $40 a month, and even though the $80,000 is paying off faster it will probably be down to a $30,000 receivable when the $40,000 hits zero. It was moving up but did not catch it.

What Can Be Done with Contracts?

Many things can be done with equity contracts. The following lists give some good ideas and in the wonderful world of investing many more could be developed. Here are a few:

1. Hang onto them and live by the conditions of the mortgage and you will eventually be paid off in one of two ways:

A. The contract will run the distance.

B. The purchaser will come up with the money (i.e. refinance) and pay off the balance owing.

2. You will have to foreclose if the buyers don't pay. In this case you could either get the house back or have your loan taken over by the next person down the chain of title. Foreclosure laws vary greatly from state to state. If you are confronted with this, obtain good legal help.

3. You can borrow against your equities. Some banks and many people will use contracts as collateral. The value put on a contract will usually be at about 50 percent of its face value. This is a great advantage because you don't have to pay taxes on this borrowed amount. It's a good way to move on to bigger and better things without paying taxes.

4. You can pledge these contracts as security for performance. For example, I wanted to buy a five-plex unit, but the man wanted $5,000 down and I only had $2,000 to give him. I promised to pay the other $3,000 in two years. I gave him an "assignment for collateral purposes only" on a $7,000 equity contract which I held. I got the best of both worlds. I was able to put very little down and tie up the units AND I was able to continue receiving the payments from the contract.

5. You can sell your contract equities. This is frequently done so let's go over some things people look for in buying contracts.

A. The first and most important thing is the yield (or how fast they are going to get their money back). The formula is simple:

Rate of Return = Net received (cash returned) for one
                 year divided by the amount invested

For example, if you purchased a $10,000 contract with $100 monthly payments for $5,000, your rate of return would be:

$$\frac{\$1,200\ (\$100 \times 12\ \text{months})}{\$5,000} = 24\%\ \text{yield}$$

if you had paid $6,000 for that contract, it would be:

$$\frac{\$1,200}{\$6,000} = 20\%\ \text{yield}$$

There are some other aspects of figuring yields to consider:

1. The return in subsequent years is different because:

    a. the payments might change.

    b. some of the cash one has invested has returned so the yield should be refigured.

    c. equity growth can be added as part of the yield, but will only be received later as a bonus when the contract pays off.

2. Balloon payments drastically change the nature of purchasing a contract, but unless received the first year, they should not be figured in the first year's yield.

3. Anyone buying and selling contracts figures yields to determine what they will give or take for the contracts. It is not, however, the only consideration. Even if it were, there are so many variables that it becomes subjective anyway. And everyone puts values on different aspects. One company might figure the first year rate of return and base all of its decision on that. Another might figure pay off time, especially balloons. Still another might only be interested in interest rates on the loans. Finally, it comes down to the old axiom, "It's worth what somebody will pay for it."

B. The second thing is the value of the property and, more specifically, the position the contract has in the value structure of the property. For example: If the property is worth $50,000 and the $10,000 equity contract you have for sale represents the amount between a $48,000 receivable and a $38,000 payable, it will be hard to sell. But on this same property, if the equity represents the difference between a $30,000 receivable and a $20,000 payable, it will draw a better price because there's plenty of protection left between the $50,000 and the $30,000.

C. The third thing that's important is where the property stands in the chain of title. Like the last point, protection is the main concern. Someone buying a contract wants to make sure he's getting the equity position he thinks he is getting. Understanding a title report and getting title insurance will alleviate this problem. Generally speaking, people who buy a contract would rather buy an equity between a receivable and a payable. This way they have equity growth and control the underlying payments—making sure that these loans get paid.

Examples

Let's look at some examples:

1. Mr. Smith owns his house outright. He wants to move so he sells on a contract of $50,000 with a $5,000 down payment. The balance is payable to him at $450 per month at 11 percent interest.

2. Mr. Harrington has a similar house but he has a first mortgage of $30,000 owed to a savings and loan. He also sells for $50,000 with $5,000 down. He lets his buyer assume the $30,000 loan and he takes his $15,000 equity on payments. But, since he's going to be in second position, he charges a higher interest rate with larger payments. The $15,000 is carried at $200 per month at 13 percent interest.

3. Mr. Davis has a similar house and he sells it just as

Mr. Harrington did, but with one change. He takes his $15,000 equity on a note secured against the house his buyers are currently living in so that he'll get his cash when they sell it. At first he wanted payments on the $15,000, but his buyers couldn't afford it so they offered to pay him interest at 15 percent which would accrue and be payable when their house closed.

4. Mr. Jones has a similar house and he, too, has a $30,000 mortgage like Mr. Harrington. He sells it for $50,000 with $5,000 down, but he holds the underlying mortgage. His payments coming in are $450 (starting interest is $420 of that, with principal being $30). His payment on the $30,000 mortgage is $300 (interest is $250 and principal is $50).

Let's look at what each one of the men has in terms of:

A. debt to asset ratio
B. ease of handling
C. marketability of his contract

Mr. Smith:

A. His debt to asset ratio is zero—which is excellent.

B. He only has one payment to worry about and calculating his taxes are relatively simple. All he has to do is:

1. calculate and claim his interest.

2. use the installment sales computation to figure out what percent of each principle payment is profit, and therefore, needs to be claimed.

C. His marketability is high:

1. He stands in first position—some companies will only buy this type of contract.

2. The payments represent a one percent repay which is good but not excellent ($45,000 at $450.00 a month).

3. The interest rate (11 percent) is okay but not the best in today's market.

Mr. Harrington:

A. His debt to asset ratio is also zero, (unless he still stands primarily liable for the loan he let his buyer assume).

B. He also has the same tax situation as Mr. Smith.

C. The ratios are the same as Mr. Smith's, so the same thing holds true, but he is in second position now. People that purchase contracts will want to make sure that:

1. the underlying mortgage is properly being serviced.

2. the equity represents true value (that they're not buying something that is over the actual value of the house).

3. they can encumber their interest

The $200 monthly payment on the $15,000 is a good yield. All of this makes for a very salable contract.

Mr. Davis:

A. His debt to asset ratio is also zero.

B. This one is very easy to handle as long as a definite payoff date is listed and some sort of a protection clause is added in case the $15,000 plus interest is not received. If this payment is received the next tax year he will qualify for the installment sales advantage.

C. Marketability—usually a mortgage with no payments has a lower value, but in this case, it would have a high value (if all else were okay, i.e. the value of his buyer's house), because of the short payoff date. If you have one like it and you need the cash you'll find a ready market of buyers because the payoff date is so short.

Mr. Jones:

A. Debt to asset $30,000 debt = 66%

$45,000 asset

This is not great, but it is certainly within the realm of normalcy.

B. Ease of handling—the only difference is that he will have an interest expense, but it is easy to figure. This sale qualifies for installment sales treatment like the others.

C. Marketability—Very good. The $150 net payment on the $15,000 equity represents a 1 percent repay. Also, there's a starting equity growth of $10 per month. All this is favorable, which means this contract will have a great deal of ready buyers.

The Slow Down and Relax Benefit

Another good thing about contracts with equity growth is that you can stop buying and selling houses (see the last chapter) and yet your equity will keep growing. Let's look at this aspect in detail, because you don't want to get caught short down the road. After a year of working this approach I had 26 contracts. My average receivable payment would come in for 23 years, and my average underlying payment would go out for 13 years. The average equity amount was $10,050 and the average net monthly payment was $94. I had a combined equity growth of $890 per month, meaning that after I collected my payments and made payments on all my houses, my net worth grew $890 each month (and that amount also increased a little month after month).

As long as there is equity between the two payments, there will be equity growth, but down the road as the underlying loans start paying off, the equity growth will slow down and then cease, and then the over-riding loans will be all that remains on the properties and the equity will start decreasing. Ostensibly, this sounds bad, but it's true only if one doesn't take advantage of the increase in payments and equity growth.

Remember:

1. You can get to this point in a relatively short period of time by doing the right things. Then you can follow the automatic pilot feature given in the last chapter of this book.

2. Once the underlying payments drop off, *you will have the excess payments to reinvest.* Every payment not going out adds to the cash you have available *for other investments.*

Purchase Contracts Back Down the Ladder

Another point to consider is this: if you decide to start buying contracts, take a look at your own underlying loans. You might be able to do quite well making discounted offers on these and paying them off. Then the total net payments coming in to you will increase even sooner. By doing this you will also consolidate your position. Your debt to asset ratio will change for the better, making you feel more comfortable and making your financial statement look better.

Calculations

To figure the monthly principal, interest and new balance use the following steps:

Step 1: Old balance × interest rate: 12 (months) = this month's interest.

Step 2: Monthly payment − (minus) this month's interest = this month's principal.

Step 3: Old balance − (minus) this month's principal = new balance.

This new balance becomes the old balance next month. If your calculator has a memory this will even be easier because the balance can be entered and adjusted internally by hitting memory minus (m −) at the end of Step 2. Then memory return (MR) will show the new balance.

Conclusion

Your only limitation for using these contract equities is your own imagination. They have value because of all they produce. I often had people with rental properties trying to trade me their rental unit for my contract equity. I was often tempted, but these contracts were the answer to what I wanted in my investment plan. Well set up contract equities make good friends.

Chapter 11

Tips on Fixing-Up

What Do You Have to Crew About

ONE of the most difficult decisions I had to make as a small investor was whether to do the fix-up work myself, use subcontractors, or hire employees.

Once I made a decision on which way to go, thinking the problem was solved, something else would always come up. Let me pose the dilemma. When I first started investing, I took the advice of others and used subcontractors. For most types of buildings this would have been fine, but remodeling has its own unique problems. Once the subcontractor started a job, almost invariably, he would find something else that needed repairing. On one occasion I had a man putting in a new toilet. Once the old one was out he could see that the floor was rotting. To do that work meant changing the original bid. Then he found that the joists had termites because of the moisture—another new bid. Now it involved the ceiling of the room below—and another new bid. I felt like a yo-yo.

Another time a subcontractor agreed to paint a room for $80. Once he started applying the paint the old wallpaper began to bubble. It would have taken too long to scrape and redo the wall so we paneled it. It took three different bids to do this job.

After going through this several times, I decided to hire my own man. Then, if anything was wrong, he would just go ahead and fix it. I soon found, though, that having employees also had its drawbacks. I'm not going to say which is better, but I will list the good and bad points of each. Each house (situation) is different. You'll have to decide.

Employees

Good Points:

1. If you can find a good employee he could take a lot of pressure off of you by running errands between jobs.

2. He has more time to learn your system and how you like things.

3. You can schedule your jobs to fit your schedule and coordinate getting your priorities done a lot easier than with independent contractors.

4. Under your direction, he can watch out for you and get the best prices possible for materials.

Bad Points:

1. It's your time they're using up. If they break down on the freeway you'll probably be their taxi service.

2. Sometimes they'll treat your priorities all the same. They'll put rental (low quality) carpeting into a nicer home. You'll have to be available to inspect their work all the time.

3. You'll have to pay all kinds of taxes and insurance for them. Be prepared to get a good bookkeeper.

4. Your goals are not the same as his. You're trying to get a house livable by Friday and they're looking forward to Friday because it's payday.

5. If they get sick or leave, the work doesn't get done until they can be replaced.

6. They may not always be honest. Remember they are handling YOUR tools and YOUR materials.

Subcontractors

Good Points:
1. Generally, they're working by the job so:
   a. They work fast because they don't get paid until it's done.
   b. They do it right the first time.
2. You can get bids and keep the price down.
3. You don't have to worry about taxes and insurance.
4. They are using, losing and abusing their own tools.

Bad Points:
1. They don't always do the quality work that they've promised. Sometimes the job has to be done completely over at their expense, but causing you time delays.

2. Once you've paid them some of the money, they might not perform as you'd expect. For example: I needed a house painted. A subcontractor (who was also a friend) gave me a bid of $375 for labor only. I would supply the paint and brushes. I told him that $375 was too low—$450 was a fair price, and I wouldn't mind paying that if he did a nice job by my deadline. He asked when he would get paid. I asked him when he would be finished and he said the following Wednesday. I told him I'd pay him that Wednesday. Wednesday came and he was only about one-third done, but he

really needed some money. The ensuing conversation was right out of kindergarten.

"You told me you'd pay me Wednesday."

"But you promised to be finished Wednesday."

"But you promised me the money today and I need it or the bank will take away my car."

I paid the money in full with a promise from him that he would complete the job by that Saturday. Six weeks later I had to pay my crew to finish the job.

This sort of thing is common.

3. They're acting in their own best interest.

You see, both ways have advantages as well as disadvantages. There were times when I only used subcontractors and, if I kept on top of them, everything worked out all right. Other times I only used employees and the same thing held true.

In either case, if I could get them to think like me then what I wanted to happen would happen. But most people aren't used to operating within someone else's time requirements.

Lock Into Definite Times

I got a bid from a man to paint a few rooms. "When can you be done?" I asked.

"Well, I'll get started tomorrow."

"I appreciate that, but when will you be done?"

"Let me see, it will take me about two days."

"That's fine, but when will you be finished?"

"Why are you so worried about that? It'll get done."

"Because I have plans for this house and I need to know. Besides, I'll have to be here at that time to pay you."

"Okay, I'll be done Thursday."

"What time Thursday?"

"3:30."

"Okay, I'll see you Thursday at 3:30."

Like I said before, it's hard to get people to work in your time plan and commit themselves.

Bids and Counter Bids

A note of caution should be taken when offering a subcontractor less than the bid he has given. I realize that this should be the normal way of doing business, but I have found that once their bid is compromised so is the quality of their work.

It got to the point where I just said yes or no to their bids. I would rather get someone else than have the first subcontractor feel slighted and then justified if his work is not up to pay.

Once subcontractors knew this the bids they gave me were usually fair. I wanted them happy doing my jobs. Sometimes I would carry it to the other extreme and offer them more if their bid was too low. When I did this I usually got better results and in better time. This is a good place to use the Golden Rule.

Doing the Work Yourself

Good Points:

1. You save money by controlling material costs and the fact that you won't have to pay someone else.

2. You control the quality of the workmanship.

3. You do the work in your own time to meet your schedules and deadlines.

Bad Points:

While you're fixing the toilet and saving $25, you

could have used that same time to purchase a house that would make you thousands of dollars. This point alone is why I never do the work myself. It would even be better to pay the highest bidder and go out there where the BIG money is.

Let's cover some other aspects of fixing up places.

How Much Work Should I Do?

Remember, the idea is to turn houses. Generally, cosmetic work will take up the value of the house, but I've found that with some houses the extra dollars spent trying to improve a place doesn't always take up the value that much more.

For example, a house in a run-down neighborhood has a top value on it—no matter how much money is put into it. So, determine the top value of the home and only fix it up to reach that point. Any more fix-up is a waste of money and time. Weigh each property. Get in and out with as little as possible. Let someone else fix it up to be "fit for a king." Once you understand this concept, the proper questions might not be, "Should I use subcontractors or employees?" but, "Should I be doing this at all?" Question yourself on each move.

Should You Live in the House?

No. Not as a general practice. If you want to remodel the house you're in, fine, but if you're thinking of moving your family from one house to another—don't. The exception, of course, is if you find a house you like better than the one you're in—go ahead and move. Remember, though, no one lives well in a dusty mess. I've seen too much hardship brought on families by living in a mess, fixing it up, then moving on to another mess. Keep your business and pleasure separate.

Bathrooms and Kitchens

If you have to fix up, start here. Women usually make the decisions on the house and that's where they look first. Pay attention to color and arrangements.

Conclusion

Weigh the following:
1. How much did the acquisition cost?
2. How much more money do you have?
3. Could this money be spent better elsewhere?
4. How much time do you have?
5. What will cleaning it up do to the value? (Many times that's all it takes to make a good profit.)
6. What is the minimum amount you could put into it to make it "cute?"
7. Are there other investors or people out there who will buy it "as is?"

Use your team of advisors to help you decide—then move on it and get it ready. And whether you use subcontractors or employees, surround yourself with good people.

Chapter 12

Tips on Selling

NOW that you have laid the proper foundation with your purchase arrangements and fixed up your property, it's time to carry through with the third phase of the A.C.E. plan. I must stress, once again, the need to avoid costly entanglements.

Have a good picture of what you want out of the house in terms of total price, monthly payments, and interest rates. Make sure that they are reasonable. In order for the house to sell quickly, you might want to make these costs a little lower than average, so you will attract a large amount of prospective buyers.

If you have plenty of offers to choose from, the chances of having to sell to someone on cluttered terms is lessened. When you have only a few looky-lous, their terms start to dominate your terms. If this happens, then some sort of unfavorable entanglements will occur.

To have as many people as possible looking and making offers, you need to advertise in the most effective way. A good realtor will really help, but make it clear what price YOU want out of it.

Newspaper ads are good. Most people look there when trying to find a house. If you advertise through the newspaper use the following as guidelines:

1. Your ads should state first that which will draw the most attention. The price might do that, but it's usually the financing information that impresses people. For example, you could start the ad with the following:

A.   Owner Contract . . .
B.   Small Down . . .
C. $2,000 moves you in tomorrow . . .
D.   No Qualifying . . .
E.   Easy Assumption . . .

This will get people's attention because it's the terms they are looking for. The balance of the ad should be just as exciting.

2. The ads should prequalify the house for the people. I've spent too much time on the phone answering questions when the information could have been put in the ad. The most common questions to an underworded ad are:

A.   How many bedrooms?
B.   What is the interest rate?
C.   What are the monthly payments?
D.   Is the yard fenced?
E.   How many bathrooms?
F.   What kind of heating?
G.   Is it near schools?
H.   Is it on one level?
I.   How large is the garage?

And a variety of other questions from lot size to bus lines; from how new the roof is to how old the house is. Be sure to include the address in the ad. When they call it helps if they've seen the outside before you meet them there. This prevents you from having to sit and wait at the house while they drive up for the first time and not stop because they don't like the neighborhood, or the outside of the house.

Take your choice. You can either answer the questions on the phone or put them in the ad. I would suggest paying an extra $5.00 or so and put in all the information that will be deciding factors for these people.

3. If you feel that the house will sell best from the outside, then list the address and the times it will be open. I have, on occasion, hired people to be there, so when someone comes, they can be shown around and given a preprinted sheet with all the pertinent information, especially your phone number. Then if they are interested, an appointment can be made for me to meet them personally.

Certainties vs. Uncertainties

From the time you buy a house and move on to fixing it up, you should remember to eliminate uncertainties. People like to hang on to their CERTAINTIES. If they have $5000 in the bank for a down payment on a house and the house you have to sell is surrounded with questions, they most likely won't buy it.

Let's suppose the bathroom needs some work. That's simple enough, but maybe all kinds of things are going through their minds. How long will it take? How much will it cost? Who can we get to fix it up? The answers to those questions exist, but sometimes that doesn't matter. With too many questions it's easier for them to walk away. Be ready with answers, but first eliminate those things that make people uneasy.

One time I had an excellent young couple that I knew were stable. They had the down payment but were leery of the basement stairs. I agreed to have the stairs repaired the next day. I was selling the house as is, so they agreed to add that cost to the price, but I was the one who took care of the problem. Everyone was happy.

Financing poses another kind of uncertainty. Obviously, most sellers want to get as much down or as high a monthly payment as possible. These terms leave a lot of questions in the buyers mind—especially with the economic climate the way it is. They don't even know if they'll have a job next year. What happens if the wife gets pregnant and has to quit work? etc.

In order to alleviate many of these questions, you should be aware of them and take as much uncertainty out of the sale as possible.

When explaining the financing terms, write it out on a piece of paper so the figures are recognizable and definite. I've carried on many negotiations on scratch paper which helped avoid questions like, "Did he say what I think he said?" Figures on paper spark negotiations and eliminate error.

If you put a house in the paper for sale and don't specifically list the terms, people are not sure whether you're charging 10 percent, 11 percent, or 15 percent for your interest rate. Also, they're not sure what the monthly payments are going to cost or how much the real estate taxes are. When they show up to start bargaining they don't know where to start—there are too many uncertainties in their life. If they have $2,000 in their checking account to put down on the house, they are literally afraid to trade the $2,000 for the house that represents too many uncertainties for them, even though it may be a good deal.

At one time I had a house for sale that I wanted to move right away because I needed $3,000 for a commitment I made on buying another house. I felt that the house was worth about $36–37,000 but, because I wanted to move the house right away, I was willing to sell it for $30,000 with the $3,000 down. A lady came to look and really seemed to like it. The second time she came to look at it, she brought a friend and they were spending all their time figuring out where to hang pictures and where to put the furniture. I was there drawing up the papers, figuring out the deal. The payments were going to be $270 a month. At that time she was paying $300 a month for rent and these payments seemed to be right for her. She was really excited until she talked with her attorney. He asked "What about this, and what about that? What about the plumbing? Is the furnace modernized?" Before she came back to get answers to these questions, she wanted to back out of the deal. There was nothing I could say to her to get her to change her mind; even though almost every one of the questions the attorney asked could be answered in the positive. She left. Within a week I was able to sell it for $36,000 with $4,000 down. She had the opportunity for a great buy, but the attorney in this case caused her to lose out.

In summary, the way to eliminate uncertainties is to keep asking yourself questions, i.e., "Would I want this?" "Can I make this easier to understand?" "Are there any uncertainties that can be cleared up?" Houses are purchased to solve people's problems. Have as many solutions on hand as possible.

People Buy for Their Reasons

Long before I started investing I learned this lesson, but real estate has thrown me some investing curves. In my early days of selling insurance I'd ask the question, "Tell me, Bill, of all that we have talked about tonight, what point caused you to buy this policy?" "I never had the chance to go to college," he would say, "and I'm going to make sure that my kids can go whether I'm here or not." I was shocked. I had given him many better reasons for buying—my company was the best, our dividends were highest and our costs were the lowest. I had just mentioned the college aspect in passing and here he was buying it for that reason.

Learn to think like your prospective buyers and do what you think they will like. People buy and sell houses for their own reasons. It's good to second guess, or find out those reasons and use it to your advantage, but sometimes their reasons will surprise you.

For example, one house I bought was a disaster. This is the house, by the way, that made me finally resolve to never deviate from my plan. It needed everything. After putting in $10,000 of my own money, I borrowed $6,000 more from the bank. After four months of working—fixing up the bathroom, painting the house inside and out, putting on a new roof, putting a cement floor in the garage, laying new carpet throughout, redoing the kitchen cabinets and every other possible thing that can be done to a house (I really made that old place look like it never did before.) It was ready to sell. After it sold, I asked the lady what made her decide to buy. I was waiting for a compliment on all the quality work that was done, so I was set back when she said, "I've always wanted a house with a double stainless steel kitchen sink." I knew she wouldn't have bought it had all the other work not been done but, heck, the kitchen sink was the one thing that was there when I bought it.

It's good to understand this principle, and it's a comfort to know that, generally speaking, a good portion of the average buyers want a lot of the same things. Keep abreast of the popular trends and make your houses appeal to a wide variety of people.

Benefits vs. Features

People buy benefits. When selling your houses, stress the benefits. For our purpose here a benefit is something that will only be derived if a person buys and uses the product. A feature stays with the product whether it's purchased or not.

For example, you walk into a car lot and a salesman says, "You ought to buy this car—it has the best engine on the market." Compare that to another salesman saying, "You ought to buy this car. You will save $415 a year in gas because it has the best engine on the market." The best engine on the market will stay with the car but the benefit of saving gas will only come if you buy and drive it.

Let's get back to real estate. "Close to schools" is a feature but, "you won't have to get up every morning and drive your kids to school—they can just walk around the corner," is a benefit. Certain kinds of heating, new roofs, full basements, big yards, deductible interest payments, fenced yards (and hundreds more) can all be stated as benefits. You'll be surprised how quickly people pick up on these things. They'll only trade their hard-earned cash for benefits.

Qualify Prospective Buyers on the Phone

Once I had advertised a house, it was exciting to start getting phone calls. I would jump up from dinner, leave company, and drop everything I was doing to go show the house. Then, they wouldn't show up, or they needed a bigger place, or it wasn't close enough to Mama.

I soon learned to ask a lot of questions on the phone.

Perhaps I had a different house that would be better, etc. I have wasted so much gas, not to mention time, that could have been avoided had I qualified the prospective buyers over the phone.

Sometimes you won't get "the whole truth and nothing but the truth," even though people think they are being honest. I can't count the times I've stated what I wanted down and, upon being reassured that the amount was no problem, I would drive over and show the house. After they fell in love with the house and it was time to draw up the papers, I was told, "The down payment is coming from my mother in New Jersey."

After several bad experiences like that, I learned to ask this leading question: "Now, if you like the house, are you in a position to buy it right away?" Having them answer that question opened up the information channel and saved me a lot of time, and them a lot of embarrassment. (I've rarely seen the relative or friend come through.)

Its Best Light

In conclusion, a house should be cleaned up and as close to livable as possible. I wouldn't suggest boiling cinnamon water and baking a loaf of bread in the oven of a vacant house to make it seem "just like home," but having it clean and ready to move into is appealing. Sometimes that's all it needs.

Chapter 13

Tips in General

THE following sections contain many things I have learned over the years. These tips are given here in an effort to help you make your investing uncomplicated. It's always advisable to keep your life uncluttered, avoiding entanglements which will slow you down.

The Eight Cylinder Approach

An investor constantly needs to ask himself "What else could I be doing with my money?" It would be easy for me to say, "Only do things according to this plan, and ignore everything else," but that would be irresponsible on my part.

Even though I do feel there is no better plan (in terms of growth and benefits), I also feel that no one should act on only a few spark plugs. The eight cylinder concept here simply means that all investment plans are considered. I would suggest becoming an expert in one (this one) but at least know of the others, and be prepared to use them all if at the time they can benefit you.

Let me give you an example. A friend of mine, named Joe, understood the tax advantages of selling on installment sales. He too views all other ways as causing time and money delays. In June he put a house up for sale, asking $50,000—one for which he paid $38,000 with $3,000 down, and then put $2,000 into fixing it up. He was asking for $6,000, but someone came along and offered him $13,000 cash for his equity and then take over his $35,000 contract. This changed the purchase price to $48,000. The buyer had the $13,000 in hand. Most of us would have taken this, but he was afraid of the taxes he would have to pay, so he hesitated. He found himself in a rut and, worst of all, he was not asking the right question—what else could he do with that additional money?

An eight cylinder approach would have him looking at this idea and seeing several alternatives. Let's see what he could have done had he taken the $13,000. He felt that it would have thrown him into a high tax bracket of around 40 percent (or $3,200 which is 40 percent of the $8,000 profit). This would need to be paid to the IRS leaving him only $4,800 ($8,000 minus $3,200).

I say get all the cash you can if someone offers it. He was planning to get his $5,000 back anyway so let's see what he could do with the other $8,000 (which he could use until tax time). He has six months left this year, plus four months next year before his taxes become due. How much can he make in ten months? He immediately bought two houses and sold them within five weeks. He purchased three more and two months later purchased three more. He sold all of these on contract except one. In February a couple wanted to cash him out of that one. He closed that deal in March—clearing $15,800.

He was once again going to have high taxes on that amount the next year, but he had cash once again to pay the taxes which were due then. He now had seven additional contracts with equities of $94,000—netting him $850 per month. He had enough cash from the February sale to pay the taxes from the deal last June and the little bit that he would have to pay on each of the installment sales. Plus he had over $6,000 more to do it again.

One other thing—he also got his original $5,000 back on the previous June sale and that, too, was reinvested.

If someone walks in with cash for a house, take it. My approach doesn't preclude this—it encourages it. What it does suggest, though, is that you look for cash in hand and not money that must come from a bank or a father-in-law in New Mexico.

Formulas in Perspective

Many moons ago I read about an old Indian guide who helped people in the backwoods. The story has it that he was surefooted, tenacious and always got his people through. The only time he didn't was when they didn't follow him. Oh, they could stop and camp here and there, and swim in the rivers, but if they got too far behind him, they became lost. Apparently he didn't look around often enough to see where they were.

If you were in the market for a guide, what criteria would you establish for choosing one? Would you want one that knew the way? Would you want one that took care of most of the problems? And would you want one that was acting FOR you?

The answers to the foregoing questions are obviously "yes." Because we choose our destination by choosing our path we all must take care to choose wisely.

Some investors live by formulas; some live by feelings alone, (or intuition) while most of us live by a combination of both. But because formulas affect us we should find the answers to the questions previously asked. And then carry it asking: a) How am I going to fit in? b) How do I start, continue and end? c) How are adaptations made, if needed?

The reason I bring this up here is because I have seen people that have known the formulas and then have gone out into the real world and blown it. One time, when I had a 5-unit place for sale for $80,000 with $8,000 down, a man looked at me and made an offer of $98,500 with $9,000 down. When I came out of shock I told him I only wanted $80,000, which was a fair price. "No," he said, "I have this formula and after I plugged the rents in and expenses it comes out to $98,500." "I know, but it's in a rotten part of town," I answered. He insisted on that amount. Either his guide was a wacko or his brain went swimming too long. You probably think I'm making this up, but it is the truth. I also thought it was so far out that I didn't want to do business with him. That was the first reason. The second reason cinched it. His formula said I would wait 6 weeks which would give him time to close another deal and then come up with the money for my down payment. I sold it to someone else.

This taught me a lesson—WATCH OUT. Caution is the password. Ironically some of the most dubious formulas are expounded in the most convincing way. A good comparison is with the ancient Greeks—the person to win the debate wasn't the one that was RIGHT or WRONG, but the one that put across his argument in the most persuasive manner.

I have had run-ins with many people and their formulas and after watching them, my suggestion is to: a) keep everything in perspective, b) keep learning and adapt information you need to *your* circumstances, c) establish check points to measure your progress.

In short—make your own formula.

Exchanges

There are plenty of books that tell the advantages and mechanics of exchanging properties. I agree that it is an excellent way to defer paying taxes. If you have an excellent realtor on your team who can handle all the mechanics, it can be an enjoyable and worthwhile transaction.

I hesitate in suggesting this for a small investor until he has some experience. The reason I say this is because exchanges can get complicated. The more people involved, the more entanglements. At one time five or six people were involved with a three-way exchange. I thought we were a bank with all the problems we were causing.

The deal never did consummate because of one small discrepancy. I wish I could have put together some of these exchanges in my early days, but of the four attempts I made, all of them fell through. There were circumstances out of my control that came up and affected them adversely.

If you want this tax advantage, do it right. Let a professional set it up and do the leg work.

Having Your Own Office

This question repeatedly comes up. Other people must wrestle with it as I did. For a long time I operated out of my basement, but after a year or so I decided to get an office. In hindsight I wish I would have followed the following guide plan:

1. Only move when you have to. If you can work at home with no interruptions, fine, but if you end up tending kids, running household errands, etc., it's time to remember that you need to concentrate on investing.

If you can have privacy in your home that would be ideal.

2. If a move is needed, make it gradually. Don't get into the biggest, nicest place you can. Move to an office where you share services with others who just want a place to hang their hats. Many buildings have small offices surrounding secretarial/receptionist services. The benefits are immense.

Somebody is always there to answer your phone; someone will greet people coming to see you, and they will be able to perform typing and copying services. This is an invaluable asset. After having my own secretary for a year I realized that she spent only one hour a day doing actual typing. I would have saved over $500 a month with the other arrangements.

Also the place I was going to rent wanted 9 cents a copy which I thought was too high. I knew the price of paper and copy toner was less than 2 cents a copy so I went out and leased a copy machine. Lease payments were $110 a month; paper and toner and maintenance were about $20 a month. I had to service the machine daily, buy the paper, call for repairs, etc., to make my 500 or so copies. I thought I was saving all this money until I multiplied 500 by 9¢ and came up with $45 not $130.

Also, there usually is a nice conference room for your use when sharing space.

Of the above that would need to be paid by you to an employee, you'd have to pay taxes on those salaries to every government agency available. Payment for these shared services is like rent. Plus if your own secretary was sick you'd be left with doing the work yourself or trying to find someone else to do it.

3. If you then need a bigger office, you're on your own. You obviously need one for certain reasons, most of which I would say are out of the realm of investing. There was nothing I was doing as an investor (even

when processing six houses a month) that couldn't have been handled by the preceding office arrangements.

In summary, move up slowly. Have your team give you feedback on these moves.

Business Cards

Just a hint here might make the difference between turning that one extra deal or not. According to the A.C.E. plan you're in the buy, fix-up, and sell business. To keep that information in front of people you should have a nice looking business card stating so.

First, why a nice looking card? It's simple; people will hang on it. If it is embossed, or has nice art work, etc., it will hang around the top drawer in their buffet until cousin George comes into town next summer and needs a place to stay. Second, state what you do! This information doesn't have to be long. Actually, it could be quite short. I saw one card that said, "Houses" under the man's name. Another one said, "I buy houses" and another one simply said, "Real Estate Investments."

Many times I would make my offer and if unaccepted I would just leave. On one house I went back a few weeks later and the man came running out. "I wanted to call you, but I couldn't remember your name," he said. "I finally had to sell the house for $1,000 less than your offer. Man, I wracked my brain for two days trying to get hold of you."

After that experience I even carried it one step further and would write them a letter a few days later restating my offer (be sure to include acceptance date) and again writing my phone number.

Whatever you want your card to say and however you want it to look is important, but it's more important to just have something to leave with people. Remember, "Out of sight, out of mind."

P.S. Just for fun you might want to read about Robert J. Ringer's business card in *Winning Through Intimidation*.

Notary Publics

Being a notary public and having friends that are the same could save you countless hours. It's so convenient to be able to take one of your investor friends with you and not have to wait around for everyone to get before a notary public. Too many things can happen while waiting.

Partnerships

Whole books have been written on this subject. I'll just add a little here. "Avoid costly entanglements" takes on so much importance with partnerships. I'm not saying I'm against them. Some have been the key to success for so many people. But before entering into any arrangement consider the following:

1. Expectations vary greatly. What you say and what your partner hears can be miles apart. Over a period of time the difference in these expectation levels increases.

2. Have well defined goals.

3. Remember people's situations change. Where they might have excess cash today—tomorrow they may be hurting.

4. There is no ready market for selling limited partnerships.

Make sure you have exhausted all other possibilities before seeking out partners. Of all the people I know who have entered into partnerships, almost all of them wish they would have gone it alone—even if their growth would have been slower.

Debt Ratio

You must be careful when you are buying and selling to make sure you maintain a proper debt ratio, debt ratio mean the percentage of every dollar of assets that represents liabilities. For instance, I felt that it was in my best interest if I could keep my debt ratio under 65 percent, which means that if I had a $100,000 contract receivable, I would like all of my underlying encumbrances to total no more than $65,000. Now of course this is impossible on every transaction, but it can be averaged out over many properties. In the higher priced units it's very hard to maintain that kind of ratio.

Let's say for instance that you have two pieces of property. You sell them and have a net equity of $10,000. In one, it's a small house, your receivable is $25,000 and your payable is $15,000—you have a $10,000 equity and the debt ratio is 60 percent. But let's say this $10,000 in the other house is a receivable of $80,000 and a payable of $70,000. Your liability to asset ratio is over 87 percent. If this ratio gets way out of line, a slight dip in your market area could adversely affect you. Also if you have occasion to use your financial statement, a bad liabilities to assets ratio will stick out like a sore thumb.

For instance, let's say you have a $400,000 net worth, but it shows up as $900,000 in assets with $500,000 in liabilities. That's not bad, but if that same $400,000 showed up as $500,000 in assets and $100,000 in liabilities, it would look a lot better and I'm sure you would feel even more comfortable. Let's go to the other extreme and say that it shows up as $3,000,000 worth of assets and $2,600,000 worth of liabilities. That ratio is totally out of line and if you are like me, you wouldn't be sleeping too well at night.

It is easy to keep control in this area. Just weigh each transaction to see how it looks individually and as a part of your total picture.

Carry Legal Forms and Deeds

You never know when a good deal will pop up. I made it a habit to carry all necessary deeds with me. Even if for no other reason than to show the people what we could be signing at the title company. It would be helpful to really be familiar with these forms. If people ask you questions, the answers are often on the forms. For example, when I made an offer, I would constantly be asked how they were protected, and what would happen if I sold the house to someone who didn't make them the payments. I would pull out the appropriate form and go over those provisions, which would ease their fears.

It's also nice to know this information for your own benefit.

Publisher's Note

Mr. Cook publishes a monthly newsletter for real estate investors called, *The Money Machine Newsletter*. It is the country's "what to do," "how to do it," "what's happening" newsletter for the real estate investor who wants to be successful in today's market. Each month includes a message from Mr. Cook, questions and answers, an update on the latest happenings in the real estate world, a feature story, frequent guest writers, and a monthly calendar of seminars and conventions across the country.

For subscription information, write:

> Investment & Tax Publications
> P.O. Box 1201-M
> Orem, UT 84057

or call 1-801-224-3500.

Chapter 14

Getting the Equity Out of Your House

ONE of the questions I most frequently receive is "How do I get the equity out of my house?" Another variation of that question is this: "I'm paying too much in taxes. How do I use my equities to buy tax write-offs?" It's with these questions in mind that this chapter will be directed.

A Myth Put to Rest

Let's once and for all put to rest the concept that your only asset for starting your investment plan is the equity in your house. It's there all right, and I'm not going to ignore it, but I will put it in its proper light.

That is your house. It's the one you're working so hard for. The following sentence makes very little investment sense until you look closer: "I want my own house to be free and clear." Ostensibly it looks like you're not maximizing the potential of mortgaging your house to the hilt for the purpose of leveraging into other properties or investments.

Once you look deeper you realize how important it is to have this one nest egg, this one piece of earth that is yours. Therefore if the equity in your home must be used, try to do it for a temporary time only.

If You Must

If you feel that your personal residence is your only source of investment funds, there are a few ways to accomplish freeing up the money. However, please don't read this section and run out and start doing this without reading the balance of this chapter.

Before the alternatives are listed it needs to be stated that I realize the complexity of the economic situation. Many of the traditional approaches have changed, but let's list several ways and maybe something can happen with one or more in tandem.

Refinance New Mortgages

Banks will let you refinance your home up to a certain amount of its fair market value. Eighty percent is common these days. If your house is worth $70,000 you may get a loan up to $56,000 (maybe higher in some areas). If your current loan balance is $40,000, this move will free up $16,000. Not bad for a few hours of paperwork, or is it?

Let's look at the negative side and then put it in perspective. This new loan means three things are going to change:

(1) The amount of interest will go up.

(2) The amount of the monthly payment will increase.

(3) The terminology of the new loan papers will probably change. If it follows the trend, much more will now be in the bank's favor.

Are you willing to pay the price? Do you want to trade what you now have for this new set of figures? Obviously the answer to this needs to be put in perspective, and the best way to do that is by asking another question. *What else could you do with the money?*

Where's Your Priority?

This is an important question that needs frequent asking. It helps prioritize so many things:

- Can I make more money with what I'll get out?
- Am I willing to pay the price in the meantime?
- Can I pay off this excess loan with my profits?
- What happens if the expected profits aren't there or are longer in coming than anticipated?
- Do I need the whole amount or can I get by with less?

If you can safely answer these questions you may proceed in several ways. All of the ways involve some type of additional mortgaging of your house. You could:

- Refinance with a new loan for the whole amount.
- Place a second or third mortgage on the property (Note: the terms of this type of loan are usually more stringent, but these terms only apply to the actual amount of this loan. The first mortgage remains intact with no change.)

HERE'S
TO YOU,
RACHEL
ROBINSON

A Richard Jackson Book

BOOKS BY JUDY BLUME

The Pain and the Great One
The One in the Middle
   Is the Green Kangaroo
 Freckle Juice

Tales of a Fourth Grade Nothing
Otherwise Known as Sheila the Great
Superfudge
Fudge-a-mania

Blubber
Iggie's House
Starring Sally J. Freedman as Herself
Are You There God? It's Me, Margaret.
It's Not the End of the World
Then Again, Maybe I Won't
Deenie
Just as Long as We're Together
Here's to You, Rachel Robinson

Tiger Eyes
Forever . . .
Letters to Judy:
   What Kids Wish They Could Tell You

HERE'S TO YOU, RACHEL ROBINSON

JUDY BLUME

Orchard Books ~ New York

SIDE BY SIDE by Harry Woods. Copyright © MCMXXVII Shapiro, Bernstein & Co., Inc., New York. Renewed. All rights reserved. International copyright secured. Used by permission.

Orchard Books
95 Madison Avenue
New York, NY 10016

Manufactured in the United States of America
Book design by Rosanne Kakos-Main

The text of this book is set in 11 point Meridien.

10 9 8 7 6 5 4 3 2 1

Library of Congress Cataloging-in-Publication Data
Blume, Judy.
    Here's to you, Rachel Robinson / Judy Blume.
        p.   cm.
    Summary: Expelled from boarding school, Charles' presence at home proves disruptive, especially for sister Rachel, a gifted seventh grader juggling friendships and school activities.
    ISBN 0-531-06801-3. ISBN 0-531-08651-8 (lib. bdg.)
    [1. Brothers and sisters—Fiction.   2. Family problems—Fiction.   3. Gifted children—Fiction.   4. Friendship—Fiction.]   I. Title.
PZ7.B6265He   1993
[Fic]—dc20   93-9631

To Amanda

HERE'S
TO YOU,
RACHEL
ROBINSON

ONE

Trouble in our family is spelled with a capital *C* and has been as long as I can remember. The *C* stands for Charles. He's my older brother, two years and four months older to be exact. Ever since the phone call about him last night, I've felt incredibly tense. And now, at this very minute, my parents are driving up to Vermont, to Charles's boarding school, to find out if he's actually been kicked out or if he's just been suspended again.

I tried to take a deep breath. I read an article about relieving tensions in *Psychology Today*. You take a deep breath, then count to ten as you slowly release it. But as I inhaled, I caught the scent of the fresh lilacs on Ms. Lefferts's desk and I started to cough. Ms. Lefferts, my seventh-grade English teacher, looked over at me. She was discussing the three most important elements in making a biography come alive for the reader. When I coughed again, she crossed the room and opened two windows from the bottom, letting in the spring breeze.

The class was restless, shifting around in their seats, counting the hours till school let out so they could enjoy the first really warm day of the year. But the clock on the wall read 10:17. The day was just beginning. And the date on the chalkboard said FRIDAY, MAY 8. Still seven weeks of school to go.

I forced my mind back to class.

"So now that we've come to the end of our unit on biographies," Ms. Lefferts was saying, "I have an assignment for you." She walked back to her desk and stood there, looking at us, a half smile on her face. She knows exactly how to get our attention. She makes good use of pregnant pauses. I once used that expression in class and have been paying for it ever since. Now I would know better. Now I would say *dramatic* pauses.

"I want you to write a biography of your own lives," Ms. Lefferts continued. "Not an *autobiography*, but a biography. Who can explain the difference?" She took a hair clip out of her desk drawer and held it between her teeth while she gathered her streaked blond hair into a ponytail. She looked around the room as she fastened it, waiting for someone to respond to her question.

Max Wilson raised his hand.

"Yes, Max?" Ms. Lefferts said.

"An autobiography is about the life of a car," Max said.

The class cracked up. Ms. Lefferts didn't.

"Get it?" Max asked. "Auto . . . biography."

"Yes, Max . . . I get it," Ms. Lefferts said. Then she sighed deeply.

I cannot believe that just a few months ago I liked Max Wilson. I actually spent the entire seventh-grade dance with my head nestled on his shoulder. We even kissed in the parking lot while we were waiting for our rides home. What a revolting thought! Now I understand that I never really liked Max, the person. It's just that he is the only boy in seventh grade who's taller than me.

"Rachel . . ." Ms. Lefferts said.

I snapped to attention. Ms. Lefferts was calling on me even though I hadn't raised my hand. I hate when teachers do that. But I said, "The difference between a biography and an autobiography is that in an autobiography the writer is writing about his or her own life. In a biography the writer is writing about the life of someone else."

"Exactly," Ms. Lefferts said. "Thank you, Rachel." Then she went on to explain that she wants us to write a short biography of our own lives, as if we don't know anything about ourselves until we go to the library to do research. "And try to hold it to five pages, please."

Ms. Lefferts never says a paper *has* to be at least five pages. She uses reverse psychology on us. And it always works.

I began to think about my biography right away. Luckily my French teacher was absent, and the substitute told us since she doesn't know one word of French, we could use the period as a study hour. I opened my notebook and started writing, ignoring the kids who were using the period to torture the substitute.

RACHEL LOWILLA ROBINSON
A Biography
Part One—The Unexpected Visitor

Rachel Lowilla Robinson was born tall. The average infant measures nineteen inches at birth but Rachel measured twenty-three. She was the third child born to Nell and Victor Robinson, following Jessica, who was four, and Charles, who was twenty-eight months. The Robinsons had planned on only two children, so Rachel was, as they sometimes put it, the unexpected visitor.

From her mother, Rachel inherited her height and her curly auburn hair. From her father, dark eyes and a love of music. Although her mother was from Boston and her father from Brooklyn, the Robinsons settled in Connecticut to raise their family, in an area of cluster housing called Palfrey's Pond, located just one hour from New York City by train.

Nell Robinson liked to say Rachel was mature from the day she was born. "She was born thirty-five," Mrs. Robinson joked with her friends. But obviously that wasn't true. Rachel was born a baby, like everyone else. She just did things a little earlier. For example, at eight months Rachel was walking. At eighteen months she was speaking in three-word sentences. She could read at three and at four she could pick out tunes on the piano. Her favorite was the theme from "Sesame Street," which Jessica and Charles watched on TV every day. Rachel's first memory was of Charles biting her on the leg, right above her knee. She was barely two at the time.

By first grade it occurred to Rachel that she was different. As her classmates were learning to read, she was finishing the Beverly Cleary books and starting the *Little House* set. As they were learning to add and subtract simple numbers, she enjoyed adding up long columns of figures, especially the register tape from the supermarket. This difference did not make her happy.

I was careful, in Part One, not to tell too much. I told just enough to show Ms. Lefferts I've given serious thought to this assignment. And even though I tried to use interesting details, little-known facts and humorous anecdotes—the three most important elements in making a biography come alive for the reader—I was not about to share the private details of my family life. I was not about to discuss Charles.

The bell rang before I had the chance to start Part Two. I didn't notice until then that I hadn't had any trouble breathing while I was writing. I guess *Psychology Today* is right when they tell you to get your mind off whatever is making you feel tense and onto something else. I picked up my books and went to the cafeteria to meet Stephanie and Alison for lunch.

"What's wrong?" Steph asked, the second I sat down. She was already halfway through a bologna sandwich.

"What do you mean?" I said.

"You're doing that *thing* with your mouth."

"I am?" Last year the dentist made me a kind of retainer to wear at night, to keep me from clench-ing my jaw, but I left it at Steph's in January and haven't seen it since. My parents still don't know I lost it.

"You get an A *minus* or something?"

"No," I told her.

"Then what?"

"Charles."

"Again?"

I nodded and began to peel a hard-boiled egg. All three of us bring our lunch. We're convinced we'll live longer that way.

"Why doesn't Charles ever come home?" Alison asked, chewing on a carrot stick. She's small and delicate and eats so slowly she hardly ever has time to finish her lunch. But that doesn't bother her. Hardly anything does. She's probably never had trouble breathing in her entire life. She's probably never even felt tense. We are total opposites, so it's amazing that we're friends. "I mean, doesn't he *want* to?" she continued.

"I guess not." I salted my egg, then bit into it.

"I don't get it," Alison said. She's never met Charles, since he left for Vermont last August and she didn't move here from L.A. until Labor Day. Actually Steph met Alison first and they hit it off right away. She didn't even tell me Alison's adopted or that her birth mother's Vietnamese until school started. I used to worry that Steph, who's been my best friend since second grade, would forget about me. Actually, I still do. But at the moment it seems to be working out okay, even though I know she and Alison prefer each other's company to mine.

"There's nothing to get," I told her. "Except that he's impossible! Now, could we please change the subject?"

"Impossible how?" Alison asked, ignoring my request.

"Rude and obnoxious."

Alison looked over at Stephanie to see if she agreed. Stephanie nodded. "He's definitely rude." Steph took a mirror out of her backpack and set it on the table. She opened her mouth wide to make sure food wasn't caught in her braces. Stephanie is the least self-conscious person I know.

"How'd he get that way?" Alison asked.

I was really getting annoyed and Alison could tell. She offered me her bag of potato chips. "How does anybody get that way?" I said, reaching in and grabbing a handful.

TWO

When I got home from school, my cousin Tarren was at the house. She's twenty-two and has a ten-month-old baby, Roddy. She could tell I was surprised to see her. "Nell and Victor had to go to Vermont," she said, using my parents' first names. "It has something to do with Charles," she added, as if I didn't know.

"Jess and I could have managed on our own," I told her, irritated that Mom had asked her to come over without discussing it with me.

Tarren bent down to tie her running shoes. She's tall, like all the women in our family, but her hair is black and her eyes blue. Jessica and I were bridesmaids at her wedding two years ago. Now she's divorced. She and Bill, the guy she married, didn't get along even though they went together all through high school and two years of college. Tarren says Bill couldn't accept adult responsibilities, like being a father. He moved out west after the divorce and spends all his time hang gliding. His picture was on the cover of *Hang Glider* magazine a few months ago. He looked like some sort of strange prehistoric bird.

"Nell asked me to spend the night," Tarren said, "since tonight is Jessica's junior prom and all. . . ."

I had totally forgotten about Jessica's prom. I'd be devastated if it were my junior prom and Mom and Dad were away because of Charles.

"I promised we'd take lots of pictures," Tarren said. "I brought my new camera." She grabbed it off the kitchen counter. "It's a PHD. The guy at the store claims you can't take a bad picture with it." She pointed it at me. "You know what PHD stands for?" she asked. *"Press Here, Dummy!"* She laughed as she pressed but I jumped out of the way.

"Rachel! That was my last shot."

"Sorry."

"I guess it doesn't matter. Nell said you've got two rolls of film in the fridge."

I couldn't believe that in the midst of a family crisis Mom would remember we had film in the refrigerator. I guess Tarren could tell what I was thinking because she said, "Nell is the most amazing woman!"

I've heard that expression more times than I can count. It's true Mom is a successful trial lawyer, but

I don't see what's so amazing about that. I expect to do just as much with my life.

"Between you and me," Tarren continued, "I think it's grossly unfair that Nell has to spend so much of her time worrying about your brother. A lot of kids would jump at the chance to change places with him. He doesn't appreciate what he has. That's his problem!"

I didn't feel like talking about Charles, so I told Tarren I had homework and went up to my room.

Later the two of us had supper in the kitchen while Jessica soaked in a bubble bath upstairs. Tarren likes to hear about school since she's studying to be a teacher. So I told her about the biography and what Max Wilson had said in class. She laughed and laughed. She'll probably be a good teacher. She wants to teach fourth grade, which should be just right for her. We ate standing at the counter—tuna right from the can, lettuce leaves pulled off the head and, for dessert, frozen Milky Ways left over from Halloween. We're lucky we didn't break our teeth on them.

"Is this how you eat every night?" I asked, thinking of the way we sit down to dinner, the table set with place mats and pretty dishes.

"Rachel," Tarren said, "when you have a ten-month-old to worry about, *plus* papers and exams, you just don't have time to think about meals. If my mom doesn't fix supper, I'm happy grazing. When Roddy's older, it'll be different. I'll have a teaching job and my own place and . . ." Her voice drifted off for a minute. "But not everyone can be a wonder woman like your mother."

"Dad helps. He does all the grocery shopping."

"Well, I'm a single parent. There won't be anyone around to help me."

"Maybe you'll get married again," I suggested, causing Tarren to choke on her Natural Lime Spritzer, which she was swigging straight out of the bottle.

"Pul-eeese . . ." she said, wiping her mouth with the back of her hand. She sounded exactly like one of my friends.

We could hear Jessica rustling in her magenta taffeta prom dress before we actually saw her. She let me try it on last week. It fit perfectly. Jess and I could be doubles except she has a major case of acne. She uses a heavy medicated makeup that hides some of it on good days. On bad days nothing can hide it.

As Jess came down the stairs, Tarren snapped away. I was surprised when Jess posed for the camera. Usually she refuses to have her picture taken. But tonight she put her arms around me, as if I were her date, and twirled me across the room until we were both laughing our heads off and so dizzy we fell back onto the sofa.

"You two are so great!" Tarren said. "You remind me

of me and my friends when we were your age." She turned serious. "Enjoy it now," she told us, "because life isn't always all you thought it'd be." She paused for a minute, then added, "I speak from experience."

Neither of us knew how to respond. Finally Jessica cleared her throat and said, "Tarren . . . didn't you say you have to run over to the library?"

"Well . . . yes," Tarren answered, "but only for a little while."

"Why don't you go now?" Jess suggested. "The library closes at nine."

I found it strange that Jessica was suddenly so anxious for Tarren to go to the library.

"I've just got to pick up some books," Tarren explained to me. "We're studying the gifted and talented child this month."

I felt my face turn hot.

"I won't be long," she said.

As soon as she was gone, Jessica let out a sigh and raced upstairs. Ten minutes later she returned transformed in Mom's slinky black dress, satin heels and dangling earrings. She'd put on dark, wine-colored lipstick and had pinned her hair back on one side, letting the rest fall over her face.

I almost passed out. "Jessica . . ."

She held up her hand. "Don't say it, Rachel. We'll have pictures of me in pink."

"But Mom will—" I began again.

"Mom's not here, is she? And if someone at school tells Dad, it will be too late. The prom will be over."

Dad teaches history at the high school and coaches the track team. Someone will definitely tell him about this. Someone will say, "That was some outfit your daughter wore to the prom, Victor!"

A car horn tooted. Jess took a quick look out the window. "My chariot," she said.

I followed as she ran down the front walk. "And not a word about this to anyone," she called over her shoulder, tripping on Mom's heels. "Understand?"

Her friends Richie, Ed, Marcy and Kristen whooped and whistled when they saw her. Jess says she has the best friends ever. She says she can tell them anything. But I think they were surprised tonight.

"Get the camera, Rachel," Jess called. I ran inside for Tarren's PHD and snapped one group photo before they all piled back into the car.

I tried to imagine the three of us—Stephanie, Alison and me—going to our junior prom four years from now. Will we go in a group like Jess and her friends, or with individual dates? Jess says it's better to go in a group. There are fewer disappointments that way. I don't know. I think it would be more romantic to go with someone you really like. But if it came down to Max Wilson or my friends, I would definitely choose my friends.

As they pulled out, I called, "Drive carefully!"

"We always do," Jess called back, laughing.

I watched them drive away. Then I went back into the house, wondering what Mom will say if she finds out Jess wore her black dress. *She'll probably blame herself,* I thought. *She'll probably say Jess is* acting out.

THREE

cting out is exactly the expression Dr. Sparks used to describe Charles's behavior. He's the psychologist who evaluated him last year, the one who suggested he go away to school.

I admit it was a great relief when Charles left for Vermont last August—even though boarding school is a luxury we can't really afford, not with three kids who will soon be ready for college. I know my parents sometimes feel guilty about the decision to send him away to school. But I don't. Now I can invite my friends over without worrying.

I never told anyone I'd read Dr. Sparks's report. I'd found it by chance on the dining room table, mixed in with Mom's legal pads and reference books, while I was searching for a letter from music camp. It said Charles was *acting out* as a way of getting the attention he craved. Well, I could have told my parents that for free!

Thinking about Charles made me feel weak, so I took the last piece of watermelon out of the refrigerator and sat at the kitchen table slurping it up while I waited for Tarren to return from the library. When I finished, I collected the seeds and stood halfway across the kitchen. Then, one by one, I tried spitting them into the sink. Stephanie had a party on the last day of school last year and spitting watermelon seeds from a distance was one of the games we played. I was hopeless, missing the target every time. Even though I think it's incredibly stupid, I've been practicing in secret ever since. Tonight I hit my target eight out of eleven times.

The watermelon reminded me of dinner last night. We'd sat down to eat early, as soon as Mom had walked in, because Jess was in a hurry to get back to school. She and Ed were on the decorating committee for the prom. They were transforming the gym into some kind of futuristic fantasy with a hundred silver balloons and yards and yards of tinsel.

We'd been talking about the prom all through dinner, but just as we were finishing the watermelon Mom said, "Guess who's on the governor's short list for Superior Court?"

I had no idea what she was talking about, but Dad pushed back his chair, practically leaped across the table and lifted Mom out of her seat. "I've always wanted to make it with a judge," he said.

They kissed, then Mom told him, "You'll have to wait till the end of the month to find out."

"Find out what?" I asked.

"I've been nominated for a judgeship," Mom said.

"A judge?" Jessica asked. "You're going to be a judge?"

"Maybe," Mom said.

"What would that mean?" I asked. "Would you have to quit your job at the firm?"

"Yes," Mom said. "Being a judge is a full-time job."

"I can't imagine you as a judge," Jess said.

"I can," I told her. "Mom would make an excellent judge."

"I didn't say she wouldn't," Jess said.

"Would you get murder cases?" I asked Mom.

"That would depend on which court I'm assigned to," she said. "If it's criminal court, I could get murder cases. If it's domestic court, I'd get divorces and child custody cases, and if it's civil court . . ." She paused. "But it's too soon to think about the details. First we have to see if I'm actually appointed."

My mind was racing. What if Mom gets criminal court and sends a murderer to jail and he escapes and finds out where we live and comes after her. . . . I'd read about a case like that in the paper. Maybe we'll have bodyguards to protect us like the President. Not that I want to live with bodyguards. And I certainly don't want to be escorted to school every day. I don't think that would go over very well with my friends. Probably they won't want to come to my house if that happens. Probably their parents won't even let them!

Jessica brought me back from my *what ifs* when she jumped up from the table. "I'm going to be late! Be home around ten," she called as the screen door slammed.

Mom flinched. She hates it when the door slams.

It was my night to help clean up the kitchen. Mom makes out lists every Sunday night—household jobs, groceries, errands, appointments. Steph is envious of the chalkboard in our kitchen with the dinner menu printed on it every day. She never knows what's for dinner until her mother gets home from work with some kind of takeout. If it were up to Dad and Jess, our household would be chaotic. But Mom says if you're organized, everything in life is easier. I agree. Except maybe dealing with Charles.

I started clearing the plates off the table. When the phone rang, I ran for it, sure it was Stephanie or Alison. I wouldn't tell them anything about Mom being a judge yet. I'd wait until it was definite.

But it wasn't Alison or Steph. It was Timothy Norton, the director of the Dorrance School. I put my hand over the receiver and whispered to Mom and Dad, "It's about Charles."

Dad turned off the water at the sink and dried his hands on his jeans. I held the phone out to him as Mom raced upstairs to pick up the extension in their room. I felt my dinner sloshing around in my stomach. Yet from the tone of Dad's voice, I didn't think it was as serious as last time, when Mr. Norton called to tell us about Charles's accident.

That was last January, right after the holidays. Charles had gone for a joyride on his teacher's Yamaha. It was a wet night and he'd lost control, skidding across the road and crashing into a tree. He'd wound up with cuts and bruises plus a gash in his leg requiring twelve stitches.

Still, they said he was lucky because he hadn't been wearing a helmet and he could have been killed. I am somewhat ashamed to admit this, but at the time I'd let that thought run through my mind. *He could have been killed.* Then I'd pushed it away. I don't want Charles to die. Dying is too final. My parents would blame themselves and never get over it. Besides, he's my brother. I'm supposed to care about him. Even though the teacher didn't press charges, Charles was suspended for a week. But he didn't come home. He went to Aunt Joan's house in New Hampshire, instead.

A minute after Dad hung up the phone, Mom came back into the kitchen. She'd aged ten years in ten minutes. She thinks she's good at hiding her feelings because she doesn't talk about them. But she can't fool me. I can read her thoughts by the changes in her face. The crease in her forehead was deeper, her mouth was stiff and her shoulders hunched.

Dad put an arm around her. She gave him a pained look.

"What?" I asked.

Mom didn't answer.

"What?" I said again, this time to Dad.

"He hasn't handed in his papers and he refuses to take any exams," Dad explained. Then he went back to the sink, turned the water on full blast and began to scour the lasagna pan as if his life depended on it.

"What does that mean?" I asked Mom. "Will he have to do ninth grade a third time?"

"Absolutely not!" Mom said, pulling herself together. She stood tall and erect and looked me straight in the eye. "And he *didn't* repeat ninth grade. The system at Dorrance is different from public school. You know that. It was in Charles's best interest to start over as a freshman."

Mom marched across the kitchen and started loading the dishwasher, with all the dishes facing the same direction. She can't stand how Dad does it, shoving things in any which way.

"He's always been too young for his class, emotionally," Mom continued, building her case as if she were in court. She's full of excuses when it comes to Charles.

"And I don't want you to discuss this with anyone, Rachel."

"Mom!" I was annoyed that she thought I needed reminding.

"We should have held him back a year before first grade," Mom said, drumming the counter with her fingertips, "but who knew then?"

"Nell . . ." Dad said. "Rachel doesn't need to worry about this."

They looked at each other for a minute. Then Mom said, "You're right." But she kept drumming the counter. It was amazing how one phone call about Charles could change everything.

"This doesn't mean he's coming home, does it?" I asked. My mouth felt dry, as if I couldn't swallow.

"We won't know until we meet with Mr. Norton at Dorrance," Dad said.

"You'd better call for a substitute," Mom told Dad. "And I'll have to cancel my deposition." She opened a kitchen drawer, pulled out a pad and pencil and began to make a list. Without even looking up, she said, "Let the cats in, would you, Rachel. They're scratching at the screen."

I held the screen door for Burt and Harry, then bolted from the room with them at my heels. I raced up the stairs and locked myself into my room, throwing open all the windows. The night air smelled like summer. I wished it really *were* summer. I wished I could go to music camp tomorrow. Then I wouldn't have to think about Charles or what might happen if he came home.

I took my flute out of its case, sat at my music stand and began to play a Handel sonata. Music takes me someplace else. To a world where I feel safe and happy. Sometimes I make mistakes but I can fix them. Sometimes I don't get exactly the sound I want, but I can find it if I keep trying. With music it's up to me. With music I'm in control.

FOUR

Tell me more about Charles," Alison said.

It was Saturday morning and the three of us—Stephanie, Alison and me—were walking along the water's edge at the town beach. It's not an ocean beach. It's on the Sound. In fourth grade we had to memorize the difference between a sound and a bay. It's funny how you remember things like that.

The weather was still balmy but more humid than yesterday, and we wore shorts and T-shirts for the first time since last September. A few people on the beach were in bathing suits, working on an early tan. I hate baking in the sun. My skin gets freckled, my eyes sting and sometimes I get sneezing fits.

I've decided Alison's fascination with my brother has to do with the fact that until now she's been the only child in her family. Actually she's still the only child. Her mother is pregnant but the baby isn't due until July.

"Well, for one thing, Charles has a great sense of humor," Steph told Alison. "That is, when he wants to." She paused for a minute. "And he's extremely cute."

"Really?" Alison asked me. "I didn't know he was cute."

"I refuse to participate in this conversation!" I told them both.

Maizie, Alison's small, furry-faced dog, was digging up a bone buried in the sand. When we first met Alison, she told us her dog could talk and Stephanie believed her. Steph is incredibly gullible. She believes anything you tell her. She even believed her father was away on a business trip when it was painfully obvious to the rest of us her parents had separated.

Alison turned to Steph. "If Charles comes home from boarding school, will he finish ninth grade at Fox?" She acted as if Steph had all the answers. I never should have told them my parents went to Vermont. I never should have told them anything. My mother was right. This is family business. You can't expect anyone else to understand.

"Maybe he'll be in Jeremy Dragon's class," Alison said to Steph. I loved the way they were carrying on this conversation as if I weren't there.

"Oh, that'd be perfect!" Stephanie said, jabbing me in the side. "Right, Rachel?"

"I find that a totally revolting idea!" I said. Jeremy Dragon is our name for the best-looking boy in ninth grade. He wears a chartreuse satin team jacket with a black dragon on the back. I'm the only seventh grader in his math class.

"But it *is* possible," Alison said.

"Anything's possible!" I admitted. My mind was filling with *what ifs*. What if Charles comes home today? What if he *does* have to do ninth grade again, and at *my* junior high? What if he makes friends with Jeremy Dragon and Jeremy Dragon starts hanging out at our house and Charles humiliates me in front of him and my parents won't listen and . . .

"Rachel . . ." Stephanie sang, waving a hand in front of my face. "Where are you?"

I don't know why but as soon as Stephanie said that, I took off. I ran as fast as I could, with Maizie at my heels, barking.

I could hear Alison and Stephanie laughing and shouting, "Rachel . . . what are you doing? Rachel . . . wait! Ra . . . chel!"

There was no way they could catch me. My legs are twice as long as Alison's. And Steph isn't fast enough. Only Maizie could keep up with me. I kept running, from one end of the beach to the other. Finally I collapsed on the sand, totally out of breath, with a stitch in my side.

We went to Alison's house for lunch. Leon, her stepfather, made us grilled cheese and tomato sandwiches.

Alison's mother, Gena Farrell, was at the counter squeezing lemons. Suddenly she put her hands on her belly and said, "Ooh . . . Matthew's playing soccer this morning." Gena is a famous TV actress with her own series. But at home she acts like a regular parent. Alison says her pregnancy is a surprise to everyone since she's forty years old and the doctors told her long ago she'd never be able to have biological children. That's why she adopted Alison.

"Let me feel," Leon said. He put his hands on Gena's belly. "Good going, Matthew. That's a goal!"

They talk about the baby as if he were already born. Gena's had tests to make sure he's okay. That's how they know it's a boy. His full name will be Matthew Farrell Wishnik.

Before we finished lunch there was a rumble of thunder. Maizie whimpered and hid under the table. After lunch, while the rain poured down, the three of us watched a movie. Alison's family has a great collection of tapes. By the time it was over, it was close to four and the rain had stopped. I looked out the window and saw Dad's Explorer parked outside our house.

"I have to go," I said.

"Promise to call right away and tell us what's happening," Alison said.

But I wasn't making any promises.

FIVE

The front door to our house was open. I called hello but no one answered. I ran upstairs, looking for Mom or Dad. Instead I found my worst fears coming true. Charles was in my room, at my desk!

I stood in my doorway, frozen. For just a minute I saw Charles the way Steph does—as a boy with dark hair, dreamy hazel eyes and a scar on his forehead. The scar makes him look interesting, not just handsome. Suddenly Grandpa Robinson's voice popped into my head. "Too bad the boy got all the looks in your family, Victor," he once told Dad. I was incredibly hurt when he said that, even though I was only eight.

Charles began to read aloud from my biography. "Rachel is credited with having discovered the vaccine, now widely used, to prevent hair balls in lions."

"Put that down!" My heart was pounding but I spoke slowly and quietly.

"Hair balls in lions?" Charles asked, acknowledging my presence. He didn't seem concerned that I'd caught him red-handed. "Hair balls in lions?" he repeated, laughing.

"I *said* put that down!" I sounded just like my mother when she turns on her lawyer voice. But that wasn't enough to stop Charles. He kept right on reading from Part Two of my biography, the part I call "Rachel, The Later Years." I'd handwritten it on one of Mom's legal pads early this morning. I'd enjoyed inventing my three brilliant careers—first as a veterinarian doing research on large cats in Africa, then as a musician with the New York Philharmonic, and finally as a great stage actress specializing in Shakespeare. I'd also given myself a husband and two children, all wildly successful.

"Her son, Toledo . . ." Charles paused, looking at me. "You named your son for a town in Ohio?"

"Spain, you idiot!" I tore across the room and reached for my biography. "Toledo, Spain!" I'm taller than Charles, but he's fast and he held the pages high above his head. Every time I grabbed for them, he'd transfer them to his other hand and dance around the room.

I felt so desperate I kicked, catching him on the shin. Then I dug my nails into his arm. I've never had a physical fight in my entire life. But I would have kept it up if he hadn't yelled, "Cut it out, Rachel . . .

or kiss your biography good-bye." He had both hands on my paper now, ready to rip it in half.

I didn't doubt that he'd do it. And there was no other copy. Even though I'd meant to enter it in my computer, I'd been rushing to meet Stephanie and Alison and figured I'd do it later. Tears stung my eyes but I would never cry in front of him. I would never give him that satisfaction!

I backed away and stood at the foot of my bed, my hands grasping the white iron rail. "You mess that up and you're dead!" I told him.

"Then you'll have to rewrite your biography," he said. "At thirteen Rachel Lowilla Robinson murdered her brother, Charles. She spent the rest of her life in jail. All eighty-four years of it."

"No," I said. "It would go more like, Since the judge and jury agreed that her brother provoked her, Rachel was acquitted and lived happily ever after."

"You won't get off that easy," he said. "They'll get you for manslaughter, at the very least."

"I'm a juvenile," I told him. "At the most I'll get probation."

"I wouldn't count on that."

"Really," I said. "Well, let's go and ask Mom, since she's just been nominated as a judge."

I could tell by the expression on his face I'd caught him by surprise. *Good!* He laid my biography on the desk. "Isn't that something!" he said. "Another milestone for our extraordinary family." He flopped in my favorite chair and draped his legs over the arm. "So . . . are you surprised to see me, little sister?"

"I'm never surprised by you," I said, which was a big lie. His moods can switch so fast you never know what to expect, which is the single worst thing about him. "When are you going back to school?" I asked, trying to sound as if I didn't care. "Or were you actually kicked out this time?"

"Expelled, Rachel. The expression is *expelled.*"

"Were you *expelled* on purpose?" I asked, wondering what exactly this would mean.

"Yeah. I missed you so much I couldn't wait to come home." He inspected his arm where I'd dug in my nails. He could have smashed me. But that's not Charles's style. Instead he gave me his best, dimpled smile. "You've done a real job on your room. What color do you call this?"

"Peach," I answered.

"Peach," he repeated, looking around. "Maybe I'll switch rooms with you. This one is bigger than mine. And since I'm older, I should have the bigger room, don't you think?"

Was he serious? I couldn't tell. This *used* to be his room. When we were younger, Jess and I shared her room. But then Charles campaigned for the small room on the first floor, and when Mom and Dad finally agreed, I got this one.

Aunt Joan sent my bed and the wicker furniture from her antique shop in New Hampshire. And Tarren gave me the rag rug for my birthday. I'm not about to give up my room! But Mom and Dad wouldn't ask me to, would they?

Now I felt totally confused, the way I always do around him. I wanted to scream, *Go back to school! Go anywhere! But leave us alone!* Except in our family we don't scream. We swallow hard, instead.

Charles stood up and stretched. "I think I'll go down and unpack. My room has several advantages over yours. . . ." He walked in front of the bed, where I was sitting. He put his face close to mine and I could smell onions on his breath.

"Besides," he said, "if I had to sleep in a room with peach walls, I'd puke." He made a disgusting retching sound, and as I jumped back, he laughed.

When he was gone, I closed the bedroom door, lay down on my bed and cried.

Mom and Dad tried to make Charles's first supper at home a festive occasion, even though being expelled from school isn't normally an event to celebrate. Charles came to the table wearing a T-shirt that said I DON'T NEED YOUR ATTITUDE . . . I HAVE MY OWN. None of us commented. Dad grilled chicken with mustard sauce and Mom made Charles's favorite coleslaw, so full of vinegar it choked me. But Charles loved it. The sour taste agreed with him.

In the middle of dinner he said, "So I think I'll drop out for a while . . . maybe get a job or something."

"That's not an option," Dad said.

"You have to be sixteen to drop out, don't you?" I asked. "And your birthday's not until November."

"Aha . . ." Charles said. "The child prodigy speaks."

I hate it when he calls me that. It makes me feel as if I've done something wrong, something to be ashamed of.

"It's just a matter of finding the right school," Mom said to Charles softly.

Charles exploded. "There is no right school for me! Don't you get it by now? I'm allergic to school!"

"Excuse me," Jessica said. "I've got to pick up my prom pictures before Fotomat closes."

"Excuse me, too," I said, shoving back my chair. "I have a ton of homework."

Charles shook his head. "Those daughters of yours need to be taught some manners," he told Mom and Dad. "They shouldn't be allowed to leave the table when the rest of us are still eating. If I didn't know better, I'd think it has something to do with me. I'd think they're not really as glad to see me as they pretend."

"They might be if it wasn't for your attitude," Mom said.

"Attitude?" Charles said, looking down at his T-shirt. "If we're talking attitude here—"

But Mom didn't wait for him to finish. "Just stop it, Charles!"

"Nell . . ." Dad said, quietly. "Let it go."

"Right," Charles said snidely. "Let it go, Mom. We don't want to upset Dad, do we?"

Later, I think we all regretted how badly dinner had gone and we gathered in the living room. "What's this?" Mom asked, examining the red marks on Charles's arm where I'd dug my nails into his skin. They were sitting next to each other on the small sofa.

"Harry," Charles said, using the cat as an excuse.

"I don't like the way it looks," Mom told him. "Put some peroxide on it."

"Yeah . . . yeah . . ."

"I'm serious, Charles. It could get infected."

Charles smiled at me.

Dad perched on the sofa arm, next to Mom, and Jess passed around her prom pictures. As she did, she gave me a private look, letting me know she'd already removed the group shot showing her in Mom's slinky black dress.

"Oh, Jess . . ." Mom said, studying the pictures. "That shade of pink is perfect on you."

"Magenta," I said.

Everyone looked at me.

"Well, it's more magenta than pink, isn't it?" I asked.

"*Magenta*," Charles said, making me wish I'd never heard the word. "Glad to know you're keeping up with your Crayola colors, Rachel."

Before I could think of something to say back, Dad held out one of Jessica's pictures and said, "Brings back memories, doesn't it, Nell?"

Mom said, "In my day you had to be *asked*."

Dad put his arm around Mom's shoulder and nuzzled her. "If they could see you now, those guys would be eating their hearts out."

"Good," Mom said, smiling at him.

Mom isn't beautiful like Alison's mother but she is very *put together*. She wears classic clothes and her hair is always perfect, whether it's loose or tied back. She says grooming is more important than looks. I hope that's true because when Mom was young she was awkward—too tall like me—and had a serious case of acne, like Jess.

"So, Jessica . . ." Charles said, studying one prom picture after the other. "Do they still call you *Pizza Face*, or is it mostly *Jess the Mess*?"

Jessica grabbed the pictures out of his hand. "Asshole," she hissed. "I wish you'd never been born!" She started from the room in tears, then turned back to face him. "And I hope you get the worst zits ever. I hope they swell and ooze and hurt so bad you go to bed crying every night!"

"Thanks, Jess . . ." Charles called, as if Jess had given him a compliment. "I appreciate that."

Mom ran after Jessica, and Dad said, "Dammit, Charles . . . we're a family. Could we please try to act like one?"

"I am trying," Charles said. "It's just that my sisters are so sensitive they can't even take a joke."

SIX

I lay in bed for a long time that night, stroking Burt and Harry, as I listened to Jess crying in her room. I don't understand Charles. I don't understand how he can be so cruel and hateful.

Unfortunately cystic acne runs in our family. Mom and Dad actually met at a drugstore, buying the same medicated skin cream, when they were first-year law students at Columbia. They started going together right away and were married the week they graduated. Mom says Dad is the first person who ever talked to her about acne. Everyone else shied away from the subject. It made them too uncomfortable.

Until then, Mom never even went out with a guy. Looking back, she says her acne was a blessing in disguise. It freed her to concentrate on schoolwork. She won a scholarship to college and another to law school, and she always graduated with honors. But she never kissed a guy until she met Dad and she was twenty-two at the time! I'm glad I've already had my first kiss. Not that I'm proud of having kissed Max Wilson, but at the time it seemed like the right thing to do.

There are a lot of things in life I consider unfair and cystic acne is one of them. I'm not talking about your basic teenage acne. I'm talking about painful lumps and bumps that swell and distort your face. I don't know what I'll do if I get it. Jess has tried antibiotics but they haven't helped much. Mom is always saying, "It cleared up before my thirtieth birthday," as if that will help Jess feel better. Imagine waking up every day with your problem right there on your face for the whole world to see! And having to deal with stupid guys calling you *Pizza Face* and *Jess the Mess*.

I consider Jess one of the bravest people I know. She gets up and goes to school five days a week. She has friends. She even manages to have a sense of humor.

When I finally did fall asleep, I tossed and turned and had bizarre dreams. I woke at dawn, sweaty and anxious, so I crept down to the kitchen and made myself a bowl of Cream of Wheat, with just a drop of brown sugar and milk. Whenever I feel my stomach tying up in knots, I eat comfort food—bananas, mashed potatoes, cooked cereal.

I was thumbing through the Sunday paper and feeling better when Charles waltzed in, humming to himself. "Good morning, little sister," he sang, as if we were old friends. "Did you get your beauty sleep?" He looked at me, then answered his own question. "I guess not."

I mumbled a few choice words under my breath.

"What was that?" he said.

"Never mind."

He began pulling out baking pans, mixing bowls and ingredients from the refrigerator.

"What are you doing?" I asked.

"It's Mother's Day, Rachel."

"I *know* it's Mother's Day."

"So . . . I'm going to bake something special for our dear old mom."

"Since when do you know how to bake?"

He shook his head. "There's so much you don't know about me."

That was certainly true. I never would have guessed Charles would remember Mother's Day. I thought about the gift Jess and I had bought for her—a subscription to *Metropolitan Home*. Mom's always saying she needs to redo the living room, if only she could find the time. We hope this will encourage her.

I read the rest of the paper while Charles baked. I have to admit, when he pulled a scrumptious-look-ing coffee cake out of the oven forty-five minutes later, I was pretty amazed. He tested it with a toothpick, then set it on a cooling rack. The smell made my mouth water.

I watched as he prepared a steaming pot of coffee, poured a pitcher of orange juice, and arranged it all on a tray. At the last minute he plucked a flower from the bunch on the table and set it on top of his cake. Then he took the Sunday paper, including the section I was reading, folded it up and tucked it under his arm. Before he started out of the room, he looked at me. "Impressed?" he asked.

He knew I was, even though I didn't say a word.

A minute later Jessica came into the kitchen, still in her nightshirt, her hair disheveled, her face covered with dark green goo that smelled faintly of seaweed. She yawned.

"What are you doing up so early?" I asked.

"Couldn't sleep." She opened the refrigerator and stuck her head inside. "I just met our *nightmare* on the stairs."

"He was bringing Mom breakfast in bed . . ." I told her, "in honor of Mother's Day!"

"Oh, God . . ." Jess said from inside the refrigerator. "He's such a hypocrite!"

"Suppose they don't find another school for him?" I asked. "What do you think will happen? I mean, he won't finish ninth grade at Fox, will he?"

"Mom and Dad are smart. They'll figure out something."

"But I've got to know now!"

"There's no way you can know, Rachel. And worrying about it isn't going to help." She backed out of the refrigerator and touched her face to see if the mask had hardened yet. It hadn't.

"Does that mean you think he's going to stay here?" I asked.

"It's his home, isn't it?" she said. "Mom and Dad are his parents, aren't they? They can't just *give* him away."

"Maybe they could send him to live with someone else," I suggested.

"Like who?"

"I don't know . . . Aunt Joan? She took him when he was suspended."

"That was for a week," Jess said. "Don't get your hopes up." She stuck her face back inside the refrigerator.

Mom came downstairs, beaming. "Charles baked a fabulous coffee cake," she said to me. "You've got to try it. It's light and fluffy and the topping's perfect." Then she noticed Jess. "Jessica, please close the refrigerator. Everything will spoil."

Jess touched her cheek. This time she was satisfied. The seaweed mask had set, leaving her with a hardened green face and white circles around her eyes. She looked like a green raccoon.

"Maybe I'll get a job as a baker," Charles said, following Mom into the kitchen.

"That could be a wonderful summer experience for you," Mom said, "if you don't have to go to summer school."

"I wasn't talking about a *summer* job."

"We've already been through that," Mom reminded him. "Let's not spoil our day."

"Oh, right!" He thumped his head with the back of his hand. "Today is Mother's Day . . . a family holiday. I hope my sisters remember that."

"Excuse me," I said. "I'll be in my room, practicing."

"Practicing?" Charles sneered.

"The flute!" I shouted.

"Oh, the flute," he said. "I thought you had something more exciting in mind."

"Grow up, Charles!" Jessica said, following me out of the kitchen.

"I'm trying . . ." he said, "I'm trying. . . ."

"Maybe you need to try harder," Mom told him.

"Push, push, push . . ." Charles said. "That's our family motto."

Mom ignored him and called after us, "Please be ready by eleven, girls. We're going to see Gram then."

Gram is Mom's mother. Her name is Kate Carter Babcock and she's seventy-six. She had a stroke a year ago and has lived at a nursing home ever since.

I get very depressed when we go to visit. *What's the use?* I think. *What's the use of going through a whole lifetime, then winding up like Gram?*

Gram can't talk. The stroke affected the left side of her brain. She makes sounds, not anything we can understand, though. They tried therapy for a while, but when she didn't respond they stopped. I don't know if she understands what we say, or even if she recognizes us. I like to think she does.

Today, when we got there, Gram was dressed for company. The nurse had brushed blush on her cheeks, and it stood out against her pale skin in two uneven circles. She sat in her wheelchair, facing the window that overlooks the garden. She had a soft, pastel-colored blanket across her lap. I recognized it as one of Roddy's baby blankets. When he was born, Tarren received so many she brought half a dozen to the nursing home.

I was glad Gram's chair was turned to the window, because one time we came to visit and someone had left her facing the blank wall. Mom was furious. She'd gone straight to the director to complain.

Mom opened the white florist's box we'd brought and took out a small orchid corsage. She slid it onto Gram's wrist. "Happy Mother's Day," she said, kissing Gram's cheek.

"Happy Mother's Day," Jess and I repeated in unison.

Then Charles stepped forward and kneeled beside Gram's chair. "Hey, Gram . . . remember me . . . your one and only grandson?" He paused for a moment. "So, how's it going?"

Gram turned her head toward Charles. Her eyes seemed to focus on his face. After that it was as if the rest of us didn't exist.

We took Gram for a stroll around the grounds. The tulips and daffodils were in full bloom, and the dogwoods were about to flower. I guess if you have to be in a nursing home, it's better to be in one with pretty gardens.

Mom pushed Gram's wheelchair. Dad hung back. I think visiting Gram reminds him of his own parents, especially his father. After Grandpa Robinson died, when I was in fourth grade, Dad went to bed for six weeks. I was very scared at the time, thinking he was going to die, too. That's when I started running through my *what ifs* at bedtime. My stomach was always tied up in knots. I went to the school nurse every day. Finally my teacher called Mom and asked her to come to school. The next day I was taken to Dr. Klaff for a complete medical checkup. Dr. Klaff said there was nothing physically wrong with me, except that I needed to learn to relax.

Then one day, just as I was getting used to the situation, Dad got out of bed and decided to change his life. He didn't want to be a lawyer anymore. He wanted to be a teacher. So he went back to school to get a degree in education, then got the job teaching history at the high school. We never talk about that time in our lives.

As we walked with Gram, Charles kept up a steady one-way conversation with her. "Yeah, I'm doing really well at this school, Gram. Dorrance . . . that's what it's called. I'm probably going to be class president next year and I've already made the varsity track team. That's how it is with us . . . we always have to be the best! But I guess you know that, Gram. . . . I mean, you're the one who raised Mom, right?"

"Charles . . ." Mom said, warning him.

"Yeah, right . . ." Charles answered.

Gram seemed mesmerized, as if the sound of Charles's voice were enough to make her day. I couldn't help wondering what she was thinking. Did she understand he was feeding her a pack of lies?

An hour later, as we said good-bye to Gram, Charles turned away from her wheelchair with tears in his eyes. When he caught me watching, he walked off by himself.

Gram made a few sounds. Maybe she was calling to him. Who knows? But the nurse had a different interpretation. "We're ready for our dinner, aren't we?" she asked Gram in singsong.

"Will you please not address her in that tone of

voice," Mom said to the nurse. "Will you please talk to her as if she were a healthy person!"

"But she's not, is she?" the nurse replied tartly.

Mom was about to pounce but Dad reminded her this is the best nursing home in the area. There's a waiting list to get in and if Mom makes a fuss again, the director will call, threatening to expel Gram. Wouldn't that be something . . . Charles and Gram expelled in the same week! Mom backed off and headed for the car.

The rest of us followed. Charles walked behind me, deliberately stepping on the backs of my shoes, pulling them off my feet. I thought about sticking out my foot and tripping him, but I didn't feel like making a scene. So I moved away and walked closer to Mom. She put her arm around my shoulders and said, "Don't be sad, honey. Gram's had a long life. And she's not suffering. We should all be grateful for that."

SEVEN

By Monday morning I was seething. And all because of Charles!

So at the bus stop, when Dana Carpenter, a ninth grader who also lives at Palfrey's Pond, said, "I hear your brother's back," I wasn't exactly thrilled.

"Is he going to the high school next year?" she asked.

"I really don't know."

"I hope he does . . . he's so cute . . . and I love his sense of humor." Dana has been going with Jeremy Dragon since Christmas. They fight a lot and sometimes break up, but they always get back together. So why this sudden interest in my brother?

The bus came along then and I got on with Stephanie and Alison.

"Now I'm *really* curious," Alison said, as we took our usual seats. "I've got to meet this brother of yours!"

"How can you be so cruel and hateful?" I spoke

louder than I'd intended and some kids turned to look at me. So I lowered my voice to a whisper. "You're supposed to be my friend."

"I am your friend," Alison said. "And I think it's cruel and hateful of you to accuse me of being cruel and hateful, because I'm not!" She looked at Stephanie, who kind of shrugged at her.

"I just don't think I can take any more of this!" I felt very weak and leaned back against my seat, closing my eyes for a minute.

"Any more of what?" Alison asked.

"I think she's depressed about her brother," Stephanie told Alison, as if I couldn't hear.

"I know that," Alison said. "I'm not stupid." She fussed with her bag for a minute. She carries this huge canvas tote stuffed with all kinds of junk. She pulled out a roll of Lifesavers and offered one to Steph, then to me. I shook my head. Steph popped one into her mouth.

At the next stop Jeremy Dragon got on the bus. "Hey, Macbeth . . ." he said as he passed us. Last Halloween the three of us went to his house dressed as the witches from Shakespeare's play. When Jeremy came to the door, instead of saying *trick or treat,* we'd recited a poem.

Double, double, toil and trouble;
Fire burn and cauldron bubble.

And ever since, he's called us Macbeth. Sometimes it means all three of us—sometimes, like in math class, it's just me.

When we were moving again, Alison said, "I wonder what *my* brother's going to be like?"

"Your brother's going to be a baby," Stephanie reminded her.

For some reason that made me laugh. But my laugh came out high-pitched, not at all like my regular laugh.

"I wasn't trying to be funny," Steph told me. "I was just making a point."

"Are you saying that baby brothers aren't as depressing as older ones?" Alison asked.

"Not *all* older brothers are depressing," I said. "Just some."

Stephanie sighed. "Maybe you should see Mrs. Balaban."

"The school counselor?" I asked.

"Yeah," Steph said. "I saw her once . . . when I found out . . ." She hesitated for a moment. "When I found out my parents were separating."

"You went to Mrs. Balaban?" Alison said, as if she couldn't believe it.

Stephanie nodded.

"So did I!" Alison told her.

"You?" Steph said to Alison, as if *she* couldn't believe it. "Why did *you* go to Mrs. Balaban?"

·50·

"Because of the . . . when I found out about the . . ."

"Pregnancy?" I guessed.

"Right. . . . When I found out my mother was pregnant."

"How come you didn't *say* anything about seeing Mrs. Balaban?" Steph asked Alison.

"How come *you* didn't?" Alison asked Steph.

"I thought we were talking about *my* problem," I said, and they both looked at me.

The next morning Mrs. Balaban sent a note to my homeroom teacher, saying she wanted to see me. I was really angry. How could Alison and Stephanie betray me this way? If I want to see Mrs. Balaban, I will. But that's *my* business and nobody else's. I intended to tell them exactly that at lunch, which is our first and only period together except for gym, which we have twice a week but not today.

I stopped at Mrs. Balaban's office on my way to the cafeteria. "I'm Rachel Robinson," I said. "You wanted to see me?"

"Oh, Rachel . . . yes . . . I'm very glad to meet you," she said. "Sit down."

Mrs. Balaban is young and good-looking. The boys think it's great to be called to her office. One time she brought her baby, Hilary, to school. The girls oohed and aahed over her, while the boys oohed and aahed over Mrs. Balaban.

"I only have a minute," I said, standing in front of her desk. "I have to go to lunch."

"Well, let's see how fast I can explain this to you." She poured some sparkling water into a mug decorated with Beatrix Potter rabbits. "Want some?"

"No thanks."

She took a long drink. When she finished, she burped softly, her hand covering her mouth. "Sorry," she said. "Have you heard anything about Natural Helpers, Rachel?"

"I've heard of Natural Lime Spritzers," I answered.

She laughed. "This isn't a drink. It's a program we're going to try next fall. It's called Natural Helpers."

I felt my face turn hot. That's the kind of mistake Stephanie would make, not me. And it happened because I was worrying instead of listening.

"It's a kind of outreach program," Mrs. Balaban continued. "You know . . . kids helping other kids."

I waited to hear what this program had to do with Charles.

Mrs. Balaban took another swig from her cup. "I asked the teachers to recommend a group of mature seventh and eighth graders . . . people other kids would relate to . . . and you were one of them."

"So this doesn't have anything to do with . . ." I began.

"With . . ." Mrs. Balaban repeated, looking at me.

"Never mind. I was confused for a minute. I thought you wanted to see me because . . ."

"Because . . ."

I was so relieved this didn't have anything to do with Charles, I started to laugh.

"What?" she asked, curious.

"Nothing," I said, trying to keep a straight face.

She twirled her wedding band around on her finger. "Do you think you'd be interested in participating in this kind of program, Rachel?"

When I didn't respond right away, she said, "Of course I want you to take your time and think about it. Because the training will be fairly intense. And I know you're already involved in other school activities, not to mention your schoolwork."

"Schoolwork is no problem," I said.

She shuffled some papers on her desk. "Straight A's," she said, smiling up at me. She must have had my transcript in front of her. "Very impressive. But you know, Rachel, there's nothing wrong with a B now and then."

"I prefer A's," I said.

She laughed. "Remember, I don't want you to feel pressured to take this on, unless it's something you really want to do . . . okay?"

"Okay."

"We're having an introductory meeting next week, and Rachel . . ."

"Yes?"

"There's no rule that says Natural Helpers can't have their own problems . . . so if there's something on your mind that you'd like to talk about . . ."

"No," I said, "there's nothing."

"But if there ever is . . ."

"I have to go now," I told her. "This is my lunch period."

When I got to the cafeteria, Stephanie and Alison were already eating.

"Where were you?" Steph asked.

"Mrs. Balaban," I said.

"You actually took my advice?" she asked.

"Not exactly . . ."

Steph turned to Alison. "I knew she'd never admit she took *my* advice!"

My life at home is falling apart and Mrs. Balaban wants me to help other kids. What an incredible joke! What makes her think kids would come to me with their problems? I'm not very popular, except right before a test when everyone suddenly needs extra help. And when Steph's parents were separating, she didn't even *tell* me and I'm supposed to be her best friend! We had a huge fight when I found out she'd been lying to me. We didn't speak for seven weeks. And did Alison come to me when she found out her mother was pregnant? No. She went directly to Stephanie. So, it seems to me Mrs. Balaban doesn't know much about finding Natural Helpers!

That night I had too many *what ifs*. I knew I'd never get to sleep if I couldn't clear my head. So I went down to the kitchen to make myself a cup of herbal tea.

Charles was at the table, stuffing his face with cold mashed potatoes and leftover salmon with a big glob of mayonnaise on top. He'd refused to have dinner with us earlier. The thought of all that mayonnaise at ten o'clock at night was enough to gag me. I looked away and thought about going back upstairs. But then I changed my mind. Just because *he's* in the kitchen doesn't mean I can't have my tea. I took a few deep breaths and put the kettle on. While I was waiting for the water to boil, I opened the cupboard where we keep the teas and chose Grandma's Tummy Mint. Burt and Harry were sniffing around the table, begging for salmon.

"Come on, you guys," Charles said to them, with a mouthful of mashed potatoes. "Not while I'm eating."

"Cold mashed potatoes are disgusting," I muttered.

"To each his own," he said.

I didn't respond.

"You know . . . I'm worried about you, Rachel."

"You're worried about me?"

"Yeah . . . it's not normal for a girl your age not to have friends."

"I have plenty of friends."

"So where are they? How come they never come over?"

I chose my favorite mug, decorated with pink and lavender hearts, and poured boiling water over my tea bag. Then I set the mug down so the tea could steep. It's amazing how few people know how to make a good cup of tea. They think they can hand you a cup of hot water with a tea bag on the side and that's it.

"I asked you a question, Rachel."

"My friends are none of your business," I told him.

"I think you're trying to hide something."

I spun around. "I am *not* trying to hide anything. And I don't have to explain my friendships to you!" I knew better than to continue this conversation. So I took my tea upstairs, to the privacy of my own room.

The next day I asked Stephanie and Alison if they wanted to come over after school.

"Sure . . ." Alison said. "Will Charles be there?"

"Probably," I told her. "But don't get into a long conversation with him. Don't start telling him about your dog and how she can talk."

"Would he believe me if I did?" Alison asked.

"No, but he'd lead you on and then he'd never let you forget you said it."

"Fine . . . I won't say anything," Alison said.

"No . . . that would be even worse. Then he'll think you *can't* talk."

"Okay . . . I'll just say one or two things."

"And nothing personal," I told her. "Don't tell him your mother's pregnant."

"Got it," Alison said. "Nothing personal."

"And no questions!"

Alison repeated that. "No questions."

"You, too," I told Steph.

"All right," Steph said. "Stop worrying! I've known Charles since I was seven . . . remember?"

"I'm not worrying," I said.

The cats were sleeping outside the kitchen door when we got home. Burt woke up and stretched when he heard us. Harry didn't even move. I gave them fresh water from the outside faucet. Then I opened the door. Charles wasn't in the kitchen, so I poured three glasses of cranberry juice and set out a box of Dutch pretzels.

"The way you eat pretzels is so weird," Stephanie said to me.

"To each her own," I answered. It's true that I have a special way of eating pretzels. I like to lick off all the salt first. Then, when the pretzel is very soft, just before it's actually soggy, I chew it up. I didn't always eat pretzels that way. But a few years ago I broke a tooth on one, and ever since I eat them very care-fully.

"Well . . . are we going to see him or not?" Alison finally asked.

"All right," I said. And I started down the hall to Charles's room, with Alison and Stephanie right behind me. I knocked and called, "Charles, I'm home with my friends!"

We waited but he didn't answer.

"Maybe he's not here," Steph said.

"I couldn't be so lucky," I mumbled on the way back to the kitchen. Just when I decided he probably wasn't home he appeared, fresh out of the shower, barefoot, with wet hair. He was wearing cutoffs and a T-shirt that said ELVIS IS DEAD.

"Well, well, well . . ." He smiled, surveying the scene.

I said, "Alison, this is my brother, Charles."

"You're Charles?" Alison said, like she couldn't believe it. What was she expecting . . . Dracula?

"None other," he answered, turning on the charm. "And who are you?"

"Alison Monceau." She practically drooled. "From L.A. I've heard a lot about you."

"I can imagine," Charles said. "I'm one of my sis-ter's favorite subjects."

"Not from Rachel," Alison said quickly. "Rachel doesn't like to talk about you."

"What?" Charles said. "Impossible! Rachel, is this true? You don't talk about me anymore? You don't tell people how I bit you on your leg when you were two?"

"He bit you?" Alison asked me. Before I could answer, Stephanie waved her arms, trying to capture Charles's attention. "Hey," she called, "remember me?"

He looked her up and down. "No!" he said. "I don't believe it! This can't be Stephanie Hirsch!"

Stephanie suddenly grew self-conscious, touching her hair, her mouth, then crossing her arms over her chest. She tried to smile at him without showing her braces.

He was doing such a number on them! And they were just eating it up. Fools! I wanted to shout. He's just using you. He's just playing games.

"I was beginning to think the child prodigy had no friends," Charles said, making me cringe. "Why, just last night I accused her of being friendless. Right, Rachel?"

"That's it!" I said. "The party's over!"

I opened the screen door and let it slam behind me, expecting my friends to follow. But they just stood there, enthralled by my brother, until he said, " 'Parting is such sweet sorrow . . .' " and disappeared down the hall. As soon as he was gone, Stephanie and Alison burst out laughing.

"I don't see anything funny!" I told them from the other side of the screen door.

"That's your problem, Rachel," Stephanie said. She pushed the screen door open and she and Alison joined me outside. "Maybe if you treated him better, he'd treat you better."

"Why are you taking *his* side?" I asked. "You're supposed to be *my* friend."

"I am your friend," Steph argued.

"No," I said, "a friend is someone you can depend on!"

"You *can* depend on me. It's just that you always think everything's going to be a disaster!"

"Not everything," I told her. "Just *some* things!" But it was useless. They'd never understand. I turned and ran to the top of the hill. Then I lay on the grass with my arms hugging my body, and I began to roll. I rolled all the way down, like I used to when I was small, stopping myself just short of the pond.

Alison and Steph, thinking I was playing some game, followed, rolling down the hill after me, laughing hysterically. Steph stopped on her own, but I had to grab Alison or she'd have rolled right into the water. When she stood up, I steadied her. "Well . . ." I said, "are you satisfied?"

"About what?" she asked. Sometimes Alison is so dense!

"About Charles," I said.

"Oh, yeah . . . I guess." She and Steph exchanged looks. "I mean, based on what I just saw, I can see how he'd be a pain as a brother . . . but as a boy . . ."

I held up my hand. "I don't want to hear it, Alison!"

"All she's saying is—" Steph began.

But I didn't let her finish. "I am not interested in either of your opinions about my brother."

"It's getting hard to be around you, Rachel!" Steph said. "You're so . . . intense!" She turned to Alison. "Come on . . . let's go." And they walked off together.

I wanted to call after them, to tell them I needed them. But I couldn't find the words.

Instead I went home and rearranged my dresser drawers, folding and refolding each sweater, each T-shirt, each pair of socks. Then I started on my closet. When everything was in order, when everything was perfect, I sat down at my music stand, picked up my flute and began to play.

EIGHT

I handed in my biography. I thought of taking out the section about inventing a vaccine to prevent hair balls in lions, but I didn't. Just because Charles found it wildly funny or even peculiar doesn't mean anything. Because Charles is peculiar himself.

He stays up all night watching reruns of old sitcoms on TV—"The Munsters," "Gilligan's Island," "The Brady Bunch." He goes to bed at sunrise and sleeps away half the day. It's easy to avoid him on this schedule. Maybe that's why he does it. Maybe he's trying to avoid us. He doesn't even join us for dinner, which is fine with Jessica and me. But it bothers Mom and Dad. They think eating dinner together is the single most important part of family life. They've been seeing Dr. Sparks. They want Charles to see him again, too, but so far he's refused.

"That quack!" Charles shouted at Mom a couple of

nights ago. "He knows *nothing*! You're blowing your money on him."

"Fine," Mom said, without raising her voice. "Then we'll find someone else. Someone you feel more comfortable with."

"Don't count on it," Charles told her.

At the dinner table we don't talk about him. Jess and I try to keep the conversation light, but you can tell Mom is stressed-out and Dad's not himself, either. He tries not to let us see he's distracted, but he can't fool me. I've seen him gobbling Pepto-Bismol tablets. And I've heard him talking quietly with Mom late at night, long after they're usually asleep. I've stopped asking them about Charles and what's going to happen, but I haven't stopped wondering if we have to live this way until he's eighteen.

On Monday my biography came back marked A+, and in the margin Ms. Lefferts wrote, *Excellent work, well thought out, delightful reading. See me.* When I went up to her after class, she said, "Rachel, I had no idea you were interested in the theater."

She was referring to my imagined career as a great actress. I'd written that Rachel died onstage at the age of ninety-seven. It was weird writing about my own death, but I suppose if I absolutely have to die—and death is a fact of life, isn't it?—then ninety-seven isn't bad, especially if I'm able to work right up to the end. Besides, since I'm just thirteen now, that gives me another eighty-four years to figure things out.

Ms. Lefferts was in one of her hyper moods, talking very fast, using her hands to punctuate every word. "I'm going to be advisor to the Drama Club next year and I certainly hope you'll join."

"Well . . ." I began.

But she didn't wait for me to finish. "I know you're busy. I recommended you for that helping program myself. . . . What's it called again?"

"Natural Helpers," I said.

"Yes, Natural Helpers . . . but the Drama Club could be a very exciting experience for you. We're going to do a fall play and a spring musical."

"I'll—"

"That's all I'm asking. That you give it your serious consideration. Because we really need people like you . . . people with a *genuine* interest in theater."

"It sounds—"

"Oh . . . and I forgot to mention we'll be going to New York to see at least two plays."

"Will we go by train or bus?" I asked.

She seemed surprised by my question. "I haven't worked that out yet. Do you have a preference?"

"Yes," I told her. "I prefer the train." I didn't add that I get motion sick in cars and buses but not on trains.

"Well . . ." she said, "I'll keep your preference in

mind. I'm hoping to get tickets to a contemporary drama and a Shakespearean comedy."

"Shakespeare is my favorite," I said.

Ms. Lefferts put her hand on my shoulder and squeezed lightly. "Mine, too, Rachel. Mine, too."

What am I going to do about all these activities? I wondered as I got into bed that night. Mom says the trick is to know your own limits. But I don't know what my limits are. I wish my teachers wouldn't expect me to do everything!

I decided to make a list. In one column I wrote down the activities I'm participating in now — Orchestral Band, All-State Orchestra, Debating Team, plus a private flute lesson each week and forty-five minutes of practice a day. In the other column I wrote down the activities I'm thinking about adding next year — Drama Club and Natural Helpers. Also, Stephanie wants me to run for eighth-grade class president. She's already volunteered to be my campaign manager and she's thought up the perfect slogan — *Rachel Robinson, the Dare to Care Candidate.*

I tried to figure out how many hours a week these activities would take, not counting president, but until tomorrow, when I go to the introductory meeting of Natural Helpers, I won't really be able to come up with an exact figure. I wonder if it's even possible to handle so many activities. I wish I could be a regular person for just one year! But then Mom would be disappointed. She'd say it's a crime to waste my potential. I wonder if she's ever wished she could be a regular person.

I turned off the light and lay down. Burt snuggled up against my hip and Harry at my feet. I closed my eyes, but my mind was on overtime. What if class president isn't allowed to participate in other activities? What if Natural Helpers turns out to be a full-time activity? What if I get a part in the school play, which means rehearsals every afternoon, when I'm supposed to be at Debating Club preparing for an interschool match and Orchestral Band is rehearsing for the spring concert and my flute teacher says I haven't been practicing enough and my grades start slipping and everybody says I'm not doing my job as class president because I'm too busy doing other things and I am impeached by the class officers? Being impeached would be even worse than being expelled. Being impeached would probably make the local papers!

Suddenly I felt my heart thumping inside my chest. I sat straight up, frightened. The cats looked at me as I leaped out of bed. But then a voice inside my head reminded me to stay calm, to breathe deeply. I began to count backward from one hundred. That's it . . . count slowly . . . very slowly . . . that's better . . .

The panicky feeling passed, leaving me drenched

with sweat. I lay back down and closed my eyes. *Psychology Today* says one good relaxation technique is to imagine yourself in a serene setting, like a beautiful tropical island with a white sand beach and palm trees swaying gently in the warm breeze. Yes. Okay. I'm on an island, swinging in a hammock, when this incredibly handsome guy comes up to me. He's carrying a book of Shakespeare's sonnets. He sits beside me and begins to read. After a while he reaches for my hand, looks deep into my eyes and, not being able to resist a moment longer, kisses me. It is a long, passionate kiss . . . without tongues. The idea of having someone's tongue in my mouth is too disgusting to contemplate.

I must have fallen asleep then, but when I awoke in the morning I had a gnawing ache in my jaw.

The next afternoon I went to the introductory meeting of Natural Helpers and nearly passed out when Mrs. Balaban presented someone named Dr. Sparks. Could he be *that* Dr. Sparks? I wondered, as I slid lower and lower in my seat. How many psychologists named Dr. Sparks can there be in one town? He must be the same one! Suppose he recognizes my name and asks if I'm related to Charles? Suppose he tells Mrs. Balaban that with my family situation I shouldn't be a Natural Helper?

I worried all through the meeting. I hardly heard a word he said.

But when the meeting ended, Mrs. Balaban thanked Dr. Sparks and he left without addressing any of us individually. I felt so relieved I let out a low sigh. Only the girl next to me seemed to notice. Then Mrs. Balaban told us we should think long and hard about becoming Natural Helpers. "I'll need your answer by the last day of school," she said. "And remember, it's a significant commitment. Helping others always is. You'll have to be aware and involved all the time."

Aware and involved all the time, I thought as I sat in the dentist's office after school. By then my jaw was killing me. I opened and closed my mouth, hoping to relieve the pain.

Unlike most of my friends, I'm not afraid to go to the dentist. I have very healthy teeth. I've had just two small cavities in my entire life. Besides, our dentist, Dr. McKay, is also a stand-up comic. He performs at the Laugh Track, a comedy club on the highway. He tries out his material on his patients, so in this case you might say, going to the dentist is a lot of laughs!

"So, Rachel . . . how do you get down from an elephant?" Dr. McKay asked as he adjusted the towel around my neck.

"I've no idea," I told him.

He tilted the chair way back. "You don't . . . you get it from a duck."

I laughed, which wasn't easy to do with my mouth

open and the dentist's hands inside. I hate the taste of his white surgical gloves.

"Hmm . . ." he said, poking around. "Are you wearing your appliance?"

I tried to explain that I'd lost it, but he couldn't understand me. I guess he got the general tone, though, because he said, "So, the answer is no?"

I nodded.

"Well, you're clenching your jaw again."

I tried to act surprised. I said, "I am?" It came out sounding like *Ah aah?*

"Uh-huh . . ." he said. "And grinding your teeth, too."

Grinding my teeth? That definitely did not sound good.

"Everything all right in your life?" he asked.

I wiggled my fingers, indicating so-so.

"Still getting all A's in school?"

I wish people would stop acting as if there's something wrong with getting all A's. I waved my hands around, our signal for letting me sit up and rinse. After I did, I said, "This doesn't have anything to do with school."

"Maybe not, but I'd still like to see you learn to relax. And so would your teeth."

People are always telling me to relax, as if it's something easy to do. When Dr. McKay finished cleaning my teeth, he moved the chair to an upright position. "I'm going to do an impression," he said.

I assumed he meant an impression of someone famous. So I was surprised when he said, "Open wide, Rachel . . ." and he slid a little tray of flavored goo into my mouth.

On the way out of Dr. McKay's office I met Steph, who had an appointment with the orthodontist in the next office. "How do you get down from an elephant?" I asked. I hardly ever tell jokes because no one laughs when I do. I don't know if this means my comic timing is off or people just don't expect me to be funny.

"How?" Steph said.

"You don't. You get it from a duck."

Steph just looked at me.

"It's a joke," I said. "Down . . . as in feathers. Get it?"

"Oh, right . . ." Steph said. "Now I do." But she didn't laugh. Then she said, "Did you hear about Marcella, the eighth-grade slut?"

"No, what?"

"She got caught in the supply closet with Jeremy Dragon."

"Is this a joke?"

"No. Why would it be a joke?"

"I don't know. The way you set it up, I thought you were going to tell a joke."

"No, this is a true story," Steph said. "It was the

supply closet in the arts center. When Dana found out she went crazy, yelling and screaming in front of everyone!"

"Really?"

"Yes . . . then Jeremy goes, 'How come it's okay for you but not for me?' And Dana shouts, 'What are you talking about?' Then Jeremy goes, 'You know what I'm talking about!' And he walks away, which makes Dana so mad she takes off his bracelet and throws it at him. It hits him in the back of his head. So he turns around and goes, 'Thanks, Dana!' Then he picks up his bracelet and puts it in his pocket."

"You were actually there?" I asked. "You actually saw this happen?"

"No," Steph said. "But everybody's talking about it. Everybody knows!"

"What was he doing in the supply closet with Marcella?"

"What do you think?" Before I had a chance to respond, Steph answered her own question. "Pure animal attraction!"

"Yes, but the difference between humans and animals is that humans are supposed to *think*," I explained, "not just react."

"But let's say you were alone in a supply closet with Jeremy Dragon . . ." Steph said. "Wouldn't you react?"

"I don't know."

"Well, I do. I'm reacting just thinking about it, like any normal person."

"Are you suggesting I'm not normal?"

"I didn't say that."

"It sounded like you did."

"Well, I didn't."

"Good, because I'm as normal as you!"

"If you say so."

"What do you mean by that?"

"Lighten up, Rachel, will you?" Stephanie said, shaking her head. "You're never going to make it to eighth grade at this rate."

I wanted to ask Steph exactly what she meant by that remark, but she went into the orthodontist's office before I had the chance. It's not as if I wouldn't want to be alone with Jeremy Dragon. But I'd choose someplace more romantic than a supply closet at school!

NINE

When Alison came over that night, I asked if she'd heard about Jeremy Dragon and Marcella. "Steph told me," she said. "I feel bad for Dana." She walked around my room touching things—the framed photos on my dresser, my collection of decorated boxes, the needlepoint pillows on my bed. "I'd do anything for a room like this." She sounded as if she were in a trance.

Since she goes through this routine every time, I decided to call her on it. "Okay," I said, "on Saturday I'm coming over and we're going to organize your room."

"Oh no," Alison said, "it wouldn't work!"

"Why not?"

"I'd never be able to keep it like . . . this," she said, opening my closet door, "with all my clothes facing the same direction, and my shoes lined up in a row."

"It's easy!" I told her. "You just have to put away your clothes when you take them off."

"But you know how I am. You know I never put anything away until my closet is empty and all my clothes are piled on the floor."

"You can do it if you want to."

"I want to . . . but I know myself. I'm too tired at night to care."

"Then you should go to bed earlier."

"That's what my mother says."

"I don't mean to sound like your mother, but you'll never know until you try."

"No, I'd just wind up feeling bad." She sighed. "Maybe someday. Maybe next year, okay?"

I shrugged. "Whenever."

"Besides," she said, looking around, "Steph says it isn't normal for a teenager to have a room as perfect as this."

"Stephanie said that . . . about me?"

"Not about you," Alison said, backing off. "About your room. We were just talking, you know, about this article in *Sassy* and . . ." I waited while she painted herself into a corner. "Steph didn't mean it personally or anything."

"I cannot believe Stephanie told you I'm not normal."

"She didn't say that!"

"You know what Stephanie's problem is?" I asked.

"Stephanie confuses *normal* with *average*. It's true that the *average* teenager doesn't keep her room as neat as I keep mine. But just because it isn't *average* doesn't mean it's not *normal*."

I absolutely detest the word *normal*. I detest the way Stephanie throws it around. And, I admit, sometimes I do wonder about myself. There's no question, I'm different from most kids my age. I don't know how to explain it. Maybe when my mother jokes to her friends that *Rachel was born thirty-five,* she knows what she's talking about. Maybe I won't find out until I actually *am* thirty-five. Maybe then I'll be more like everyone else.

Alison was running her hand over the books on my shelves. "So, can you recommend something good? I have a book report due on Friday and I forgot to go to the library."

"They're all good," I told her. "It just depends on what you're in the mood for."

"Something about a girl who lived a long time ago."

"Historical fiction," I translated. "Let me think . . ." My books are arranged alphabetically by author so I know exactly where each one is. I pulled two off my shelf—*Summer of My German Soldier* and *A Tree Grows in Brooklyn*—and handed them to Alison.

"I'll take this one," she said, thumbing through the first.

"Good choice," I told her. "I think you'll like it." I wrote down Alison's name, followed by the title and author, in my library notebook. Even though every one of my books has a bookplate on the inside cover, some people forget to return them. They don't mean to. It just happens. This way I know who's got what. As I was putting away my notebook, Charles opened my bedroom door. "You know you're supposed to knock!" I said.

But he paid no attention. "I was hoping for a quick game of *torture*," he said, standing in the doorway.

"We are *not* interested!" I tried to force him out by closing the door but he blocked it.

"What's *torture*?" Alison asked.

"*Torture* is having a conversation with my brother. *Torture* is enduring his witty comments."

Alison didn't get it. But Charles pushed past me and said, "An excellent definition, Rachel." He looked at Alison. "You just don't know how refreshing it is to live with a child prodigy."

Alison didn't get that, either. She sat on the edge of my bed, not knowing what to say. Charles smiled at her. She smiled back, clearly flattered by his attention.

"So, what's your ethnic heritage, California?" he asked.

"None of your business," I told him, answering for Alison.

"I don't mean to pry," Charles said to her smoothly, "but I'm very interested in ethnic heritage, given my background."

What background? I wondered.

"Well, I'm adopted," Alison said. "I don't know anything except that my birth mother was Vietnamese."

"I'm adopted, too," Charles said. "I wish our family were as open about it as yours."

"What are you saying?" I asked, totally shocked. "You're not adopted!"

"You mean you never guessed?" he asked me. "You never put two and two together?"

"You're lying!" I shouted. Then I turned to Alison. "He's lying!"

"Here are the facts," Charles said quietly to Alison, as he sat beside her on my bed. "I'm one-eighth Korean, one-eighth Native American, one-quarter Irish, one-quarter Eastern European, and one-quarter Cuban."

"How would you know all that if you were adopted?" I asked.

"I've seen the papers."

Alison was confused and so was I. "Get out of my room!" I shouted at Charles, holding the door open. "Now!"

"Good-night, California," Charles sang as he left. "Until next time . . ." He blew her a kiss.

I slammed the door after him. "I'm sorry," I said to Alison. "He's so obnoxious."

"No . . . it's okay," she said.

"It's not okay! He's playing with your mind."

"Maybe he is adopted."

"He's not!"

"You're younger," she said. "Maybe you just don't know. Some people don't talk about it."

"It's not possible!" I said, feeling lost. "Grandpa Robinson said—" I stopped in midsentence. "I mean, he looks like my father . . . don't you think?"

"Not really," she said.

But Mom and Dad would never keep such a secret, would they? No, they believe in honesty. On the other hand, Mom is a very private person. She holds everything inside.

As soon as Alison left, I went directly to my parents' room and knocked on their door.

Dad called, "Enter. . . ." He was grading papers at his desk. I heard water running in the bathroom. Mom was probably taking a shower.

I pulled a small chair over to Dad's desk and waited for him to look up from his work. When he did, he said, "What can I do for you?"

"I have a very important question," I said.

"Okay . . . shoot."

There was no easy way to do this. I focused on Mom's collection of glass bottles. There are eleven of them sitting on top of her dresser, each with a silver top.

"Rachel . . ." Dad said.

I looked at him, then back at Mom's bottles. Finally I managed to say, "Is Charles adopted?"

Dad didn't answer right away. He reached for my hand. "I know it must feel that way to you . . ."

"It doesn't feel that way to me," I said, "but that's what he just told Alison! He told her he's one-eighth Native American, one-eighth Korean, one-quarter Irish and . . ."

Dad started laughing.

"I don't find it funny at all!"

"He's not adopted," Dad said. "He probably just feels that would explain things."

"Are you absolutely sure?" I asked.

Dad stroked my arm. "I was there at his birth, honey. I held him in my arms, same as I held Jessica and you when you were born. Not that I wouldn't love any of you just as much if you were adopted . . ."

"It's cruel to lie to someone who really is adopted, trying to make her think they have something in common."

"I'm not excusing him," Dad said, "but maybe he likes Alison and is trying to impress her."

"What do you mean by *likes*?"

Dad kind of smiled and said, "You know . . . boy meets girl . . ."

"You mean likes her *that* way!" I didn't give Dad a chance to respond. I jumped up. "That's out of the question. She's my friend. My friends are off-limits to him. You've got to do something, Dad! You've got to get him out of my life!"

"Rachel, honey . . ." Dad stood, too, and wrapped me in his arms. "It's going to be all right. I know these are difficult times . . ."

"So were the Crusades!" Mom said, coming out of the bathroom in her purple robe.

TEN

Charles has a tutor. His name is Paul Medeiros and he's tall, about six feet, with dark hair and dark eyes. He wears rimless glasses. He's Dad's student teacher. He's going to come to our house every afternoon for two hours. This means Charles will *not* be finishing ninth grade at my school. What a relief!

When I met Paul a few days ago, he was wearing jeans and a black pocket T-shirt. He had a pencil smudge on the side of his face. He said, "So you're Charles's older sister."

"No," Charles told him, "this is my *baby* sister." Charles was wearing a T-shirt that said ALL STRESSED UP AND NO ONE TO CHOKE. I felt like choking him!

"She doesn't look like a baby," Paul said.

"Looks can be deceiving," Charles said. "She's just thirteen." He said *thirteen* as if it were the plague.

I could see the surprise on Paul's face. But I liked

him for not making a big thing out of it. "Then you're the musician?" Paul asked.

"Well, I love music but I'm not that good," I told him.

"She's only a child prodigy," Charles said.

"Charles . . . I am not!" I wish he would stop calling me that! I've met real prodigies at music camp. Some of them are only ten or eleven and they're already studying at Juilliard. It was a shock when I realized I'll never be as good as they are, no matter how much I practice.

Paul gave me an understanding smile, then playfully shoved Charles back toward his room. "Okay, time to hit the books." He turned for a moment and said, "Nice to meet you, Rachel."

When he said my name, I felt incredibly warm inside. At first I thought I was having what Mom and her friends call a *hot flash*. But I don't think you get them till you're older. I'm not sure if what I feel for Paul is pure animal attraction or not. Either way, from now on I'll have to be very careful because if Charles ever finds out—or even *suspects*—I have an interest in Paul, he will deliberately humiliate me in front of him. Not that I think Paul would let him get away with it. Still, the damage would be done.

That night I lay on my bed reading sonnets to the cats. I imagined I was onstage and the entire audience, including Paul, was mesmerized by my voice.

Suddenly I had the feeling I wasn't alone and when I looked up, Charles was standing in my doorway. "You read Shakespeare to the cats?" he asked.

"They're very good listeners," I told him. "Now please leave!"

"You know, Rachel . . . when people start reading to their animals . . ."

"Out!" I said again. "Right now!"

I could hear him chuckling even after he'd closed my door.

I began to think of Paul every night when I went to bed. Thinking about him is very relaxing. It's better than anything I've read in *Psychology Today*. My jaw hasn't hurt at all since Paul started coming to our house. But whether that's due to my new dental appliance or to Paul himself, I really can't say.

I wonder if Tarren knows him since he's graduating from the same college where she is a junior. Next time I see her I'll have to ask.

But the next time Tarren came over, she pressed a screaming baby into my arms and said, "Where's your mother?" Her eyes were red and swollen, her hair damp and matted around her face.

Mom was at the dining room table, working on what could be her last big jury trial before she is appointed a judge. "Tarren, what is it?" Mom asked, pushing back her chair.

Tarren threw her arms around Mom and cried, "Aunt Nell . . . my life is just one big mess! I don't think I can take it anymore."

Roddy continued to scream. Mom said, "Rachel, take the baby into the kitchen and give him a bottle or something."

Tarren pulled off her shoulder bag and passed it to me. "There's a bottle inside."

I took Roddy into the kitchen, but since there's no door between the kitchen and the dining room I could still hear everything.

"All right," Mom said to Tarren. "Now calm down and tell me what's going on."

Tarren sobbed, "I got another ticket . . . for speeding. I was only doing sixty-seven, but they gave me points." She blew her nose. "If I lose my license I won't be able to get to school and if I can't get to school I'll never graduate, and if I don't graduate and get a teaching job I'll never be able to support myself and Roddy and I'll never get out of my parents' house, or have my own life, or . . ." She was crying again.

Mom sounded firm. "Listen to me, Tarren. We've been through this before. You are responsible for your own actions."

"But it was a mistake," Tarren cried. "I didn't know I was going over the speed limit."

"We all make mistakes," Mom told her. "The point

is, you can't fall apart every time something goes wrong. You've got to learn to be strong!"

"I don't know how to be strong, Aunt Nell. I want to be like you . . . you know I do . . . but I just don't know how."

"Then you're going to learn, right now," Mom said. "You're going to start by telling yourself, This is not a life-threatening situation. This is not a serious problem."

"It's not?" Tarren asked.

"No, it's not!" Mom said.

Roddy lay in my arms, sucking on his bottle, his fingers playing with my hair. I love Roddy. I love the way he smells and feels. I love his sweetness.

"And I don't want to hear you sounding like your father, Tarren," Mom continued. "Your father still hasn't learned to be strong, and he's forty . . ." Mom hesitated.

"Forty-four," Tarren said.

"Yes, forty-four," Mom repeated. Mom says Uncle Carter takes after Grandfather Babcock, who drank too much and wasted his money on get-rich-quick schemes. I never knew Grandfather Babcock. He died when Mom was just nineteen. I think she worries that Charles will turn out like him or Uncle Carter.

"Life is an obstacle course," Mom said.

I know Mom's obstacle speech by heart. *We all have to make decisions. I'm not saying it's easy. But you don't have to collapse every time you come face-to-face with an obstacle.*

"An obstacle . . ." Tarren repeated, her voice trailing off.

As Mom and Tarren were talking, Charles breezed into the kitchen. "Hey, Roddy, baby . . . how's it going?" He lifted Roddy off my lap and held him high over his head. Roddy shrieked, loving it.

"He just finished a . . ." I began to say, but by then it was too late. Roddy spit up half of what I'd just fed him, right on Charles's head.

Charles shoved Roddy back at me and ran for the sink. He turned on the faucet full blast and stuck his head under it. When he'd had enough, he turned off the water and shook his head like a dog who's been for a swim. Roddy clapped his hands and laughed. Then Charles laughed, too. "Very funny, Roddy," he said. "Ha-ha-ha."

"Aa-aa-aa," Roddy sang back.

"So what's tonight's catastrophe?" Charles asked, with a nod in Tarren's direction. He grabbed a kitchen towel and wiped his face.

"A speeding ticket," I said.

"She thinks Mom can fix it?"

"I don't know."

"Lots of luck," Charles said. Then he waved at Roddy and left.

This is what it must be like to have a regular brother, I thought. Someone you can laugh with, someone who talks to you naturally, without being sarcastic or cruel. Someone you can face every day without feeling you are walking on eggs. Why can't Charles be that kind of brother all the time?

Tarren looked less anxious when she came back into the kitchen. "I don't know what I'd do without you, Aunt Nell." She hugged Mom. "You're the most supportive person in my life. I hope someday I'll be more like you."

"You'll be fine," Mom said. "You can handle whatever life throws your way. Remember . . . obstacles, not problems."

"Right," Tarren said. "Obstacles." She reached for Roddy.

"You are about the luckiest girl alive," she told me. "You have the most wonderful mother in the entire universe!"

It's funny how people think life would be perfect if only they had different parents.

ELEVEN

Jessica has hardly been home this week. She and her friends are looking for summer jobs. I saw them downtown this afternoon, while Steph, Alison and I were shopping for shorts and T-shirts. Jess and Kristen were inside Ed's car. They seemed to be having a heavy discussion, so I didn't wave or anything.

Later, when we sat down to dinner, Dad asked Jess how the job hunt was going. Jessica put down her fork. "I've been all over town. I've answered every help-wanted ad in the paper and I always get the same reaction. They take one look at my skin and say, 'Nothing available now.' One woman even whispered, 'Come back when your skin clears up, dear.' Can you believe it! I mean, is that discrimination or is that discrimination? I'm thinking of suing."

Jess caught the look that passed between Mom and Dad. "Well, why not?" she asked them. "You can sue for sex discrimination and race discrimination and other discriminations, so why *not* skin discrimination?"

Mom said, "It's a temporary condition, Jess. Painful, but temporary."

"Does that make it okay for people to treat me like a freak?" Jessica asked. "Maybe my skin will never clear up. Maybe no one will ever hire me for anything. Maybe I'll just wear a face mask for the rest of my life!"

"An interesting idea," Dad said, and we turned to him. "I mean," he said quickly, "the idea of discrimination based on a skin condition."

Jessica sat up, her eyes bright.

"Or could it be viewed as a disability?" Dad asked Mom.

Mom mulled that over while she chewed, then swallowed whatever was in her mouth. "The law says you can't discriminate against someone because of a disability," she said. "If we could prove that acne is a disability . . ."

"So you'll take my case?" Jessica asked Mom.

"As a judge I wouldn't be able to represent you, Jess."

We all stopped midmouthful and turned to Mom, who flushed.

"You heard?" Dad asked.

Mom nodded. "Today."

"Why didn't you say something?" I asked.

"I was waiting for the right moment," Mom said.

"Well," Dad said, "this calls for a special toast." He poured himself half a glass of wine and held it up. "To Nell Babcock Robinson, who will bring her sense of fair play and justice to the bench!"

Jess and I joined Dad in his toast, raising our water glasses to Mom. "Will you still have to finish your big case?" I asked.

"Yes, but this will be my last one as a trial lawyer." Then she said, "It'll mean a substantial cut in income."

"We'll manage," Dad said.

I love you, Mom mouthed at him.

I love you, too, Dad mouthed back.

"Does this mean we're not going to decide about my lawsuit?" Jess asked.

Mom snapped back to reality. "What I started to say, honey, is . . . as a judge I wouldn't be able to handle your case. Dad can talk to his friends at the Employment Rights Project. They might have some ideas for you."

"But not you!" Jess exploded. "Not my own mother, the greatest trial lawyer who ever lived. I'll bet you'd help Tarren, though, wouldn't you?"

Mom winced.

"Jessica . . ." Dad said, touching her hand.

"What?"

"That's not fair."

"Exactly!" Jess said.

Mom started to say, "Don't you think I know . . ."

But Jess got up from the table and marched into the kitchen with her plate.

Mom's face tightened but she continued to eat, taking very small bites.

Dad tried to reassure me. "She'll be all right," he said, knowing I was thinking about Jess. "She's just upset over not getting a job."

I nodded, trying not to show how close to tears I was, trying to eat the rest of my dinner exactly like Mom, cutting my food into tiny pieces so I barely had to chew.

On Friday night Stephanie invited Alison and me to her house for supper. Steph's mother came home from work with two pizzas—one plain and one with the works. She put them into the oven in their boxes, then went upstairs, calling, "Be down in a jiff."

Mrs. Hirsch is a lot younger than Mom. Her name is Rowena and she has permed hair and big eyes. She dresses in clothes that look like costumes. One day she'll wear a long peasant skirt—the next she's in western gear. She used to look more like your basic working woman, but since she and Mr. Hirsch split up she's become more exotic.

Steph's house is cluttered, with piles of magazines and papers waiting to be read, and odd pieces of furniture that don't make any sense, like the sink in the foyer. Mrs. Hirsch has taken off the cabinet doors in the kitchen, so everything, including cereal boxes, is right out in the open. Steph's father is the complete opposite of her mother. You wonder how they got married in the first place but not why they've split up.

Stephanie's brother, Bruce, is ten. He's a worrier, like me. He should have been *my* brother. "What's new?" I asked him, as we sat around the kitchen table.

"Only good news, Bruce!" Stephanie warned. "Nothing about the rain forest, endangered species, global warming or the homeless. We don't need any of your gloom and doom tonight."

Bruce thought that over and finally said, "The Mets beat the Cards ten–zip."

"You call that news!" Stephanie said.

"Yeah, I call that news," Bruce told her. "I call that very good news."

"I wonder if my brother's going to be a baseball fan," Alison said.

"Your brother's going to be a baby," Steph said.

"I wish you'd stop saying that!" Alison told her. "I was talking about when he's older."

Mrs. Hirsch came back into the kitchen wearing tight jeans and a lacy top. She pulled the pizza boxes out of the oven. They were beginning to smell like burned cardboard. She set them on the table and told us to help ourselves.

"Yum . . ." Alison said, taking the first bite.

As much as I enjoy pizza, I can't eat it without thinking about Jess and those obnoxious boys who call her Pizza Face.

As if Mrs. Hirsch could read my mind, she suddenly asked, "How's Jessica?"

"She's trying to get a job," I said, "but so far she hasn't had any luck."

"Tell her to give me a call," Mrs. Hirsch said. "I'm looking for someone intelligent and responsible." Mrs. Hirsch owns a travel agency in town. It's called Going Places.

"Jess is very intelligent and responsible," I told Mrs. Hirsch.

"I know that," she said. "I wouldn't expect anything less from your family, Rachel." She turned to Alison. "And how's it going with *your* mom? Is she feeling okay?"

"She says she feels fat," Alison said. "She can't see her toes in the shower."

Mrs. Hirsch laughed. "When is the baby due?"

"July eleventh."

"Tell your folks if there's anything I can do, just give me a call," Mrs. Hirsch said. "Now, who's ready for a second slice?"

We all answered at once.

When we'd polished off both pizzas, Stephanie carried a plate of brownies to the table. "Well . . ." her mother said, "as long as you're all here together, I may just run out for an hour or two."

"Where to?" Steph asked.

"To see a friend."

"What friend?"

"Really, Steph . . ." Mrs. Hirsch said, with half a laugh.

"Really, what?" Steph asked, shoving most of the brownie into her mouth at once.

"If you don't want me to go out, I won't," Mrs. Hirsch told her.

"Did I say that?" Steph looked around the table. "Did anyone hear me say that?"

None of us answered.

"I just want to know *what* friend you're going to see," Steph continued. "And I want a number where I can reach you. You *said* we should always have a number, just in case, remember?"

"Yes," her mother said, "I remember."

Alison and I exchanged glances as Mrs. Hirsch pulled the phone book out of a drawer and thumbed through it. She jotted down a number and handed it to Steph. Steph looked it over, then asked, "Who is Geoff Boseman?"

"A friend," Mrs. Hirsch said.

"I never heard of him."

Mrs. Hirsch sighed. "He's a new friend."

"You mean this is a date?"

"Not unless you call two friends having coffee together a date."

"I do if one is a man and one is a woman."

"You're overreacting, Steph," Mrs. Hirsch said. She dropped a kiss on Bruce's cheek, but when she tried to kiss Stephanie, Steph ducked and Mrs. Hirsch wound up kissing air. She gave Alison and me a kind of embarrassed smile. "I'll be back in two hours, at the latest. Keep everything locked." She grabbed her purse and headed for the kitchen door.

When she was gone, Stephanie said, "You think I was overreacting?"

"Yes," I said.

Then Steph looked at Alison, who nodded and said, "She's separated. She's allowed to have dates. But even if she was still married, she could meet a friend for coffee, or even dinner."

"A friend that Bruce and I have never heard of?"

"I've heard of him," Bruce said.

"You've heard of Geoff, with a *G*, Boseman?" Steph asked him.

"Yeah. Isn't he the guy Mom met at the gym?"

"The gym!" Steph said. "She's having coffee with some guy she met at the gym?"

"On the StairMaster," Bruce said.

"The StairMaster?"

"I think that's what she said."

"I can't believe this!" Stephanie said to the ceiling.

"Lighten up," Bruce told Steph. Exactly what Steph is always telling me.

"Yeah," Alison said, "stepfathers can be the best. Look at Leon."

"I don't *need* a stepfather!" Stephanie said.

"Isn't this conversation premature?" I asked. "I mean, one cup of coffee does not necessarily lead to marriage." As soon as I said it, I realized my mistake. Natural Helpers are supposed to listen carefully, not just to the spoken but to the unspoken. We're supposed to acknowledge feelings. But did I acknowledge Stephanie's feelings? No, I did not. And did I size up the seriousness of the situation and offer support and encouragement? *No.* If I'm going to be a Natural Helper, I'm going to have to learn to be a better friend.

At eight, Steph and I sat down to watch Gena's TV show. It's called "Franny on Her Own," and it's the only show on TV I watch regularly. Actually it's not as bad as most half hour comedies. It doesn't have a laugh track and it's not stupid. Gena plays an intelligent woman who comes to live in the city after years in the country. It's a kind of city-mouse, country-mouse story. They finished shooting for the season before she looked pregnant. Alison says Gena would rather stay home with the baby next year, but it's hard to give up that kind of salary.

"This is so embarrassing," Alison said as the show began. "I don't see why you want to watch it."

"Because your mother is the star!" Steph explained. "We know her."

"Why don't you tape it instead?" Alison said. "Then we could do something interesting."

"It's just half an hour," Steph told her. "You can read or something if you don't want to watch."

"Or play computer games with me!" Bruce said. "I couldn't care less about your mother's TV show."

"You're on!" Alison told him, and the two of them ran up to his room while Steph and I laughed over "Franny on Her Own." It felt good to laugh with Steph again. According to *Psychology Today,* laughter is the best medicine.

TWELVE

Jessica got the job at Going Places. She'll be working full-time over the summer but just three afternoons, plus Saturdays, for now. After her first day of work she was bubbling with excitement, not just about the job but about Mrs. Hirsch. "*Rowena* . . . isn't that the most romantic name?" she said on Monday night. She was on the living room floor surrounded by travel brochures. "She's so warm."

"Who is?" Charles asked. He was passing through with a copy of Stephen King's latest book. Stephen King is his hero. Maybe he can go live with him in Maine!

Jessica looked up at Charles. "I was talking about Rowena Hirsch, my boss."

Mom came through then, with a mug of coffee. "What about her?" she asked.

"I was just saying how *warm* she is," Jess repeated.

"How sincere. She's completely different from anyone I've ever known."

Mom raised her eyebrows but didn't comment.

"I'm thinking of becoming a travel agent," Jess said. "I mean, not right now, but later, when I finish college. I'd love to travel."

"Travel agents don't get to travel," I told Jess. "They arrange for other people to travel."

"Rowena doesn't travel much because she has kids at home," Jess said. "But there's another agent at her office who travels all the time. She writes a newsletter, reporting on hotels and stuff like that."

"You've only been working one day," Mom reminded her.

"You can tell a lot in one day," Jess said.

"A travel agent," Charles said. "That suits you, Jess."

"What do you mean by that?" Jessica asked, suddenly wary.

"I mean I can see you as a travel agent. You'd be very . . . competent."

Jessica didn't answer him. It's always hard to know when he's coming in for the kill.

"I'm glad you enjoyed your first day on the job," Mom said, "but shouldn't you be working on your English paper now?"

"It's not due until Friday."

"That doesn't give you much time."

Jess gathered up her travel brochures.

"And you've got the SAT's on Saturday morning," Mom reminded her. "I hope you've explained that to Rowena."

"I have . . . but they're just for practice."

"Still, you want to do your best, don't you?"

Jess muttered something under her breath and headed upstairs.

Charles tsk tsked. "It's not easy running your children's lives, is it, Mom?"

Mom gave him a look but didn't answer his question.

After Jessica's second day of work it was, "I love the way Rowena dresses. She has such style." The two of us were in the bathroom, brushing our teeth before bed. "And she built the business on her own. She's a real role model for today's young women."

"She's not that great," I said, annoyed at the way Jessica was gushing.

"I guess you really don't know Rowena the person, Rachel. You only know her as Stephanie's mother."

"You can tell a lot by how someone treats her children," I said. Not that I've ever seen Mrs. Hirsch treat Steph or Bruce badly, but she's not as perfect as Jessica thinks, either.

By the end of Jessica's first week of work we were all sick of hearing about Rowena and we'd pretty much tuned her out until she said, "And Rowena thinks I should be taking Accutane now." Mom and

Dad were at the kitchen table finishing their coffee and going over the household bills. Jess and I were drying the pots and pans from dinner. "She doesn't see any point in waiting and neither do I. She even gave me an article about it. Here . . ." Jess said, pulling a folded page from a magazine out of her pocket and shoving it under Mom's nose. "Her nephew's acne cleared up six weeks after he started taking it. *Six weeks!* And he hasn't had any side effects at all." She looked from Dad to Mom, then continued, "And with my salary I can pay for it on my own. Rowena even said she'd give me an advance, if I need it."

"Where did you get the idea we can't afford Accutane?" Mom asked.

"Well, it's expensive," Jess said. "And you've been making such a big thing out of your *substantial* cut in income now that you're going to be a judge."

"It's the serious side effects that concern me," Mom said, "not the cost. Our insurance would cover the cost."

Jess exploded. "The truth is, you don't want me to take it. You've never wanted me to take it!"

"Jessica, that's just not true," Mom said. "Accutane isn't a drug to take casually. Maybe Rowena doesn't know that. I'm going to call and straighten this out right now!"

"Nell . . ." Dad said.

"Don't *Nell* me," Mom told him, storming out of

the kitchen. Dad followed her into the living room.

"Welcome to another evening of fun and games with the Robinsons," Charles said, appearing out of nowhere. He opened the freezer and pulled out an ice-cream sandwich.

"Just shut up!" Jessica shouted.

Charles smiled and went out the kitchen screen door, letting it slam behind him.

"I wish I lived at Rowena's!" Jess said to me.

"You sound like Tarren," I told her. "And you know how much you love it when she gets going over Mom."

"This has nothing to do with Tarren!" Jess said.

"Why are you angry at me?" I asked. "What'd I do?"

"I'm *not* angry at you. I'm angry at *them*," she said, with a nod in the direction of the living room, "for not taking me to someone else when Dr. Lucas said I should wait before I take Accutane. And now I find out I've been suffering for more than a year just because Mom has some warped idea that bad skin makes you a stronger person."

"Mom never said that."

"She doesn't have to say it, Rachel. You've heard it often enough, haven't you? *Looking back*," Jess said, in a perfect imitation of Mom, "*I realize I am where I am today because I had very little social life during my teens due to bad skin. Bad skin has . . .*"

She stopped when she saw Mom standing in the doorway, listening. Then she ran from the room.

"How can she possibly believe that?" Mom asked. "Doesn't she know that I, of all people, sympathize and identify?"

I wasn't sure if Mom was talking to me or to herself.

On Monday afternoon, while I was sitting on our front steps waiting for Paul to give Charles his break, Tarren drove up. She looked very pretty in a summer dress and sandals, her dark hair pulled back, her cheeks flushed. "I have to leave Roddy for a few hours. Can you watch him? Please, Rachel, it's urgent."

"An obstacle?" I asked, looking into her car, where Roddy was napping with his pacifier in his mouth.

Tarren thought that over. "Not exactly," she said. "More of a . . ."

"A what?" I asked.

"Well, I guess you could call it an obstacle. A romantic obstacle." She looked down and fluttered her eyelashes.

"Really?" I said, hoping for more information.

"Rachel, this isn't something I can discuss with you or your mother or anyone else."

Now I was even more curious.

"He's married," Tarren whispered.

"Who is?" I asked.

"My obstacle," she said.

"Oh." Suddenly I felt very uncomfortable.

"He's my professor, at school. We're . . . involved."

Did that mean what I thought it meant?

"I know what your mother would say and I'm not prepared to take her advice," Tarren said. "Because he's wonderful. Even if he is married. Even if it doesn't make any sense. Do you see what I'm saying?"

"I think so."

"Do I have your word, Rachel . . . that you won't say anything about this?"

I nodded.

She hugged me. "Thanks." Then she opened the car door and reached in for Roddy. "Someday I'll cover for you. That's a promise."

"Do you by any chance know Paul Medeiros?" I asked, as she lifted out Roddy.

"No, should I?"

"He's Charles's tutor . . . he's graduating this month."

She handed Roddy to me. "I don't think I know him." She opened the trunk of her car and pulled out Roddy's stroller.

"What time will you be back?" I said.

"Around six, okay? If anyone asks, just say I'm at the library."

As soon as she pulled away, Roddy woke up and started screaming. "It's okay . . . it's okay . . ." I said, patting him. I tried to get his pacifier back into his mouth but he wouldn't take it. Then I offered him a bottle of apple juice, which he knocked out of my hand. Finally I strapped him into his stroller and wheeled him, at top speed, down to the pond. But he still didn't let up.

"Want to see the ducks?" I asked, lifting him out of his stroller. He thrashed around in my arms and screamed even louder.

Stephanie saw us from across the pond and waved. "Ra . . . chel," she called, "what are you doing?"

I didn't answer. It was obvious what I was doing.

In a minute Steph joined us and took Roddy from me. As soon as she did, he grew quiet and looked around. He seemed surprised to see me. Steph talked softly to him. Then she set him down on the ground and he began to crawl toward the pond, stopping along the way to pull up blades of grass that he stuffed into his mouth. We followed, also on hands and knees, making sure he didn't actually swallow anything.

Later, Steph said, "Can I stay over on Saturday night . . . because my mother has a date with the StairMaster and I'm not about to hang around the house waiting to meet him."

"Sure," I said. "Should we ask Alison, too?"

"Yeah, that'd be fun . . . like the old days."

I wanted to ask what she meant by *the old days* but I stopped myself, afraid I might spoil the moment.

THIRTEEN

Dad is a Gemini. His birthday is June 3. According to my book on horoscopes, you can't ever *really* know a Gemini. They have two sides. One you see, one you don't. I guess the side you don't see with Dad is the side that sent him to bed for six weeks after Grandpa died.

Mom left Jess and me a list of things to do for Dad's birthday dinner on Wednesday night. Jess doesn't work at Going Places on Wednesdays. The menu was honey-glazed chicken, wild rice and sugar snaps. Jess and I baked the cake—chocolate with buttercream frosting—while Paul was tutoring Charles. We decorated it with forty-seven candles plus one for good measure.

"Well . . . doesn't this look festive!" Mom said when she got home from work. She admired the table we'd set with our best linens and dishes. We'd even used Gram's silver, which was passed down from *her* mother. It's ornate and very beautiful, but we hardly ever use it because you can't put it in the dishwasher. It goes to the first daughter in the family, so Jess will inherit it someday. Maybe she'll let me borrow it on special occasions.

"What would I do without the two of you?" Mom asked, shaking two Tylenol out of a bottle, then washing them down with a glass of water.

Jessica didn't answer. She's still angry at Mom for listening to Dr. Lucas about not taking Accutane. Her skin looks angry, too—red and broken out, with swellings on her chin and forehead. Tomorrow she's got an appointment to see the dermatologist Rowena recommended.

Mom headed upstairs to get changed, and when she came down a few minutes later, she said, "Rachel . . . get Charles, would you? Dad will be home any minute."

"Charles doesn't eat with us . . . remember?"

"Tonight is a special occasion."

"We'd have a better time without him," I told her.

"Rachel, please! We have to make an effort."

"I don't see why," I muttered under my breath.

"Because that's the way I want it," Mom said, setting another place at the table.

"Okay . . . okay . . ." I said.

Charles's room is painted lipstick red, which was his favorite color when he was thirteen, the year he persuaded Mom and Dad to let him move downstairs. Last year, before he went away to school, he taped an embarrassing poster to the wall behind his bed. It shows a woman wearing only red boots. I WANT YOU! she's saying.

Mom was offended by it but Dad convinced her Charles was entitled to his privacy. So his room was declared off-limits to the rest of us, as long as he kept it reasonably clean. But keeping his room clean has never been a problem for Charles. Jessica is the one who lives in a mess. Charles likes things in order. Once, when I was in fourth grade, I made the mistake of letting Stephanie borrow one of his *Batman* comics, and he almost killed me for taking it out of its plastic wrapper.

Now I knocked on his door and when he called, "Come in . . ." I opened it slowly, not sure of what I might find. The shades were pulled, making it very dark except for a single bulb inside the slide projector. Charles lay on his bed, a black baseball hat on his head. He was munching chips dipped in salsa and swigging Coke from a can as he flipped through a tray of slides with his remote control.

"Look at this picture, Rachel . . ." he said, as if he were expecting me. "Remember when this was taken?"

I turned to look at the screen and saw a picture of the two of us at the lake in New Hampshire, where we go every summer to visit Aunt Joan. I'm about six and Charles is eight. We have a huge fish between us. We're both laughing and pointing to it. We look happy. Were we? I don't remember.

"Mom says your presence is requested at the dinner table," I told him. "We're celebrating Dad's birthday."

He cut off the projector, jumped off the bed, smoothed out his shirt and gave me a smile. "Do I look . . . acceptable?"

I nodded.

When Dad came home, he feigned surprise. "What's this?" he asked, eyeing the festive table.

"Happy birthday!" the rest of us shouted.

We go through this with each of our birthdays. Even though we're never surprised, we always pretend we are. We sit down to dinner before we open presents. Mom started that rule when we were little. Otherwise we'd get too involved in our gifts and forget about the food.

All through dinner Charles didn't make one rude remark. *Not one.* He ate heartily, complimenting us on the food, telling Dad he didn't look a day older than forty-five. He told charming stories about birthday parties he remembered. But I couldn't help noticing there were just three wrapped gifts on the table, not four. And I wondered how Charles would feel when Dad opened something from each of us, but not from him.

After the main course Charles insisted on helping

Jess and me clear the dishes. He even scraped the bread crumbs off the table like a waiter in an elegant restaurant. He asked if there was anything else he could do.

Jessica almost fainted. "I think that's about it," she said, lighting the candles on the cake.

"Wait!" Charles called, as we were about to carry it in. "This is the stuff family memories are made of." While he ran out of the room, trying to find the camera, Jess and I looked at each other. We didn't know what to think.

Charles snapped away on our Polaroid as we sang "Happy Birthday." It took three tries for Dad to get all forty-eight candles out. Then Jess moved the cake to the center of the table and we took our seats to watch Dad open his presents.

Jess gave him a book. She'd showed it to me earlier.

"What do you think?" she'd asked.

"*The Pencil*?" I said, leafing through it, amazed that anyone had written such a book. It was four hundred pages long.

"Look at the subtitle," she said. *"A History of Design and Circumstance.* You know Dad loves anything having to do with history."

And now, as Dad opened it, he seemed really pleased. "I've been meaning to check this out of the library," he told Jess. "Thank you, honey."

I gave Dad a snow globe. Inside is a tiny skier perched on a hill. Dad loves to ski. The second it snows, he straps on his cross-country skis and off he goes, around Palfrey's Pond, through the woods, even on the roads before they're plowed. One winter he got a pair of snowshoes and tried walking to school in them.

Dad turned the snow globe upside down and shook, then watched as snow fell on the little skier. "Thank you, Rachel," Dad said quietly. "I love it. It'll keep me going till next winter."

I knew he really meant it. With Mom it's a lot harder. She doesn't like most things that other people choose for her. That's why Jess and I always decide on something from the two of us. Like the Mother's Day subscription to that magazine. The sample copy is still on her bedside table. I wonder if she's ever actually looked at the pictures inside.

Then Dad opened the final box, from Mom, which held an envelope with two tickets to a concert at Carnegie Hall this coming Saturday night. Music is Dad's thing, not Mom's, but she tries for him. They smiled across the table at each other.

"Well," Mom said, "shall we cut the cake?"

"Wait!" Charles pushed back his chair. "I haven't given Dad my gift yet." He stood up and cleared his throat. "Dad . . ." he began, then paused to clear his throat again. "Dad . . . on this night, on the anniversary of your forty-seventh birthday, I give to you the gift of living history." He paused and looked at each of us. "I give you back your roots." He paused again. "From this night and forevermore . . ."

What was he up to this time?

"From this night," he continued, "I will proudly carry forth the name of our ancestors . . . from this night I will be known as Charles Stefan *Rybczynski*."

There was a deadly silence at the table. And then Jessica blurted out exactly what I was thinking. "You mean you're changing your last name from Robinson to Ryb-something?"

"I'm not changing it, Jess," Charles explained. "I'm reclaiming my true name . . . *our* true name."

Dad had a false smile on his face. "Well . . ." he began.

But Mom interrupted. "Are you contemplating a legal name change?" she asked Charles.

"Mom . . . Mom . . ." Charles shook his head. "Ever the lawyer. Does it really matter whether or not I go through the formalities of changing my name?"

"Yes," Mom said, "it does."

Charles pulled a document out of his back pocket and unfolded it carefully. He spread it out in front of Dad. "I'll need your signature," he said, "since I'm under eighteen. But I told my lawyer that wouldn't be a problem."

"Your lawyer?" Mom asked.

"Yes," Charles said. "My lawyer . . . Henry Simon."

"You went to see Henry without discussing it with us?" Henry Simon is an old family friend. He went to law school with Mom and Dad. He practices in town.

"Don't worry," Charles said. "I set up an appointment. I wore a nice shirt."

"You had no—" Mom began.

"I explained it was a surprise," Charles said. "And Henry . . . Mr. Simon, that is . . . promised he wouldn't say anything. He didn't, did he?"

"No," Mom said. "I wish he had."

"Poor Mom," Charles said. "You're feeling left out, aren't you? But you can do it, too. You can become *Judge Rybczynski*. It's easy." He looked around the table. "You can all become *Rybczynskis*."

"No thanks!" Jess said. "Can you imagine your children trying to print that name in first grade?"

I laughed. I couldn't help myself.

"Let's not get ahead of ourselves," Charles said, which made Dad laugh, too.

"Well, Charles . . ." Dad finally said, "it's a mouthful to say and a bitch to spell. . . ."

Charles handed him a pen, but before Dad could sign his name Mom said, "Victor . . . don't you think you should sleep on it?"

"What for?" Dad asked. "If Charles wants the family name, it's his." Dad signed his name to the document, then sat back in his seat. "You know . . . I remember my grandfather telling me a story about the day he got to Ellis Island. The officials couldn't say his name, let alone spell it. My grandparents didn't speak a word of English but they understood what was happening. And they were all for it. A new country. A new life. A new name. I wonder what they'd think if they were here tonight?"

"I think they'd be honored," Charles said.

"You could be right," Dad told him.

Mom picked up the cake knife. "I guess it's time for dessert," she said, cutting into the cake as if she were trying to kill it.

Later I overheard Mom and Dad in the kitchen. "We're talking about a name that's going to follow him the rest of his life," Mom said.

"Maybe . . . maybe not," Dad told her. "And either way I still think it was better to sign, without making it into a production."

"You actually *like* the idea, don't you?"

"There's a certain strength to a name like that," Dad admitted.

"Well, I hate the whole thing! It's just one more way for him to separate himself from the rest of the family."

"He's testing us . . . you know that."

"I'm tired of being tested!" Mom said. "I'm tired

of him manipulating us. And I hate what this is doing to the girls."

I stood with my back against the wall right outside the kitchen. My heart was thumping so loud I was sure they could hear it.

"Sometimes I feel . . ." Mom continued. "Sometimes I feel such anger toward him I scare myself. Then I remember what a sweet, clever baby he was." Her voice broke. "If I didn't have those memories to fall back on, I don't think I could tolerate another day of his mischief."

"Nell . . . honey . . ."

I sneaked a look into the kitchen. Dad was holding Mom in his arms. I backed away as quietly as possible, right into Charles, who jabbed me in the sides with his fingers, making me cry out.

"What?" Dad asked, rushing into the hall.

"Nothing," I said.

Charles laughed. "Rachel's very edgy," he said. "She's worried she won't be able to spell my last name."

FOURTEEN

ow do you *spell* that name?" Stephanie said. She and Alison had come over to spend Saturday night.

"R-y-b-c-z-y-n-s-k-i."

"How do you pronounce it again?" Alison asked, unrolling her sleeping bag and placing it next to Steph's.

"Rib-jin-ski," I told her.

"That's an incredible name," Alison said.

"Why would anyone *want* such a long last name?" Steph said. She pulled a stuffed coyote out of her overnight bag. She's slept with that coyote since her father won it for her at a carnival. She says she plans to take it to college with her. She says she plans to take it on her honeymoon if and when she decides to get married.

"You'd have to ask Charles," I told her.

"Where is he?"

"Stephanie!" I said. "Don't you dare ask him!"

"But you said . . ."

"She was just kidding," Alison told Steph. "Right, Rachel?"

"I was definitely not serious!" I said.

"Is Charles home?" Alison asked.

"I believe he's in his room."

Mom and Dad had left for New York on the 4:30 train. They planned to have dinner at their favorite restaurant before the birthday concert at Carnegie Hall. Mom wore her slinky black dress, the one Jessica *borrowed* for her junior prom. Jess got home from work before they left. "How come you're so dressed up?" she'd asked when she saw Mom.

"It's a benefit," Mom told her, "for the Legal Defense Fund. There's a party after the concert."

Jess seemed nervous, especially when Mom looked in the mirror and said, "I don't know. There's something about this dress. Does it look odd to you, Victor?"

"It looks great!" Dad said. Obviously no one had told him what Jess wore to the prom.

Mom sniffed herself. "It doesn't smell like my perfume," she said.

"Whose could it possibly be?" Jessica asked, sounding defensive.

"I've no idea," Mom said. "Something just doesn't feel right."

"It shouldn't feel any different than it always feels," Jessica said. I shot her a look, hoping she'd shut up about Mom's dress, but she didn't. "It shouldn't feel any different than when you wore it to that benefit for the homeless."

"Maybe I've gained weight," Mom said, adjusting the straps.

"You never gain weight," Jess told her. "It's probably that you're not wearing those dangling earrings." Jess was talking about the earrings *she* wore to the prom.

"They'd be too much for tonight," Mom said.

When Mom and Dad finally left, Jessica let out a long sigh. "Do you think she guessed?" Jess asked.

"No, but you were acting so guilty she would have in another minute."

"I couldn't help myself," she said. "I didn't mean to say anything but the words just kept pouring out. I should have taken the dress to the cleaners."

"Mom'll probably send it after tonight. Stop worrying."

Jess looked at me and laughed. "This must be a first . . . *you* telling *me* not to worry!"

Later Jess went out with Kristen and Richie. Ed and Marcy have the flu.

A few minutes before seven, the three of us took our positions at the windows in my room facing Steph's house. Even though Steph refuses to meet the StairMaster, she is very curious about him.

At five after seven, a red pickup truck pulled up to Steph's. A guy in jeans and a leather jacket got out. A guy with a ponytail. Stephanie inhaled sharply.

"It's probably just a delivery," Alison told her.

We watched him swagger up to the front door. He wasn't carrying a package. In fact, his hands were in his pockets until he rang the bell. Mrs. Hirsch answered.

"He's probably selling magazines," Alison said.

Steph didn't say anything.

Mrs. Hirsch was wearing jeans, western boots and a fringed jacket. She linked her arm through his. They laughed as they got into his truck.

"I guess he's not selling magazines," Alison said.

"I can't believe this!" Steph finally said. "How old do you think he is?"

"Over eighteen," Alison said.

"Probably thirty," I said.

"Right," Alison said, glancing at me. "And they're probably just friends. Younger men and older women make good friends for each other. I read about it in *People* magazine."

But Stephanie wasn't listening. "And with a ponytail!" she said. "This is so embarrassing!"

If I were a Natural Helper right now, what would I do? I reminded myself of the first steps we learned at the introductory meeting. *Listen, not just to the spoken but to the unspoken. Be aware of body language.* Right now Steph had her arms folded across her chest. An angry pose, a defiant one. *Be on her side. Offer encouragement and support, but not advice . . .*

But as soon as the red truck pulled out, Steph said, "Let's play Spit!" You could tell she didn't want to talk about her mother and the StairMaster.

So for the next hour we played Spit, a card game Alison had taught us. It's meant for just two players but we've invented a way it can be played with three. I used to hate it, but lately I've learned it's an excellent way to relieve tension. It's such a fast game you can't afford the time to think—you just have to react. And it's so silly we always wind up laughing our heads off and singing "Side by Side," our theme song.

Tonight, when we got to the section that goes

Through all kinds of weather
What if the sky should fall . . .

Stephanie stopped and turned to me. "That's the perfect line for you, Rachel."

"What line?" I asked.

"That line." She sang it. "What if the sky should fall?"

"I don't know what you mean," I told her.

"You always think the sky is falling."

"I do not think the sky is falling."

"You think the worst is going to happen," she said. "And that's the same thing."

"I do not think the worst is *necessarily* going to happen!"

Alison held up her hands. "Let's not get into one of these stupid arguments," she said. "Okay?"

"Who's arguing?" I asked.

"I didn't mean it was bad or anything," Steph said. "I just meant . . ."

But we were interrupted by a sudden blast of music. When I opened my bedroom door, it grew even louder. I walked to the stairway and called downstairs, "Kindly lower the volume!" My choice of words made Alison and Stephanie laugh.

But Charles either couldn't hear me or chose to ignore my request. Now the neighbors would start calling. There are rules at Palfrey's Pond and one of them is no noise loud enough to break the tranquillity of the area. I love that word, *tranquillity.* It means peacefulness, serenity.

I looked at Stephanie and Alison. "I better go tell him to turn it down." As they followed me, the phone rang. "I knew it," I said. "Neighbors."

"Aren't you going to answer?" Steph asked.

"No," I said. "Let the machine take the message."

We paused outside Charles's bedroom door. The sound of the music was deafening. "Metallica," Alison said to Steph. They know the names of all the groups. But they don't know Bach from Beethoven.

Finally I knocked. No response. So I banged on his door with two fists and shouted, "Charles . . . turn that down!"

Suddenly the music clicked off and the door opened, just enough for Charles to have a look. Stephanie and Alison giggled nervously. They find anything having to do with Charles exciting.

"The neighbors are going to call to complain!" I told him.

"It's my warden," Charles announced. As he opened his door all the way, a pungent odor hit us. It was so dark and smoky in his room, it took me a minute to realize he wasn't alone.

Marcella, the eighth-grade slut, sat on the floor with Adrienne, a ninth grader who has a major attitude. There were also two guys I'd never seen before, swigging beer from bottles. And over in the corner, looking unhappy and out of place, were Dana Carpenter and Jeremy Dragon! What were *they* doing here?

"Macbeth!" Jeremy said when he saw me. "What are *you* doing here?"

"I live here," I told him. Why would Jeremy and Dana be at a party in Charles's room, especially since everyone knows about their fight over Marcella?

"You live here?" he asked, surprised.

"This is my baby sister," Charles said. "Rachel Lowilla, the child prodigy." He grabbed my wrist.

"Come in, Rachel . . ." He beckoned to Stephanie and Alison. "Come in, girls. We're celebrating my name change. Have a beer . . . have a joint . . . loosen up!"

"No thank you!" As I tried to pull away, Dana came up behind him and rested her hand on his arm. "Charles," she said quietly.

Charles let go of me and wrapped an arm around Dana's waist. They smiled at each other. What was going on here? "You're going to read about my little sister someday," Charles told his guests. "In addition to developing a vaccine to prevent hair balls in lions, she's going to—"

"Murder her brother!" I shouted, not waiting for him to finish. Then I slammed the door and broke for the stairs, with Alison and Steph following. When we got back to my room, I slammed *my* door and woke the cats.

"I *knew* Dana liked Charles!" Steph said, flopping in my chair.

"Some people have no taste," I muttered.

"And *he* likes her!" Steph continued.

"I thought he liked me," Alison said.

Steph and I looked at her.

"Well, he acted like he did . . . didn't he?" she asked. "I mean, that night I came over to get a book, he definitely acted like he was interested. You were there, Rachel."

I shrugged.

Alison continued, "I think what happened is he realized I'm just in seventh grade and he decided I'm too young . . . for now."

"Right," Steph said. She waited for me to agree.

There was no point in hurting Alison, so I said, "It's possible."

"Anything's possible," Alison said, using one of my favorite lines.

"Right," Steph and I said at the same time.

We were quiet for a minute, until we heard a voice calling, "Macbeth . . . where are you, Macbeth?"

Jeremy Dragon?

"Open the door," Steph whispered.

I opened it.

"Hey . . ." Jeremy said.

"Hey . . ." I said back. *I could not believe this!*

"Aren't you going to invite me in?" he asked. I stepped aside. He walked into my room and looked around. "Nice," he said. "Very . . . neat."

"Yeah," Steph said, "a hot Saturday night for Rachel is folding her socks!" Then she laughed nervously.

I could have killed her!

But Jeremy thought it was a joke. He laughed and said, "So, is that what you're doing . . . folding Macbeth's socks?"

Steph said, "No . . . we're just hanging out."

"Well, if you're just hanging out," Jeremy said, "how about a game?"

"A game?" I repeated.

"Yeah, a game . . . like Monopoly."

"You want to play Monopoly?" I asked. *I definitely could not believe this!*

"Yeah," he said. "That is, I wouldn't mind."

I looked at Alison and Steph. We were having trouble keeping straight faces. I went to my closet, reached up to my top shelf and pulled down my Monopoly set, which Tarren had given to me when I was in third grade.

The four of us settled on the floor, with Jeremy seated between me and Steph, across from Alison. He chose the little race car for his token. I took the hat.

We rolled to see who would start. Alison got the high number. None of us asked Jeremy anything about Charles's party. And he didn't volunteer any information. For the next two hours we concentrated on Monopoly. Midway through the game I went down to the kitchen and brought up a bottle of apple juice, a bag of pretzels, and a tin of cookies my aunt had sent us. Jeremy ate three-quarters of the cookies and drank half the juice.

The game finally ended when Alison built hotels on Boardwalk and Park Place and the rest of us went bankrupt. By then it was close to eleven and the three of us walked Jeremy downstairs. He didn't head for Charles's room or even call good-night to anyone at the party, which, from the sound of it, was still going strong.

I didn't want to think about Charles's party. I'm not the family warden, despite what Charles says. It's not my job to report on him to my parents. If he does something that directly affects me, that's different. If not, let them find out on their own.

"Good-night, Macbeth," Jeremy said as he went out the door and down the path. "Good game."

The three of us went back up to my room and fell across my bed, laughing hysterically. Then we were absolutely quiet. Then we began laughing hysterically again, until our sides were splitting.

I woke up sometime later to see Stephanie sitting in the window. I crept out of bed and kneeled beside her. The StairMaster's truck was parked in front of her house. "It's been there for an hour at least," she whispered. "And don't tell me they're just talking."

"It is possible."

"Please!"

"Sorry."

"I hate this!" Steph whispered, looking over at Alison, who was totally out of it in her sleeping bag. "It's so . . . disgusting!"

I nodded.

She choked up. "If she marries someone like him, I'm moving out. I'll go live with my dad."

"You can live with us," I said.

She smiled. "Thanks."

I put my arm around her shoulder. "It must be really hard to see your mother with someone like him."

"It is . . . it's so hard." Then she cried. I held her and patted her back. "Thank you," she said after a few minutes. "I think I'll go to sleep now."

I wish I could just let go and cry like that. I wish I knew how to let my friends comfort me.

FIFTEEN

At the bus stop on Monday morning, Dana said, "Just so you know . . . it's all over between Jeremy and me."

"You don't have to explain," I told her.

"But I want to. You seemed so . . ." She paused, trying to find the right word. "You seemed so *surprised* the other night."

"I was."

"You really don't know Charles, do you?" she said. "If you'd just give him half a chance, you might be . . ." She paused again, then came up with the same word. "*Surprised.*"

"He's a very surprising person," I agreed.

She shook her head at me, obviously annoyed. "I really don't understand you, Rachel. Most of the time you seem so grown-up, and then you . . ."

I glanced over at Alison and Stephanie, who were listening to every word.

"I just hope you'll try to get to know your brother," Dana continued, "because he's a very warm and intelligent person."

"If you say so."

"And would you, please, stop acting like such a bitch!" With that, she turned and marched away from me in a huff.

Now Stephanie and Alison were really cracking up. I went over to them, took each one by the arm like a mother with two small children, and led them away.

"Is she *really* going with Charles?" Alison asked.

"It sounds like *she* thinks so," Steph said.

"What about *him*?" Alison asked. "Does *he* think he's going with *her*?"

"I wouldn't know," I said. "Charles and I haven't exchanged a word since Saturday night."

That afternoon Dana rang our doorbell. "I'm here to see Charles," she said when I came to the door.

"Charles is with his tutor," I told her. "He's busy until five-thirty."

"I know that," she said, as if she knows everything about our family. "But they take a break at four-thirty, don't they?"

"Yes," I said, "but just for ten minutes."

She checked her watch. It was quarter after four. "If you don't mind, I'll wait."

"Suit yourself," I told her. But I didn't invite her inside.

"And Rachel," she said, "I'd really appreciate it if you wouldn't discuss this with Jeremy again."

"Discuss what with Jeremy?" I asked, since I've never actually discussed anything with him.

"*This*," Dana said, as if I were stupid. "Charles and me."

"I've never discussed you and my brother with Jeremy."

"Oh, please!" she said. "It's not like I didn't see the two of you coming out of math class today."

But what Jeremy had said on the way out of math class today had nothing to do with Dana.

He'd said, "I can't say I like your brother, Macbeth."

"I can't say I do, either," I'd answered.

"He's too full of himself."

"He's definitely full of something."

"He's not . . . you know . . . as *real* as you," he'd said, looking directly into my eyes. The way he said it made it sound like a compliment, but I couldn't be sure.

So Dana sat on the front steps to wait for Charles. Burt rubbed against her leg and she petted him, cooing, "Good kitty . . . sweet kitty." I turned away and went back into the house.

At four-thirty, when Charles and Paul came into the kitchen for their break, Charles asked, "Is Dana here?"

"Out front," I told him.

"You could have invited her in," he said.

"You didn't mention you were expecting company," I answered.

Paul dropped an arm around Charles's shoulder and said, "No distractions during our time together. Ask her to come back at five-thirty . . . okay?"

"Okay," Charles called, on his way to the front door. He didn't sound angry or even annoyed. I don't understand how Charles can get along so well with Paul but not with any of us. If Mom or Dad had said no distractions during tutoring, Charles would have told them where to go. But with Paul, he's a totally different person. He's keeping up with his schoolwork and even moving ahead of where he would be if he were just finishing ninth grade. Of course since he's already finished ninth grade once before, that's not surprising. But still . . . As soon as Charles left the kitchen, Paul looked at me and said, "What about you, Rachel?"

"*What* about me?" I asked.

"Do you have a boyfriend?"

"No!" I answered too quickly, feeling my lower lip begin to twitch. I couldn't look at him. Instead I said, "I have to practice now. Excuse me." And I ran from the room.

"When am I going to hear you play?" Paul called after me.

"Whenever . . ." I called back.

I wish I could let Paul know how I feel about him.

I often imagine us having deep, meaningful conversations. I often imagine us kissing passionately. Sometimes I imagine *more* than kisses. If Steph knew what I was thinking, she'd be relieved. She'd say, *So you're normal after all . . . at least in* that *way!* But she can't know. No one can. Paul has to remain my secret.

SIXTEEN

Mom lost her big jury trial on the same day I won a major debate against a ninth grader at Kennedy Junior High. Toad Scrudato, the only other seventh grader on our team, said, "Rachel, you were brilliant!" Those were his exact words. So obviously I was feeling pretty good. This was before I found out about Mom. At the time I didn't even mind that Toad's father's car broke down on the Merritt Parkway on the way home from the debate and we had to be towed to a garage, then wait an hour while a new battery was installed.

I called home at quarter to six to say I'd be late. Charles answered. I asked for Dad. He said Dad was coaching at a track meet. When I asked for Mom, he said she wasn't home yet, either. "And neither is Jessica, so that leaves me, Rachel. Do you have a message for me?" I told him about Mr. Scrudato's car but nothing else.

Then Toad and I sat on the curb outside the garage and read while Mr. Scrudato made call after call on his car phone. Toad and I have known each other since kindergarten. We're sort of an odd couple. He's always been the smallest kid in our class and I've always been the tallest, until Max Wilson moved here. But we have a lot in common intellectually.

By the time Toad's father dropped me off at our house, it was after seven. As soon as I walked in, Dad took me aside and said, "Mom lost her case. She's pretty upset."

"Should I say something?"

Dad shook his head. "You know how she is. She doesn't want to talk about it."

The same way I was when I missed *sesquipedalian* and lost the state spelling championship last year.

Still, I was surprised when Mom didn't come to dinner. It's not as if this is the first case she's ever lost.

"She's just disappointed," Dad told Jess and me as he grilled hamburgers on the patio. "She wanted to go out on a high note."

"Who?" Jess asked, as if she lived on another planet.

"Mom," Dad said. "This is a blow to her pride but she'll get over it." He sounded like he was trying to convince not only us, but himself. I must have looked strange because Dad reached out to touch my arm. "Don't worry, Rachel . . ."

Until then I wasn't worried.

Charles passed by, grabbing a roll. He flipped a

hamburger onto it and smothered it with salsa. "Is it true?" he asked, taking a huge bite. "Did the perfect litigator really lose her final case?"

Dad snapped at him. "A little compassion is in order this evening, Charles!"

"Yeah, sure," he said, with a mouthful. "I've got compassion. I'm just saying, you know, we'd all be better off if we were less competitive."

"Speak for yourself," I said.

"I always speak for myself, Rachel," he said, going out through the patio gate.

After dinner I went upstairs. The door to Mom and Dad's bedroom was open a crack. I knocked lightly. "Mom . . ." No answer. I pushed the door open and tiptoed in. She was asleep with an ice pack across her forehead. I looked around and was surprised to see her suit tossed over a chair and her shoes in the middle of the floor as if she'd kicked them off on her way into bed. "I'm sorry you lost your case," I whispered as I picked them up and put them in her closet. But she didn't hear me.

I went down the hall to my room and sat at my desk, staring out the window. I wasn't in the mood for my math homework. I wondered what my teacher would do if I came in tomorrow and used that as an excuse. *Sorry, I didn't feel like doing my homework last night.* She'd probably call Mrs. Balaban, who would send me to Dr. Sparks!

While I was sitting there, Dad came in. "Tell me about the debate."

I didn't want to talk about it now. It didn't seem right to be happy about winning when Mom was so unhappy. So I just gave him the basics.

"I'm proud of you, honey," he said. "But I'd love you just the same if you'd lost today. You know that, don't you?"

"Why do you always say that?"

"Say what?"

"That you'd love me just the same if I lost."

"Because it's true."

"That's not what I mean."

"Then what?"

I wasn't sure how to explain it. "I mean," I said, trying to find the right words, "why can't you just accept good news?"

"I guess I want you to remember that winning's not the most important thing in life."

"But it's a lot better than losing," I told him. "Just ask Mom."

He ran his hands through his hair. He does that when he's thinking. So I quickly added, "Mom would be glad I won. I don't see why you can't be, too."

"I *am* glad, Rachel. I just want you to keep it in perspective." He dropped a kiss on top of my head. "I've got to run over to the library. Be back in an hour."

When he was gone, I jotted down *Keep it in per-*

spective on my math worksheet. Under that I wrote *Victor Robinson, Tuesday, June 9.*

The next afternoon, right before school ended, I was called to Mr. Herman's office. The one time in my entire life I didn't do my homework and I've been reported to the vice principal! I felt sick. I wondered if this would go down on my permanent record. When I got to his office, Toad was there, too, looking as terrified as me. Mr. Herman told us to make ourselves comfortable but neither of us moved an inch. Even though he has a friendly smile, Mr. Herman's size makes him formidable. Kids call him the sumo wrestler.

"Good news," he said. "You've both been recommended for Challenge, a new program for junior high students who excel academically. If your parents give permission, you'll be taking courses in math and science at the college next year."

As he explained it to us, I began to feel like I couldn't breathe. Another program to separate me from my friends! When he asked if we had any questions, I managed to say, "Do we *have* to?"

"Have to what, Rachel?"

"Do this?"

Toad looked at me as if I were totally insane. But I didn't care. I felt light-headed and grabbed hold of the back of a chair facing Mr. Herman's desk.

"It's entirely up to you," he said. "It's an honor just to be asked."

"A person can't do everything just because she's asked," I told him.

"A good point," he said.

I definitely could not breathe! I closed my eyes and forced myself to count backward from one hundred.

Mr. Herman never noticed. He went right on talking. "Well, I guess this has really caught both of you by surprise!" When neither of us responded, he cleared his throat. "Here's a letter to take home to your parents." He handed one to Toad and another to me. "Think of this as an opportunity not to be missed."

As the bell rang, I shoved the letter into my purse. I wish I could explain to Mr. Herman and everyone else that right now I don't *need* another opportunity.

On the bus home from school Alison said, "Are you okay, Rachel?"

"Yes . . . why?"

"You look sort of pale."

Steph squinted at me. "No, she doesn't. She's always that color."

"She's usually got *some* pink in her cheeks," Alison said. "Maybe she's coming down with that flu."

"She looks fine to me," Steph said.

While they were arguing, some guy shoved Jeremy

Dragon, who was getting off at the next stop, right into my lap.

"Sorry about that, Macbeth," he said as he pulled himself up.

I could feel my cheeks burning, especially when the driver yelled at us to quit fooling around.

As Jeremy got off the bus, Alison whispered, "You're not pale anymore, Rachel!"

"I wish he'd fall onto me!" Steph said, making all three of us laugh.

The minute I got home, I folded and refolded the letter from Mr. Herman until it was small enough to fit into the secret compartment of my favorite box. Since Mr. Herman says participating in Challenge is entirely up to me, I don't have to show it to my parents. At least not yet.

SEVENTEEN

Jessica's been taking Accutane for a week. The doctor Rowena recommended told Jess about the possible side effects and gave her a booklet to read. But Jess decided to try it, anyway. I don't blame her. I'd try anything if I had her kind of cystic acne. Before the doctor gave her the prescription Jess had to sign a paper stating she would not get pregnant, because if you take Accutane while you are, it causes serious birth defects. As if Jess would be foolish enough to get pregnant even if she had a boyfriend, which she doesn't.

Jess will have to see the doctor once a month for twenty weeks. She'll need blood tests to make sure everything's going okay. She says Accutane can take up to four months to work but some patients see a difference right away. I hope she'll be one of them.

Tarren and Roddy came over for dinner on Thursday night. Tarren took one look at Jess and said, "Your skin looks . . . painful."

"Well, it's not as painful as acne," Jess told her. Her face was totally dried out and peeling. So far Jessica's only side effects are dry eyes and cracked lips. She carries a tube of medicated lip gloss with her and has to put drops in her eyes twice a day.

Before we sat down to dinner, Tarren cornered me. "Listen, Rachel . . ." she said, shifting Roddy from one hip to the other, "I wanted to thank you for that day you watched Roddy."

I nodded. "How's it going with your romantic obstacle?"

"It's going great."

I nodded again, then looked around to make sure no one was within earshot. "Have you by any chance met Paul Medeiros?" I spoke very softly. "He's a history major at the school of education."

"You've asked me about him before, haven't you?"

"I thought maybe you've met him since then."

Tarren shook her head. "Is he someone special?"

"No," I said quickly, hoping Tarren wouldn't become suspicious. "I mean, he's Charles's tutor . . . and I'm curious . . . but other than that . . ."

"Well, I don't think I know him. Do you want me to ask around?"

"No . . . forget it . . . it's nothing."

"You're sure . . . because I owe you a favor."

"I'm sure," I told her.

Charles joined us for dinner. I don't know why. He hasn't had a meal with us since Dad's birthday. He sat next to Roddy, who was in a Sassy Seat, which attached to the table.

We were having corkscrew pasta with vegetables and Mom's special lemon-and-herb sauce. The green peppers weren't cooked quite enough for me, so I moved them to the side of my plate. Tarren did the same with her mushrooms.

"Tarren," Mom said, "I'd like you to come to my swearing-in ceremony. It's the morning of June twenty-third, in Hartford. After, we'll all go out to lunch."

"Oh, Aunt Nell," Tarren gushed. "I'm honored."

I wondered how long it would take to drive to Hartford. If it's more than half an hour, maybe I can take the train. I wouldn't want to get carsick on the day Mom is sworn in as a judge.

Charles was quiet, intrigued by Roddy, who was slowly and methodically eating Cheerios. He picked up one at a time, using two fingers, brought it to his mouth, got it inside, then mashed it with his gums. He still doesn't have teeth. Tarren says he will soon.

"Was it always your goal to become a judge, Aunt Nell?" Tarren asked, as Dad served the salad.

"I really hadn't given the possibility much thought

until recently," Mom said. "But frankly, after this week, I'm beginning to think it will be a relief."

"What do you mean?" Tarren asked, wide-eyed.

"I lost a case," Mom told her. "I lost my final jury trial." She sounded wistful, almost emotional. This was the first time she'd mentioned the verdict.

"I can't imagine you losing a case!" Tarren said.

"Well, I did," Mom told her, "and I took it personally, even though I know better." She kind of sighed as she speared a tomato. "But I did my best and that's what counts."

Tarren had tears in her eyes. "That is just so moving, Aunt Nell. To know you've done your best even when you've failed."

Charles looked up, suddenly interested. Then Mom said, "I didn't exactly fail, Tarren. I lost a case that I'd rather have won, that's all. It happens." She sounded sure of herself again, like Mom.

"It's all about goals, isn't it?" Tarren asked. "In our Life Studies class we had to write down where we hope to be five years from today, then ten, then twenty. It really got me thinking."

Charles looked over at Tarren. Before he had the chance to pounce, Dad said, "What *are* your goals, Tarren?"

"Well, some of them are personal," Tarren said, with a glance in my direction, "and I'd rather not discuss them. But my professional goal is to become the best fourth-grade teacher I possibly can. To make a difference in a few children's lives."

Charles let out a snort.

Tarren leaned forward in her seat so she could look directly at Charles. "It would be a good course for you to take," she told him. "Talk about someone who needs to clarify his goals!"

Didn't she know better than to start in with him?

"My goals in life are very simple," Charles told her. We all waited for more but first Charles reached for his water glass and took a long drink. Then he wiped his mouth with his napkin. With Charles, timing is everything. Finally he said, "My main goal in life is to be Batman!"

"Really, Charles!" Mom said, as Charles lifted Roddy out of his Sassy Seat and bounced him on his lap to the theme from the Batman movie.

Roddy laughed and said, "Da da . . ."

"I'm not your da da," Charles said, "but speaking of your da da, is he still soaring?"

Tarren sucked in her breath. "As far as I know Bill is still hang gliding, if that's what you mean. We have almost no contact."

"Poor little guy!" Charles patted Roddy's head.

"He doesn't need your pity!" Tarren told Charles. "He's going to be just fine."

"That's the spirit!" Mom said, squeezing Tarren's shoulder.

"Having a runaway father is just one obstacle in his life," Tarren said. "And we all have our obstacles."

"Yeah, look at me," Charles said. "I'm surrounded by mine. My father, the *wimp* . . . my mother, the *ice queen* . . . my big sister, the *potato head* . . . and my little sis—"

Before he had the chance to finish, Jessica pushed back her chair. "I hate you!" she hissed.

"I know that, Jess . . . but you'll get over it."

Mom jumped up, her face purple with rage. "You want to hurt us, Charles? Okay, we're hurt! You want to cause pain? Fine, you have! You want to disrupt the family? Congratulations, you've succeeded!" She banged her fist on the table so hard the dishes rattled.

Roddy began to cry. Tarren snatched him from Charles's lap and whisked him into the kitchen, where his screams grew louder. By then Dad was out of his seat, grabbing hold of Mom, who had lunged at Charles, shouting, "Enough is enough!" A glass she'd knocked over rolled to the edge of the table, tumbled to the floor and smashed.

Charles folded his napkin. "Well," he said, "this pleasant evening seems to be drawing to a close."

As he began to get up from the table, Dad pushed him down again. "Stay right where you are!"

Charles looked surprised for a minute. The color drained from his face. He didn't move.

"We're not going to tolerate any more nights like this!" Dad shouted. "It's time for you to get your act together. Do you understand what I'm saying?"

Mom stood next to Dad, waiting for an answer.

Charles gave them a long look, then asked, "Is that it? Are you finished?"

"Oh, for God's sake!" Mom said, and I could feel her frustration.

"No, I'm not finished," Dad told him. "I'm waiting for you to answer the question!"

"I believe I get your point," Charles said quietly. "Now, may I please be excused?"

Dad didn't answer right away. When he did, his voice was flat. "You're excused to help clean up."

"Thank you." Charles stood, stacked the dinner dishes and carried them into the kitchen.

I ducked under the table to pick up the broken glass.

"I've had it," Mom said to Dad. "This time I have *really* had it."

"We can't give up on him, Nell."

"I'm not saying we should give up on him. I'm saying he's pushed me to the limit!"

Before I'd collected all the glass, the phone rang. "It's Stephanie, Rachel," Tarren called from the kitchen.

"Tell her I can't talk now," I said quietly, from the floor. "Tell her I'll call back."

But I didn't call Stephanie that night. And later, as I lay in bed watching the clock, I played the dinner table scene over and over in my mind, angry at myself for just swallowing everything I was thinking and feeling—for just sitting there, totally paralyzed, waiting to hear what Charles would say about me, almost disappointed that Jess stopped him before he'd had the chance to finish.

I got out of bed and crept down the hall to Jessica's room. But she was sound asleep, breathing evenly. How could she sleep after tonight? How could anyone?

My stomach was killing me. I needed something to soothe it. I moved silently downstairs with Harry right behind me. When I got to the kitchen, I flicked on the light switch and almost keeled over when I saw Charles perched on the counter, gnawing a chicken leg.

"Want a bite?" he asked, holding it out.

"You just about scared me to death!" I told him, keeping my voice low. The last thing I wanted was to wake Mom and Dad. "Why are you in here in the dark?"

"Is there a family rule against conserving energy?"

I didn't answer. Instead I filled the kettle and turned on the burner.

Charles jumped down from the counter. He opened the refrigerator, pulled out the grape juice and held it up, as if to toast me. "Here's to you, Rachel Robinson!" He swigged some juice right out of the bottle, then slammed the door. "Here's to my whole fucking family!"

"You better not let Mom and Dad hear you say that."

"Yeah, right. They'd call the language police. And the language police will drag me to the dictionary to find a more acceptable word for my family, like noble . . . like self-sacrificing . . . like—"

"You were despicable tonight!"

"Thanks, Rachel."

"Why'd you have to hurt everyone? What was the point?"

"The point was to get at the truth."

"Well, you didn't!" I told him. "You didn't even come close."

"Really."

"Yes, really! Mom's not an ice queen."

"Maybe not to you. After all, you're her clone."

"I'm not anybody's clone! And Dad's not a wimp, either."

"Then how come he went to bed for six weeks when Grandpa died? How come he couldn't make it in the real world? How come he gives the Ice Queen all the power?"

"He went to bed when Grandpa died because he was sad."

"Oh, that's sweet, Rachel. But plenty of people get

sad and they don't climb into bed and pull the cov-
ers over their heads for six weeks!"

"He wasn't happy being a lawyer, so he quit.
What's wrong with that?" I paused for a moment.
"And Mom doesn't have all the power. He's the one
who's always stopping her."

"Right . . . because he's a wimp! He'll do anything
to avoid confrontation!"

"He didn't avoid it tonight, did he? He told you
off and so did Mom!"

"You call that telling me off?" He smirked. "I call
that pathetic."

"Mom and Dad are *not* pathetic!"

"Are we talking about the same Mom and Dad?
The Nell and Victor with the bedroom upstairs at the
end of the hall?"

"I'm talking about *my* parents. I don't know about
yours!"

"When are you going to face the facts, Rachel? This
is a very screwed-up family!"

"You're the part that's screwed up."

"I don't deny it. But the rest of you . . ." He stopped
and shook his head.

"All families have problems," I said, thinking of
Steph and how angry she is at her mother for dating the StairMaster.

He laughed. " 'Happy families are all alike; every
unhappy family is unhappy in its own way.' "

That sounded familiar but I couldn't remember where I'd heard it.

Charles laughed again. "Tolstoy, Rachel. Don't tell me you haven't read him yet?"

"I plan to . . . this summer."

"I certainly hope so. I wouldn't want you to fall behind. After all, you've got to be the best."

"I like being the best!"

"What happens when you find out it's not always possible?"

"I've already found out and I'm surviving!"

He paused, as if I'd caught him by surprise. "You know something, Rachel, you've got possibilities. With a little coaching . . ."

"I don't need any coaching from you!" I told him. "I'm figuring out life by myself, thank you."

"Whatever you say, little sister." He started to walk away.

I called, "What do you want from us, Charles?"

He spun around. "What do I want?" He looked up, as if he'd find the answer on the ceiling. Then he repeated the question, quietly, to himself. "What do I want . . . ?"

I waited, but for once Charles seemed at a loss for words.

EIGHTEEN

The next night Charles didn't come to dinner. I wasn't surprised. But even without him at the table, it's become so tense it's hard to eat. The rest of us didn't have much to say until Dad announced we're going to see a family counselor, someone named Dr. Michael Embers.

"I don't see why *we* have to go to a counselor!" Jessica cried, with a nod in my direction. "There's nothing *wrong* with Rachel and me!"

"Because it's *family* therapy," Dad told her, sounding weary.

"But *Charles* is the one with the problem!" Jess argued, which is exactly what I was thinking.

Dad shoved his plate out of the way. "Please don't make this more difficult than it already is." He reached into his pocket and pulled out a packet of Pepto-Bismol tablets. He popped two into his mouth and chewed them up slowly. He looked very tired. So did Mom. I really and truly resent Charles for making them so unhappy.

"Well," Jessica said, "if we *have* to go, I don't see why we can't see a woman!"

"According to *some* people," Mom said, "there are already too many authoritarian women in Charles's life."

Does that mean us? I wondered, looking at Jessica. What a joke! Charles walks all over us. We have no authority over him!

On Monday night at six, we went to Dr. Embers's office. He shook hands with each of us, but only Charles introduced himself using two names. "Charles Rybczynski," he said. If Dr. Embers noticed Charles had a different last name, he didn't show it.

He said, "Please, sit down . . . make yourselves comfortable."

His office was arranged like a living room, with a small sofa, two armchairs, a wooden rocker and a couple of other chairs. I sat stiffly in one of the armchairs, next to Jessica, who sat in the other. Mom and Dad shared the sofa, and Charles settled in the rocker.

Dr. Embers was younger than I'd expected, with wiry light hair, washed-out blue eyes and a runner's slender body. He sat in a plain wooden chair and crossed his legs. "So . . ." he said, "you're having some problems. And you're here to find a way to resolve them."

Mom and Dad nodded.

Dr. Embers continued, "The good news is you're all healthy, intelligent people. My job is to help you understand the patterns that cause the difficulties so you can make the changes that will enable you to live together in harmony." I waited for him to give us the bad news, but he didn't.

"Okay, just to break the ice," he said, "I'd like each of you to describe in one word or phrase how you feel about being here today." He looked directly at me. "Rachel . . . why don't you begin."

"Me?" I said. "Why start with me?"

"Because you're the child prodigy," Charles said.

"You see!" I told Dr. Embers. "There's the problem!"

"You seem angry, Rachel," Dr. Embers said.

"I am angry!"

I expected him to say, *Can you tell me about that?* But he didn't. He just nodded and said, "Go on . . ."

But I couldn't. I mean, I didn't really know anything about Dr. Embers. I didn't know whose side he was on or how much Mom and Dad had told him. And I certainly didn't know if I could trust him. "I'm angry . . ." I hesitated for a second. "I'm angry because I don't want to be here."

He nodded again.

"But I've been told I have no choice," I continued. "I have to be here even though there's nothing wrong with me or my family . . . except for . . ."

"Except for?" Dr. Embers said, leaning slightly forward. His jacket fell open and I noticed he was wearing a silver belt buckle with an Indian design etched into it. Dad has one almost exactly like it.

"Except . . ." Dr. Embers said again, expectantly.

When I couldn't get the words out, Jessica did it for me. "Except for Charles!"

"Except for Charles," Dr. Embers repeated matter-of-factly.

"Yes," Jess continued. "He gets all the attention. He takes up all our time and energy. I'm exhausted just from living in the same house with him. It's like . . ." Jessica choked up. "It's like being slowly poisoned!"

Dr. Embers turned to Charles, who was rocking back and forth in his chair, a frozen expression on his face. "What are you feeling right now, Charles?"

"Nothing," Charles said. "Absolutely nothing."

But I didn't believe him.

We came home from our session with Dr. Embers with what he called a contract for family living. It runs for two weeks. By then I'll be on my way to music camp. I can't wait! In the contract we each agreed to try to respect one another's feelings, needs and concerns. We agreed to think before speaking. We agreed to exercise each day, if only for twenty minutes, because Dr. Embers says exercise is a good way to get rid of hostility. And we're not supposed to go to bed at night feeling angry. Even Charles signed the contract without any snide comments. Even he was too worn down to argue. When we got home, Dad taped it to the refrigerator.

The next day I signed up for Natural Helpers. I don't think I'd be a good Natural Helper if I came from a family with no problems. But I know what problems are. I know how they feel. So maybe I can help someone else feel better.

NINETEEN

Charles has new wraparound sunglasses. Dana gave them to him. I remember when she gave Jeremy Dragon a gold dove. He wore it pinned to his underwear. At least that was the rumor. I wonder if he gave it back to her when they broke up. I wonder if Charles will give back the wraparounds if he splits with Dana.

"So how about it?" Dad said to Charles. He was trying to convince him to go to Ellis Island tomorrow with his sophomore history classes. Ellis Island is the place where our family name was changed from Rybczynski to Robinson.

"I'm thinking about it," Charles said. He was wearing his sunglasses even though it was almost dark.

We were outside on our patio. It was very still, more like August than June. Dad lit a citronella candle to keep the mosquitoes away. Mom was working late at the office again. Now that her big trial is over, she says she has so much to finish up before she's sworn in as a judge she doesn't know how she'll ever get it done. I'm worried about her. A woman like Mom needs kids like Jess and me, who don't give her any trouble!

"I can't make you go," Dad said to Charles. "But it would mean a lot to me if you did."

I really felt for Dad, so I said, "I'll go."

"Me, too," Jessica added.

"There!" Charles said to Dad. "Why don't you take your devoted daughters instead of me?"

"This isn't an *instead*," Dad said. He looked at Jess and me. "For the two of you it would mean missing a day of school."

"Nothing ever happens the last week," Jess told him. "You know that."

"This isn't the last week," Dad said.

"It's the last *full* week," I reminded him. "Next week is all half days."

"And you're going to miss one of those to go to Mom's swearing-in ceremony," Dad reminded us.

"But, Dad . . ." Jessica argued, "Ellis Island is an example of *living* history. It's not something you can learn in a classroom."

Dad laughed. He knew Jess had him, and we knew he'd let us come. Then he looked over at Charles, who was picking up pebbles and letting them run through his fingers. "Charles?" he asked hopefully.

"I *told* you, I'm thinking about it!" Charles said.

I was thinking about Paul Medeiros, wondering if he'd be going with us. I hope so! After all, he's Dad's student teacher. Then I remembered this is a school trip and almost all school trips use buses for transportation. So I asked, "How will we get there?" I tried to sound casual, as if I didn't care one way or the other.

"There's a ferry from Battery Park," Dad said. "It's just a ten-minute trip, past the Statue of Liberty."

"No, I mean from *here* to New York," I said.

"Oh . . ." Dad said. "We've got a bus."

I knew it! I chose my next words carefully. "I could take the train and meet you in the city."

Charles pulled off his sunglasses and looked at me. "Don't tell me you still get carsick!"

"I don't want to discuss it with you!" I told him.

"Is she ever going to outgrow that?" Charles asked Dad.

"Of course," Dad told him. "When she gets her driver's license . . . if not before."

When I get my driver's license! That's three years from now. Mom used to tell me I'd outgrow it by ten, but I didn't. And for some reason the medicines that work for other people give me excruciating headaches. I *hate* getting carsick! It's so embarrassing, especially at my age. A few months ago Alison's mother invited us to visit her on the set of her TV series and I got sick on the drive into the city. We had to stop so I could throw up.

But Gena was very nice about it. She opened her purse, pulled out a pair of these things that looked like sweatbands and offered them to me. "I don't think I'd have survived the first few months of my pregnancy without my Sea-Bands."

When I hesitated, she said, "They're perfectly safe. You wear them above your wrists, with the little button pressing on your Nei-Kuan point. That's three fingers up from your wrist."

I thanked Gena and tucked the Sea-Bands into my purse. But I never wore them. Instead I slept all the way home and didn't get sick until I was in my own house.

Now I looked at Dad, hoping he'd say it would be fine for me to take the train. But before he had the chance, Charles started. "She wouldn't act like such a baby if you didn't treat her like one."

"Who are you to judge?" Jess asked him. She turned to me and said, "I'll take the train with you, Rachel."

I was so grateful I grabbed her hand.

Charles said, "What are you two . . . Siamese twins or something?"

"Yeah," Jess said. "You have a problem with that?"

"You see," Charles said to Dad. "It's always them against me. That's how it's been my whole life!"

"Oh, please . . ." Jess said. "You're not in second grade anymore, so why don't you stop acting like it!"

"You know, Jessica . . ." Charles began, "it could be a lot worse. I could be into drugs. I could be in trouble with the law. I could be a rapist or a serial killer . . ."

"Am I supposed to be grateful?" Jess asked.

"You're supposed to count your blessings."

"I do . . . every day . . . and you're not one of them!"

I waited for Dad to remind us of our contract for family living but Dana came along at that very moment, calling, "Helloooo . . . anybody home?"

Charles stood up and brushed off his hands. He opened the patio gate.

Dad called, "Be back by ten."

"Yeah . . . yeah . . ." Charles muttered.

After he was gone, Dad said, "I think she's good for him, don't you?" Jessica and I looked at each other but neither of us answered his question. Then Dad blew out the citronella candle, and Jess and I followed him into the house.

TWENTY

The weather broke overnight and the next morning was perfect, sunny and breezy. Jess and I were up and dressed at six. By the time Charles came into the kitchen Mom was gone, and it was just as well, because Charles looked like he'd slept in his clothes. "I have a sore throat," he said. "I think I should stay home."

Dad felt his forehead. "No fever."

"It could be Lyme disease," Charles told him. "My neck feels stiff."

I looked at him. There was an article about Lyme disease in yesterday's paper.

"Just get dressed, Charles," Dad said.

"I *am* dressed," Charles said. He was wearing his ELVIS IS DEAD T-shirt.

"Well then, have something to eat," Dad suggested.

"You're starting to sound just like Mom!" Charles said.

Dad pointed to the contract taped to the refrigerator and Charles shut up.

Dad dropped Jess and me at the train station in time to catch the 7:10 to New York, which was packed with commuters. When the train came along, we took seats across the aisle from a man carrying a canvas gym bag. As soon as the conductor collected our tickets and moved to the next car, the man, who was wearing a business suit, unzipped his bag and a small dog stuck out his head and looked around. Then the man pulled out a Dixie cup and fed ice cream to the dog from a spoon. Jess and I looked at each other and started laughing.

When we calmed down, I said, "Thanks for coming with me."

"I prefer the train," Jess said. "I always get queasy on the bus."

"I never knew that."

"Well, I don't get as sick as you, but with Charles on board . . ." She didn't have to finish her sentence. I knew what she meant.

When Jess pulled out her *Elle* magazine, I opened the book Dad had given me about Ellis Island. We read quietly for a while. Then I asked, "Do you think it's going to work with Dr. Embers?"

"It all depends on Charles," Jess said, holding her place in the magazine with her thumb. "On whether or not he wants to make the effort."

"What do you think?"

"I have no idea," Jess said. "But either way I'm not going to let him ruin my senior year!" She flipped through a few pages.

I wanted to tell her about the other night in the kitchen, when I asked Charles what he wanted from us and he couldn't answer. But I didn't.

"I'll tell you something, Rachel," Jess continued. "If he can't get along with us, that's his problem! I've got too much to look forward to, to let him get in my way." She flipped a few more pages, then tapped an ad for shampoo. "Just once I'd like to see a model in here with acne. Maybe someday they'll get real!"

When we got to the city, we followed Dad's directions and took the subway from Grand Central Station to Battery Park, which is at the southern tip of Manhattan. We were proud of ourselves for not getting lost.

Once we were there, we waited in line for tickets. Dad was lucky we went by train because by the time his bus pulled in, the lines for ferry tickets were so long we would have waited till noon.

When Charles got off the bus, I worried he'd make some rude remark about me in front of Dad's students but he didn't even glance my way. He was talking and laughing with a group of kids. I guess he'd recovered from his Lyme disease.

Paul was the last to get off the bus. I'd held my breath until then, afraid he wasn't coming after all. But when I saw him, I turned away quickly, so he wouldn't get any ideas. As Dad rounded up his students and led the way through the park down to the ferry dock, I hung back, feeling slightly out of place until Paul called, "Rachel . . . wait . . ."

I love to hear him say my name!

"Have you been to Ellis Island before?" he asked when he caught up with me.

"No, have you?"

"Once," he said, as we walked toward the ferry. "I took my grandparents for their fiftieth anniversary. They came here from Portugal right after they were married. Not exactly a romantic journey since they were both seasick the whole time."

Romantic journey! He said *romantic journey* to me!

"Victor tells me his father came over from Poland." Paul spoke as if we were actually having a conversation. It was weird to hear him call my father by his first name. I wonder what else he and Dad talk about. Do they talk about Charles? Do they talk about *me*? I tried to say something but felt like I had a mouthful of marbles.

We boarded the ferry with a large crowd—tourists from different countries speaking their own languages, other school classes, groups on outings, and families. We climbed to the upper deck and watched as two helicopters circled overhead. A group of Dad's students surrounded Paul, separating us. I looked around for Jessica but she was busy with friends.

I wandered around the deck, stopping when I heard a teacher scolding a boy, about ten. "Never mind Eric . . ." she told her class, "he's just looking for attention." When the ferry began to move, the other kids cheered but Eric sat down, clutching his stomach. Was he seasick already or just scared?

I sat next to him. He looked up at me. "I forgot my lunch," he said.

"Maybe one of your friends will share with you."

"I don't have any friends," he said. "Everyone hates me."

"That's really sad."

"Yeah, I know."

"You want my lunch?" I asked. Not that I wanted to give it to him, because I'd fixed things I really like. But I could always buy lunch if I had to, and he seemed so alone.

"What do you have?" he asked, perking up.

"Tuna with tomatoes and sprouts on rye."

"What else?"

"Oatmeal cookies, cranberry juice and a peach."

"I don't like any of that stuff," he said.

"Well then, I guess I can't help you."

"You're a geek!" he told me. "You're an ugly, stupid geek!"

"No wonder you don't have any friends!" I said, surprised at how angry I felt. Natural Helpers aren't supposed to get angry just because someone they're trying to help isn't grateful.

We stopped at the Statue of Liberty first. Eric and his class got off there. I watched from the deck as they marched off the ferry, two by two. When Eric turned and looked up at me, I waved. He stuck out his tongue. Well, at least I'd tried!

Our ferry waited at the statue while another group of school kids boarded. They were all wearing green foam Statue of Liberty crowns. As the ferry pulled out again, Dad began to recite the poem engraved at the base of the statue.

"Give me your tired, your poor,
Your huddled masses yearning to breathe free . . ."

A few kids in his class joined in, then a few more, until they were all reciting the poem together. When they finished, it was so quiet on deck I could hear the wind as it whipped my hair away from my face.

Next stop was Ellis Island. Dad reminded us to imagine ourselves as immigrants arriving by ship after a long, difficult journey. "You're tired, hungry, scared, but you've made it to the new country," Dad said. "You are about to start over in the land of opportunity!"

We entered the main building through a long portico and came into the Great Hall, which feels enormous. Probably thousands of people could fit in this room at once. The floor is made of white tile and the ceiling is so high it makes you feel tiny, even if you are the second tallest person in seventh grade.

If I were a thirteen-year-old immigrant girl coming into this vast hall, I know I'd have been scared, especially if I didn't understand a word of English, which most immigrants didn't.

Dad said we were free to look around on our own for an hour, then meet in front of the computers. Most kids went off in groups but I wandered by myself. I stopped at the first exhibit to look at the types of baggage the immigrants brought with them. There were trunks in all sizes. Some of them were made of wood, others of leather or what looked like cardboard. Some immigrants brought baskets as big as trunks. Some came with woven sacks in bright colors.

I closed my eyes and tried to imagine my grandfather as a little boy, clutching his mother's hand while his father carried their baggage into this Great Hall.

I climbed up the stairs to the Registry Room, where each immigrant was inspected for diseases and where some guard who couldn't pronounce or spell our family name, *Rybczynski*, assigned Grandpa and his parents the name *Robinson*.

On the third floor were display cases filled with

the immigrants' most important possessions—hand-embroidered clothes, candlesticks, bibles, photos, musical instruments. What would I take if I had to leave the country quickly, with just one small bag? My flute, definitely. Photos of my family and friends and of Burt and Harry. And my favorite books, the ones I read over and over again.

I checked my watch and discovered I'd been browsing for over an hour. I raced down the stairs and found Dad and his students gathered around Charles, who was seated at one of the computers. I pushed my way through the group until I was standing next to Dad.

Then I watched as Charles typed RYBCZYNSKI into the computer. In two seconds RYBCZYNSKI, STEFAN AND LEILAH popped up on the screen. I got goosebumps down my arms. These were my great-grandparents! Under their names was JOSEF, AGE FOUR. This was my grandfather! Charles moved the cursor down the screen to COUNTRY OF ORIGIN — POLAND.

Dad swallowed hard. He nodded several times, blinking back tears, and rested his hand on Charles's shoulder as Charles moved the cursor again, this time to DONOR — VICTOR (RYBCZYNSKI) ROBINSON.

Charles sat absolutely still, studying the screen. Then suddenly he jumped up and turned to face Dad. They looked at each other for a minute, but when Dad moved toward him, Charles took off, pushing everybody out of his way. He ran back into the Great Hall. Dad followed, calling, "Charles . . ." I followed Dad. Charles ran outside, under the portico and around to the left. He climbed up onto the seawall, where the immigrants' names are inscribed in bronze. For a minute I thought he was going to jump into the water. So did the tourists who were sitting nearby. You could hear a gasp go through the crowd. But instead of jumping, he spun around, arms outstretched, and began to recite.

> *"Give me your tired, your poor,*
> *Your huddled masses yearning to breathe free . . ."*

A guard spotted him and called, "You!"
But Charles didn't stop. His voice grew stronger.

> *"The wretched refuse of your teeming shore,*
> *Send these, the homeless, tempest-tossed to me:"*

The guard headed for him.
"Charles!" Dad called.
Charles looked right at him. His voice broke as he finished the poem.

> *"I lift my lamp beside the golden door."*

Dad stood in front of the wall. "Come down now."
Charles hesitated. Then he jumped. Dad caught

him, wrapped an arm around his shoulders and shielded him from the crowd. Charles hid his face against Dad. I think he was crying.

I felt myself choking up and looked away, confused, because I was also angry! Angry at Charles for making himself the center of attention again. Angry at Dad for loving him so completely. Angry at myself for . . . I don't know what. I tried to find Jessica. I needed to share this with her. But Jess was nowhere in sight.

"**W**here were you when we were at the computers?" I asked her later.

"Upstairs, with my friends," Jess said. "Don't tell Dad, okay?"

"You missed . . ."

"What?"

"Seeing our family name."

"Really?" Jess said. "Well, maybe I'll go back in and have a look."

"It won't be the same."

"Of course it'll be the same. It's a computer."

"No," I said. "It wasn't just the computer."

"Then what?"

I couldn't find the words to tell her what I sensed—that something between Charles and Dad had changed forever, something I could feel but couldn't explain. So I just shook my head and said, "Never mind."

"Rachel . . ." Jess said, "you're acting very weird!"

At the end of the day, as we got off the ferry at Battery Park, I told Jessica, "I'm thinking of taking the bus home. That is, if you don't mind."

Jessica looked surprised. "Really?"

I took the Sea-Bands out of my purse, where they've been since Gena gave them to me. "I've been meaning to try these," I explained. I slipped the bands onto my wrists, then moved them three fingers up exactly the way Gena had showed me. I hoped the buttons were pressing on my Nei-Kuan points.

"Do you want me to sit next to you," Jess asked, "or can I sit with my friends?"

"You can sit with your friends."

When we boarded the bus, I took the first seat. Mom says you're less likely to get sick if you sit up front and look straight ahead, out the driver's window.

Charles seemed like his old self as he got on, talking and laughing with a group of kids. He was surprised when he saw me but he didn't say anything. He just walked by, toward the back of the bus.

When Dad saw me, he looked concerned. "Rachel, are you okay?"

"Yes," I said. "I just want to try these." And I held up my wrists, showing him the Sea-Bands.

"Good for you!" he said.

After all of Dad's students were accounted for and seated, Paul got on the bus. "Is this seat taken?" he asked, tapping the one next to mine.

I shook my head. "I don't know about you, Rachel," he said, sinking low, "but I'm zonked." Then he closed his eyes and slept most of the way home, waking only when we made a sharp turn or a sudden stop.

I can't say whether it was the Sea-Bands or the distraction of having Paul Medeiros sleeping next to me, but I made it back without getting sick!

When we got off the bus at the school parking lot, Paul yawned, stretched, adjusted his glasses and said, "There's a concert at the college tomorrow night. Would you like to go?"

Would I like to go?

"Does that look mean *yes*?" he asked.

I think I nodded.

"It's at six-thirty," he said, "so I'll have you home by nine . . . in case you were worrying."

This time I found my voice. "I wasn't worrying," I told him.

TWENTY-ONE

I was bursting! As soon as we got home, I ran over to Alison's to tell Gena the good news about the Sea-Bands. But when I got there, Leon said she was resting. "Her blood pressure's up and she's supposed to stay off her feet. Only a month to go . . ."

I told him I hope Gena feels better soon, then ran up to Alison's room. She was sprawled across her bed, her head hanging over the edge. Stephanie was there, too, sitting cross-legged on the floor, jotting something down in a notebook. As soon as they saw me, Steph closed the notebook and she and Alison looked at each other as if they knew something I didn't. But for once I didn't care. I sat on the edge of the bed and gave Maizie a few pats.

Steph could tell something was up because she said, "What?"

"Oh, nothing . . . except I'm going to a concert at the college tomorrow night . . . with Paul."

"Who's Paul?" Steph asked.

I had to be careful since I'd never even hinted how I feel about him. "You know . . . Charles's tutor."

"Wait!" Steph said, holding up her hand. "If you're going to a concert, that means you can't come to the carnival with us." The Jaycees sponsor a weekend carnival every year. Steph and I always go.

"We could go Saturday, instead," I suggested.

"Dad's taking Bruce and me to the city on Saturday," Steph said.

"I'm sorry, but I can't miss this concert."

"Are you telling us this is a date?" Alison asked.

"No, it's not a date," I said, although in my mind it definitely is. "My parents would never let me go on a date with someone nine years older."

"Why not?" Steph asked. "My mother's dating someone fifteen years *younger.*"

"That's different," I said.

"Maybe to you . . . not to me."

"I don't know, Rachel," Alison said. "It sure sounds like a date."

I just smiled and kind of shrugged.

"Are you saying he already has a girlfriend?" Steph asked.

A girlfriend? I thought. For the first time I realized I know almost nothing about Paul's personal life, except that his grandparents came from Portugal. But what if he does have a girlfriend? What if she meets us at the concert? Worse yet, what if . . .

"So does he . . . or what?" Steph said.

"I don't know."

"Who cares if he does or he doesn't?" Alison told Steph. "Rachel is the one he's taking to the concert." She turned to me and asked, "What are you going to wear?"

"Wear?" I said.

She jumped off the bed and scooped up an armload of *Sassy* magazines. "You have to think about these things, Rachel," she said, dumping them in my lap.

After dinner I cornered Mom and asked if I could borrow her black dress to wear to the concert. She and Dad have no idea this is anything more than a friendly invitation. Mom said, "That dress wouldn't be appropriate, Rachel."

"But you wore it to a concert in New York . . . when you took Dad out for his birthday."

"That was different," Mom said. "That was a dress-up event."

"But, Mom . . . this is at the college!"

"I know, honey . . . but college students wear jeans, not gowns. Call Tarren . . . she'll tell you."

So I called Tarren and she said Mom was right. She also told me she'll be at the concert, with her Romantic Obstacle. "I'll look for you," she said.

I don't know how I got through the next day, our last full day of school. On the way out of math class

Jeremy Dragon said, "Hey, Macbeth . . . you going to the carnival tonight?"

"Not tonight," I told him. "Tonight . . ." I hesitated. "Maybe tomorrow night," I called. But I don't think he heard me because by then he was halfway down the hall with his friends.

I spent most of the afternoon in the tub, daydreaming about the *romantic journey* I was about to take with Paul. When I finally got dressed, I chose a long summer skirt and my favorite tank top. It's pale green and has a matching cardigan sweater. I thought about borrowing Jessica's parrot earrings but I didn't want anyone in my family, including Jess, to grow suspicious. Anyway, Jess was at work. So I wore my silver earrings, instead. My only real dilemma was whether or not to use strawberry-flavored lip gloss. I decided to go for it.

At five-thirty, when I heard the front door slam, I looked out my window and watched as Charles and Dana took off hand in hand. Only then did I come downstairs.

"Oh, there you are," Paul said, collecting his books. "I thought you'd forgotten."

Forgotten? Was he serious? "No," I said. "I just had a lot to do this afternoon." I tossed my cardigan over one shoulder the way models do in magazines.

Paul was wearing a blue denim work shirt with the sleeves rolled up. Mom and Tarren were right. The slinky black dress wouldn't have been right. I followed him out of the house, locking the door behind me. His car was parked out front. It's an old two-door Toyota, either gray or brown—it's hard to tell since I've never seen it clean. On the inside it was even worse. The upholstery was ragged. His seat was covered with an old blanket and mine was held together with duct tape.

"Slightly messy, huh?" Paul asked as we headed for the highway.

Until then I hadn't realized I'd been cleaning things up, folding papers and collecting gum wrappers and tucking them all into the side pocket of my door.

"No, it's fine. I'm just . . ." I almost said *compulsively neat* but caught myself in time and changed it to, "a natural helper."

When we stopped at a red light, Paul glanced my way and said, "I like that color on you, Rachel."

Which color? My tank top . . . my lip gloss? I didn't ask. I just said, "Thank you." Could he tell how fast my heart was beating? Did he know the palms of my hands were sweaty and I felt like either laughing or crying? I only hoped I could control myself. I stared straight ahead, grateful the drive to the college takes just fifteen minutes. "Do you by any chance know my cousin, Tarren Babcock?" I asked, trying to make small talk. "She's an education major."

"I don't think so," he said.

"She'll probably be at the concert."

"Is she a music lover like you?"

Lover! He said the word *lover* to me! I felt myself blush. "No," I said. "She's more into obstacles." I began to fan my face with my hand.

"Obstacles?" He laughed, as if I'd meant to be funny.

"Yes." I tried to laugh, too, but it came out more like a squeak.

"What kind of obstacles?"

"All kinds," I said. He seemed to think this was funnier yet. I wish I had never mentioned Tarren's name. How was I supposed to get out of this? Tell a joke, I thought. One of those jokes the dentist told me. But I couldn't remember any of the punch lines. I was totally hopeless!

"She sounds like someone I'd like to know," Paul said.

"Who?" I asked.

"Your cousin."

"Oh, I doubt it," I told him. I didn't add that he and Tarren would have absolutely nothing in common.

When we got to the college, we parked in a big field, then walked up a hill to a yellow-and-white-striped tent. There were rows of folding chairs set up inside and people were already taking seats. A girl handed us programs as we entered, and I followed Paul down the aisle to a pair of seats in the middle.

I knew I could easily be mistaken for a college student and for once I was glad. It's not just my height that makes me look older. It's my body. Mom says she was an early bloomer, too. She says in a few years my emotional maturity will catch up with my physical maturity. But I think it already has.

Outside the tent groups of students were settling on blankets on the lawn. I wished we could sit out there, too. It seemed much more romantic, even though the sun was still shining. If only the concert began at nine instead of six-thirty!

I read my program carefully. This was the last in a series performed by visiting musicians. Tonight it was the Connecticut Valley Chamber Players, with an all-Mozart program.

When the concert began, Paul closed his eyes. A lot of people close their eyes when they're listening to music. It helps them concentrate on what they are hearing. But I couldn't tell if Paul was concentrating or sleeping. Maybe he isn't getting enough sleep at night. Maybe he needs vitamins. I looked over at his hands, which were relaxed in his lap. They looked strong, manly. I imagined them touching my face, my hair. But then I began to feel very warm and had to use my program to fan myself.

The group of fifteen musicians played in different combinations for thirty-five minutes, took a short break, played for another half hour, then performed two encores. Paul applauded enthusiastically. He said, "Fantastic, aren't they?"

"Outstanding!" I agreed, even though they weren't.

Just as we were about to head back to Paul's car, I heard someone calling my name. "Ra . . . chel!" I knew it was Tarren even before I turned and saw her. She was already weaving her way through the tent to us.

"Hi . . ." she said, joining us.

"Hi," I answered. She looked very pretty. Her hair hung to her shoulders and she was wearing a low-cut sundress, showing off more than necessary.

"Well . . ." she said, giving me a nudge in the side. "Aren't you going to introduce us?"

I really didn't want to introduce Tarren to Paul. I didn't want anyone reminding him that I am just thirteen. But there was no way to get out of it, so I said, "Paul Medeiros, this is my cousin, Tarren Babcock." I spoke very fast and hoped Tarren wouldn't ask any questions.

A tall man with thinning hair came up to Tarren then, put his hand on her naked back and handed her a paper cup. "They didn't have lime spritzers," he told her. "Just plain seltzer."

"Thanks," she said, smiling up at him. That's when it hit me! This man, who looked as old as Dad, who wasn't even good-looking, at least not to me, was Tarren's Romantic Obstacle! She took a sip of seltzer, then introduced us. "Rachel, Paul . . . I'd like you to meet Professor Benjamin Byram." She said his name proudly, then gave me a meaningful smile. I'm not sure if I smiled back or not. I felt weird, knowing this man and Tarren were involved in *that* way.

Paul shook hands with Tarren's Obstacle. "I was in your class two years ago," he said. "Paul Medeiros."

"Of course," Professor Byram said. "I remember . . ." But I could tell he didn't. And so could Paul.

A small, pretty woman with lots of pale curly hair came up to the Romantic Obstacle then and linked her arm through his. "Sweetie . . ." he said, clearly surprised. "I thought you said you couldn't make it tonight."

"Well," she told him, "the meeting didn't last as long as I thought, and it was such a beautiful evening I asked the sitter to stay."

Tarren looked stricken—the way my father had the night Charles called him a wimp. "This is my wife, Francesca Hammond," the Obstacle said to all of us.

Francesca beamed at Paul. "Paul Medeiros! How good to see you. Where've you been hiding?"

"You two know each other?" the Obstacle asked his wife.

"Well, of course," Francesca said. "Paul is one of my prize students."

Tarren looked like she was about to be sick. She'd

turned a kind of grayish color, and one hand went to her throat. I don't think anyone noticed but me.

Francesca and Paul went right on talking. "I hear you've accepted a job teaching in Westport," she said.

"Yes," Paul said.

"That's wonderful! Come in next week and we'll have lunch. I want to hear all about it." Then she turned to her husband and said, "Darling, the baby-sitter . . ."

The Obstacle checked his watch and said, "Got to run. Nice to see you again, Paul. Glad to meet you, Rachel." He turned to Tarren and held out his hand to shake hers. "If I don't see you again, have a wonderful summer. It's been a pleasure having you in my class."

He had to pull back his hand because Tarren wouldn't let go. Then he and his wife walked away, arm in arm.

Tarren watched them for a minute, then burst into tears.

"What?" Paul asked.

Tarren just shook her head and tried to stifle her sobs by covering her mouth with her hand.

I patted her back.

"Don't tell me . . ." Paul said. "Another of Professor Byram's conquests."

Tarren looked at him. "Conquests?" she managed to ask.

Paul put his arm around her waist. "Come on," he said to me. "Your cousin needs some cheering up."

Tarren leaned against Paul as he led her to his car. I got in back, by myself. *She* sat up front, next to him.

We went to a diner and took a booth, where Tarren cried and Paul passed her napkins from the dispenser so she could blow her nose. When she shivered in her sundress in the air-conditioning, I handed her my sweater. She pulled it around her shoulders. Paul dropped a couple of coins into the jukebox on the wall and selected four songs, all hard rock, which totally shocked me. Slowly Tarren began to recover. She felt hungry, she said, and she and Paul smiled at each other, then ordered hamburgers and fries while I sipped a peppermint tea.

"He was never right for me," Tarren cooed to Paul over the apple pie and ice cream they shared for dessert. "I know that now."

"You were wasted on him!" Paul told her.

"It was like . . . I couldn't help myself," Tarren said to him. They spoke as if I weren't there, as if I were invisible. I hate being treated that way!

On the drive home I think they were holding hands. But I didn't care anymore. I just wanted it to be over. I just wanted to be alone in my room.

Finally we pulled up in front of my house. I leaned

forward and thanked Paul for taking me to the concert.

"My pleasure," he said.

"See you, Rachel," Tarren said as I got out of the car.

At the last minute I leaned back in through her window and said, "Give Roddy a kiss for me."

I knew she hadn't had the chance to tell Paul she was divorced, with a baby. Well, too bad!

TWENTY-TWO

I will never forgive Tarren for ruining what should have been the most romantic night of my life! She's such a fool, jumping from one Romantic Obstacle to another. I raced up to my room and closed the door, praying that Mom and Dad wouldn't ask any questions. I was halfway undressed when Mom knocked on my door. "Rachel . . ."

I didn't feel like explaining anything to her now.

When I didn't respond, she knocked again. "Rachel . . . there's someone here to see you."

Paul! He realizes he's made a major mistake. He wants me, not Tarren!

"It's a boy," Mom continued. "Jeremy something. Should I tell him you're already in bed?"

Jeremy . . . here? I began to get back into my clothes. "No!" I told Mom. "Tell him I'll be right down."

"Okay," Mom said. "But it's getting late."

Why would Jeremy Dragon come to my house on a Friday night at nine-thirty? It didn't make sense. Nothing made sense!

I had to shoo Harry out of the bathroom sink so I could splash my face with cold water. Then I fluffed out my hair, put on more strawberry lip gloss and flew down the stairs. I opened the front door but didn't see him.

"Pssst, Macbeth . . . over here."

I followed the sound of his voice to the maple tree.

"Hey," he said. He was wearing his dragon jacket. "How come you're all dressed up?"

"I just got back from a concert."

"Who was playing?"

"The Connecticut Valley Chamber Players."

He didn't act like that was unusual. He said, "You're really into music, huh?"

I nodded.

He smiled at me. "How about a walk?"

"Sure," I answered.

"Don't want to run into . . . you know . . . them."

Charles and Dana were about the last people I wanted to run into, too.

"So," he said, fishing something out of his jacket pocket. It was his token race car from Monopoly. "I meant to give this back to you right away . . . then I forgot . . . sorry."

"That's okay. Nobody's played since that night."
Our hands touched as he gave me the car.

We walked around the pond. I was glad it was dark
so none of the neighbors, including Stephanie and
Alison, could see us. When we got to the tree where
the raccoons live, Jeremy stopped walking and faced
me. "Macbeth . . ." His voice was hoarse.

"What?" I think I sounded alarmed.

He leaned toward me and before I even knew what
was happening, his lips were on mine.

"I've wanted to do that for a long time," he said.

"Really?"

"Yeah . . . ever since Halloween when you came to
my house reciting that stupid poem. I liked the way
your mouth twitched."

"It does that when I'm nervous."

"Like now?"

I touched my mouth. Was it twitching and I didn't
even know? He took my hand away. "It's very kiss-
able . . . you know?" He put his arms around me,
pulled me close and kissed me again. My legs felt so
weak, I thought I might fall over.

On our third try, I kissed him back. I felt a surge go
through my whole body. My mind went blank for a
minute. Never mind animal attraction, this was *elec-
trical* attraction! When I came back to earth, I asked,
"What does this mean?"

"Mean?" he said. He held my hand and we

started walking again. "It doesn't mean anything. It was . . . you know . . . just a couple of kisses."

No, I wanted to tell him! I don't know. This is all new to me. This is nothing like kissing Max Wilson at the seventh-grade dance. But I didn't say anything.

He walked me home. We kissed one more time in the shadows. Then he smiled and said, "See ya . . ."

Just when you think life is over, you find out it's not. Just when you think you'll never be foolish enough to fall for somebody else, it happens without any warning! I hope this doesn't mean I'm going to be like Tarren, jumping from one Obstacle to the next. I don't think it does. I don't think it means anything except life is full of surprises and they're not necessarily all bad.

TWENTY-THREE

The next morning Stephanie called. "How was the concert?"

"Boring."

"What do you mean by *boring*?"

"You know . . . the music wasn't that good and everyone there was ancient . . . over twenty, at least. I couldn't wait to get home!"

"So I guess you're glad it wasn't a date."

"Very!" I paused, lowering my voice. "I have important news but I can't tell you over the phone."

"Well, what are you waiting for? Come right over!"

"I kissed Jeremy Dragon!" I threw myself backward onto Steph's bed, falling on top of about thirty stuffed animals. "Not once," I told her, "not twice, but four times!"

Steph's mouth fell open. "Rachel . . . I'm so jealous!" I love the way Steph says exactly what she's feeling without worrying about it. "How did this happen?" she asked.

"I don't know. It was so bizarre. He came over to give me back a Monopoly piece and it just . . . well . . . happened."

"Does this mean you're going together?"

"No. It doesn't mean anything. It was just a . . . couple of kisses."

"Did you react?"

"You *must* be joking!"

"Rachel!" she squealed. "I can't believe this!"

"You think *you* can't!"

Mom was sworn in as a judge on Tuesday morning. I think Charles was disappointed when he introduced himself to the governor as Charles *Rybczynski* and the governor didn't say anything. I wonder if he's going to get tired of his new name.

Tarren wore a white suit and three-inch heels. She looked very . . . adult. She thanked me over and over for introducing her to Paul. They've been seeing each other every night. She says he's wonderful with Roddy. I don't want to hear about it. I made sure I wouldn't be sitting next to her at lunch.

Mom seems relieved now that she's the Honorable Nell Babcock Robinson, though she still doesn't know which court she'll be assigned to. I think she's also relieved Charles has a summer job working at the bakery in town. No one has said for sure what school he'll be going to next fall, but Jessica and I think there's a good chance it will be the high school, which means he'll be living at home. I'm trying to learn from Jess, who says we should stop thinking about him and just let Mom and Dad work it out with Dr. Embers. *I wish!*

Charles seems less angry since Ellis Island but I can't say he's changed. He's probably never going to change. He'll probably take pleasure in annoying me my whole life.

With Jessica it's completely different. We're always going to be close, no matter what. Still, I was upset when she said, "I heard about that program at the college."

"What program?"

"Challenge. Toad's brother told me."

"Oh." Until now I'd managed to put Challenge out of my mind. "You're not mad, are you?" I asked.

"Why would I be mad?" Jess said. "I learned long ago not to compete with you, Rachel. If I did, I'd just wind up resenting you and that wouldn't be good for either of us. Besides, no matter what happens at school you're still my *little* sister." She laughed and gave me an elbow in the ribs.

"Don't mention anything about Challenge to Mom or Dad, okay?"

"How come?"

"Because I haven't decided if I'm going to do it."

"Why wouldn't you do it?"

"I have my reasons," I told her. "So promise you won't say anything."

"You know I won't."

On the last day of school we got out at ten because the ninth graders were graduating at noon. When I passed Jeremy in the hall, he was carrying his red cap and gown.

"So, Macbeth . . . you hanging around this summer or what?"

"I'm going to music camp," I told him.

"Play a song for me, okay?"

"Sure."

"See you in September."

"I'll be back the end of August."

Some of his friends came along then, slamming into him. As they dragged him away, he looked back at me and waved. I waved, too. I can't believe I actually kissed him! And that come September, I might kiss him again.

"Nice that you and Jeremy get along so well." I spun around. It was Dana, dressed in her cap and gown. But her cap wasn't fastened yet and she had to hold it on with one hand.

"Nice that you and my brother do," I said.

I didn't want to go to the bakery after school but Alison insisted. She still has a *thing* for Charles. He was working behind the counter, wearing a white apron over his

T-shirt and jeans. "Well, well, well . . ." he said, "if it isn't the triumvirate! What brings you here?"

"Hunger," I told him.

He plucked a dog biscuit out of a jar and held it up. "These are quite savory. They appeal to all sizes and breeds."

"Woof, woof . . ." I said.

Steph and Alison tried not to laugh. They each bought a giant-size chocolate chip cookie. When Charles handed Alison her change, he said, "I'm still waiting for you, California."

"What about Dana?" I asked.

"Dana is my date *du jour*," he said, using the French expression. "But California is something else."

Alison had this ridiculous look on her face. I hope that's not how I looked when I was with Jeremy. "Come on . . ." I grabbed her by the hand and led her away. Steph followed.

"Good-bye, my lovelies," Charles called after us, giving Stephanie and Alison both a profound case of the giggles.

When we were outside, Steph bit into her cookie and said, "He just likes to tease you, Rachel!"

"Because you take everything so seriously," Alison added, breaking her cookie in half and sharing with me.

"I don't take *everything* seriously!" I told them. "Just *some* things."

On the way home I invited them to my house for

lunch. I felt safe knowing Charles was at work. Before we went inside, Alison said, "Guess what? As soon as Matthew's born, we're going to L.A."

"But you'll be back in time for school, right?" Steph asked.

"I think so," Alison said. "I hope so."

"But Alison . . . you have to be!" Steph said. "You're running for class president." As soon as she said it, she clapped her hand to her mouth. She and Alison exchanged a look. "We were going to tell you before you left for camp," Steph said.

"We were just waiting for the right time," Alison added.

"I mean, you acted like you didn't want to run," Steph said, making excuses. "You acted like you were only doing me a favor." She paused for a minute. "And Alison's so popular. She has a real chance of winning."

"We just thought the Dare to Care Candidate was too good to waste," Alison said.

I didn't know what to say! It's true I was going to tell Steph I can't run because of all my other activities. But I hadn't told her yet. And I certainly never imagined she'd find herself another candidate and give away the slogan she thought up for *me*.

"You're not mad, are you?" Alison asked.

"Let's just say I'm surprised," I told her.

"I want you to work on my campaign," Alison said. "You will, won't you?"

"If I can fit it into my schedule," I said, sounding

as snide as Charles. "I'm going to be really busy between Natural Helpers and Challenge."

"What's Challenge?" she asked.

"It's this program at the college for —"

But Steph didn't let me finish. "You're going to college?"

"No, it's for eighth and ninth graders. It's like . . ." I tried to find a way to describe it. "It's like enriched math . . . except . . ."

"It's for geniuses!" Steph said.

"We're not geniuses."

"It's for prodigies!" Alison said, trying out Charles's favorite word.

"We are *not* prodigies!"

"Even so," Alison said, sliding her arm around my waist, "I love having such a smart friend!"

A born politician! I thought.

"And you'll still work on my campaign, right?" When I didn't answer, she said, "Steph . . . tell Rachel you *want* her to work on my campaign."

"Dah!" Steph said. "Who'd want Rachel!" Then she tackled me to the ground and Alison jumped on top of us.

TWENTY-FOUR

On Sunday morning I carefully packed my flute in its case and tossed my last-minute stuff, like my hairbrush and Walkman, into my backpack, along with *Anna Karenina*, the novel Charles quoted the night we had our private talk in the kitchen—the one that begins, "All happy families are alike . . ."

This is the first time I'm going to camp by bus with everyone else. I've always gone by train before. I put on the Sea-Bands and adjusted them. I hope they work! But what if they don't? What if I get sick and the driver won't pull over and . . . I stopped myself. I'm not going to get sick! Mom and Dad promised we'd be at the bus early enough for me to get a seat in the first row.

I walked around my room one last time, stopping to touch the box with the secret compartment. It's always hard for me to leave, even when I really want to. I'd said good-bye to Jess last night. Now that she's working at Going Places six days a week, Sunday is her only chance to sleep late. She says she expects her skin to be clear the next time she sees me. I hope she's right.

I went down to the kitchen to get a box of crackers for the road, just in case. Charles was standing at the counter, wolfing down a bowl of cold leftover pasta.

"What am I going to do without you for six weeks, Rachel?"

"Yeah . . . who'll you torture?" I asked.

"I don't know . . . it won't be easy." He swallowed a mouthful, then puckered up. "Kiss your big brother good-bye?"

"I sincerely hope you're kidding."

"Would I kid you, little sister?"

"You would if you could."

"I'll be counting the days till we're together again."

"Me, too," I said. "I hope they go really slowly."

"Rachel, is this possible . . . you're developing a sense of humor?"

"Anything's possible!" I told him. Then I walked out the door, laughing to myself.